LOVE
in Winter
WONDERLAND

PRAISE FOR LOVE IN WINTER WONDERLAND

'Gorgeous writing, witty dialogue, a magical setting
and two characters you'll fall head over heels for.'
Jennifer Niven, author of *All the Bright Places*

'A screen-worthy holiday romance.'
Joya Goffney, author of *Excuse Me While I Ugly Cry*

'A story so charming and fun it will whisk you away.
It has TikTok sensation written all over it!'
Laura Jane Williams, author of *Our Stop*

'I devoured this delicious YA rom-com.
A treat to read any time of year.'
Katherine Webber, author of *Twin Crowns*

'Charming, heartwarming and perfect cosy reading,
complete with the perfect holiday soundtrack!'
Ciara Smyth, author of *Not My Problem*

'Full of warmth, humour and joy. A delightful read!'
Michelle Quach, author of *Not Here to be Liked*

'A dazzling love letter to bookshops,
and the power of community.'
Adiba Jaigirdar, author of *Hani and Ishu's Guide to Fake Dating*

'A wonderfully warm love story.'
Candice Brathwaite, author of *Cuts Both Ways*

'A warm and cosy read that pulls you into the perfect winter
romance. Abiola has given us all a gift to swoon over.'
Benjamin Dean, author of *The King is Dead*

'The most joyful, cosy and swoon-worthy love story.'
Kate Weston, author of *Diary of a Confused Feminist*

LOVE in Winter WONDERLAND

ABIOLA BELLO

Simon & Schuster

First published in Great Britain in 2022 by Simon & Schuster UK Ltd

1 3 5 7 9 10 8 6 4 2

Simon & Schuster UK Ltd
1st Floor, 222 Gray's Inn Road
London
WC1X 8HB

www.simonandschuster.co.uk
www.simonandschuster.com.au
www.simonandschuster.co.in

Simon & Schuster Australia, Sydney
Simon & Schuster India, New Delhi

A CIP catalogue record for this book is available from the British Library.

PB ISBN 978-1-3985-1687-8
eBook ISBN 978-1-3985-1688-5
eAudio ISBN 978-1-3985-1689-2

Typeset in the UK by M Rules
Printed and bound by CPI Group (UK) Ltd, Croydon, CR0 4YY

MIX
Paper from
responsible sources
FSC® C171272

To my dad, you are by far one of the greatest gifts I've ever had x

ONE

Trey's playlist: 'Let It Snow' by Boyz II Men

Seventeen days till Christmas

I'm about two seconds away from committing murder.

'But I thought it was two for one? I saw the deal in the bookshop window down the road,' the white woman with blonde highlights says.

She means Books! Books! Books! It's on the tip of my tongue to point out that we're clearly a different bookshop, but instead I flash my best smile – all white teeth. Next to her, her daughter's eyes flicker with interest.

'Don't get me wrong, I love a bargain as much as the next person, but we're independent.' I say 'independent' *real* slow. 'So you're helping the community when you buy from Wonderland. Plus, we're a Black-owned, family-run bookshop.'

Now the woman looks uncomfortable, catching eyes with her daughter, who huffs and says, 'Mum, it's fine. Just pay.'

The women looks like she's struggling to decide what to do. I bet now she thinks that if she doesn't support the bookshop I'll think she's racist. Truth is, I just think she's cheap.

'Look, I'll even throw in a couple of bookmarks.' I grab two from behind the counter and hand them to her. One says *Indie Bookshops Rule!* and the other says *Black Lives Matter*. We're such a subtle family.

The woman's eyes widen when she reads them. Then she reaches into her purse, pulling out her bank card, and I have to stop myself from punching the air in celebration. With this sale, we've reached our daily target, and Mum agreed that, if we did, I can leave early for Bebe's Christmas party. Bebe Richards is one of the girls in my friendship group at college, and one thing about her is she knows how to throw down. I have no idea why she's having a Christmas party on a Wednesday, over two weeks before Christmas Day, but I don't care. Anything that's not the bookshop or coursework sounds good to me.

'Thanks for shopping at Wonderland,' I say as I hand the woman her books with a grin. 'Merry Christmas.'

'And you.' She smiles back, but it looks forced. Her daughter, on the other hand, gives me a wink before they walk off. I smile and shake my head.

'Flirting with the customers again?' Dad walks up to the till and opens it, staring at the money and scratching the back of his head.

'We're on target. Slam dunk!' I shoot up my arms and flick my wrists, pretending to dunk like Kobe.

'Wasn't it busier this time last year?' Dad looks around the bookshop and I follow his gaze.

He's right. It's kind of quiet, but I'm sure it will pick up once it gets closer to Christmas. Dad's been paranoid ever since Books! Books! Books! opened. He thinks they've stolen all of our customers and tells me so after every shift. But we've been doing okay, and I think part of that is down to my epic playlist: 'The Best Christmas Songs by Black Artists' – '8 Days of Christmas' by Destiny's Child, 'This Christmas' by Chris Brown ... and is it even Christmas without Mariah?

'Relax, Dad.' I put an arm round him. We're pretty much the same height now at six foot one, and with my wide-set eyes, broad nose, strong jawline and lean physique I'm my dad thirty-odd years ago.

Dad huffs in response.

'I'm leaving soon, but I can do a quick tidy and chat to some customers first,' I say.

Dad shuts the till and points in front of him. 'If those kids aren't buying, tell them to scat. How many times do I have to remind you, Trey? We're not a library. One day the bookshop will be yours and you can't have customers loitering around.'

I don't want the bookshop, I want to say, but – like always – I swallow it down. Wonderland was created by my great-grandad and is my family's legacy. It's the first and only Black-owned, independent bookshop on Stoke Newington High Street. Dad grew up here, and all he wanted to do when he was a kid was take over and be the boss. I want to be a singer, selling out arenas, but there are two problems. The first is my parents assume that Wonderland is my future, and I don't want to disappoint them. I pray all the time that my little brother Reon will be up for the task of running the bookshop. The second problem is I have a fear of singing in front of large crowds. I even get nervous when it's a small one. But if I close my eyes, or have a couple of drinks for Dutch courage, I can sing no problem. Part of my New Year's resolution is going to be to enter singing competitions, because I want to overcome my fear and really see where singing could take me, even though I know how hard it is to break into the music industry.

The loitering kids are gone now, but they've carelessly left a few books on the floor – no wonder Dad wanted them out. I return the books to the shelves and check in with a few customers to make sure they're okay before circling the rest of the shop.

I start quietly singing along to 'Let It Snow', which is playing through the speakers.

'Ooh, sing it, DeVante,' Boogs calls over at me as he walks into the shop.

I laugh. 'Wrong group, genius.'

'Is it?' Boogs frowns. 'Isn't this Jodeci?'

'Boyz II Men.' We dap, and I hug the petite girl in the colourful patchwork coat next to him. 'Hey, Santi.'

Santi flicks her long braided twists over her shoulder and raises her eyebrows. 'DeVante?'

'How would you know?' Boogs says. 'All you listen to is Coldplay.'

Boogs and Santi go back and forth and I shake my head. Boogs, real name Dre Deton, is my best friend. He moved to Stoke Newington just over a year ago. There was a rumour going round he used to be part of a gang in his old ends. The rumour was true, but we hit it off straight away. He's all light-skinned, light eyes, breaking girls' hearts with his pretty-boy face and fire dance moves (hence the nickname Boogs, short for Boogie), but that was until he met Santi Bailey. Technically, I got them together, because I'm dating Santi's twin sister, Blair. Identical twins with non-identical personalities – Santi dresses like she was a hippy in a past life, and she's always asking me for book recommendations, whereas Blair is a walking ad for Pretty Little Thing, and I can count on one hand the number of times we've spoken about books. On paper, I'm better suited to Santi, but somehow Blair and I work. I guess opposites really do attract.

Santi turns back to me. 'Have you got the new Estee Mase?'

'Yeah, it's by the tills,' I reply.

She wanders off and Boogs whispers, 'Don't let her buy it. I already got it for her.'

My eyes narrow. 'You did? Wait? From where? I haven't seen you in here recently.'

Boogs rubs his face. 'Don't get mad, but I bought it from Books! Books! Books!'

'You *what*?' I stare at him in disbelief.

'I know, but you had sold out . . .' Boogs says sheepishly.

'Not cool, man. It'll be your own people.' I shake my head.

'My bad, bro. So what have you got Blair?'

I frown. 'For what?'

Boogs looks at me like I've grown two heads. 'The twins' birthday is tomorrow.'

What? No, that can't be right. I take out my phone and look at the calendar. *Shit!* Today is December 8th.

Boogs whistles. 'She's gonna kill you.'

He's not lying. I can't buy her a book because she won't read it, plus she'll know it's from the shop so she'll think it's free. The high street is rammed because of Christmas, and nothing decent that I can afford online will come in time.

'What did you get Santi?' I ask, hoping against odds that Boogs has made a half-hearted effort.

'That Estee book and some wellness hamper I found on Etsy. You know she's not fussy about presents – unlike your girl.'

I groan. How did this happen? It was only last week that I was talking to Blair about her birthday, but with working overtime at the bookshop and all the Boxing Day sale prep it must have slipped my mind. She's going to be pissed if Santi has a better present than her. Blair thinks that because we were together first, we should set the standard, which makes no sense to me. But it means that any time Boogs does something romantic for Santi, Blair expects me to go bigger.

'I'll think of something,' I mumble. 'At least she's not coming to the party tonight, so she can't grill me.'

'Blair didn't tell you?' Boogs says. 'Santi said Blair changed her mind. She's coming tonight.'

Before I can reply, Santi walks over to us holding the Estee Mase book. Boogs and I glance at each other and Santi notices.

'What present did you get Blair?' Santi asks.

I smile. 'It's a surprise.'

'That's code for he forgot,' Boogs whispers.

Bro code! I shoot him a death glare.

'Trey!' Santi says. 'That's terrible.'

'Boogs bought it from Books! Books! Books!' I quickly say, and Boogs actually gasps.

Santi puts her hands on her hips. 'I can't believe you would do something like that!'

I spot Mum walking into the office and follow her, a smile creeping over my face as I hear Santi laying into Boogs. Santi's pro-independent shops and Boogs deserves to be cussed out with his disloyal self. Mum looks startled when she sees me at the door and quickly shields the letter she's reading. Her black, shoulder-length hair, which is usually immaculate, is tied in a messy ponytail.

'Trey, baby, you scared me.' Mum takes off her glasses and rubs her eyes.

I don't think she's been sleeping very well. I've been hearing her and Dad having hushed conversations late at night, but every time I ask her what's up she brushes me off. I tilt my head to look at the logo on the letter in her hand.

'Who's Raymond and Raymond?' I ask.

Mum follows my gaze and folds up the letter. 'Don't worry about it.'

'Mum, come on.' I sit down opposite her. 'If something's wrong, you can tell me.'

Mum looks down at the letter and doesn't respond. I have an urge to snatch it from her and read it for myself, but I value my life too much to do that, so instead I just wait. Mum eventually looks up and sighs. 'Raymond and Raymond are developers.'

I frown. 'Developers? I don't understand.'

'The bookshop's not doing too well, Trey. We're not hitting the numbers like we used to, and we're a month behind on mortgage and supplier payments.' She puts her hand to her forehead. 'Customers just aren't spending enough and Raymond and Raymond have offered to buy Wonderland before we completely sink.'

Behind on the mortgage? I mean, I know Wonderland hasn't been super busy, but I had no idea things were this bad.

'What's Dad said?' I ask, concern creeping into my voice.

'He doesn't want to hear it.' Mum tuts. 'But if we can't get back on track by Christmas, I don't think we have any other choice but to sell to Raymond and Raymond. At least then we can get some money for this place.'

I don't know what to say. Sell Wonderland? How did we get into this mess? For months Dad has been saying how quiet the shop's been and I've dismissed him every time, when I should have been working harder and trying to bring in more sales. What would we even do without the bookshop? This is our livelihood, our legacy. I don't want to run Wonderland, but I can't imagine it not being in my life. And what would my parents do for money? Mum could go back to nursing, I guess, but what about Dad? Wonderland is all he's ever known. Selling the shop would destroy him.

Mum reaches for my hand. 'I don't want you to stress, baby. I'm sure we'll be able to find a way to fix things.' I want to believe her, but she sounds uncertain. 'Anyway, don't you have a party to go to?'

I ignore her question. 'I can stay and help with sales.'

Mum stands up with her arms outstretched and I follow suit. She has a small frame, but I find myself folding into her hug as if I'm a little boy. I thought I wanted to know what was happening at Wonderland, but now I wish I hadn't asked. The idea of losing this place makes me feel like someone is squeezing and twisting my stomach.

Mum pulls away and looks at me. 'It's Christmas. Go and have fun with your friends, okay?'

She pats my arm and I nod, but I'm not in the mood to party any more.

TWO

Ariel's playlist: 'Santa Baby' by Eartha Kitt

We pull up outside Bebe's house and I peer out of the car window in disbelief. It's three storeys high and is covered in Christmas lights, like a scene from a film or a Kardashian's Instagram post. I've never been to one of Bebe's parties, but I know they're legendary. The pictures alone on social media are enough to make anyone feel like a loser if they're not invited. And I'm not usually invited. But this time my best friend, Annika, who's Bebe's cousin, managed to get me and Jolie added to the guest list.

Annika leans over me to take a look at the house. Her long black weave snakes down her back. 'I told you this side of my family were rich and extra.'

The taxi driver taps his wheel impatiently, waiting for us to get out.

'I still don't get why she's having a party on a Wednesday,' I say. I've got an early class tomorrow and I've already planned not to stay long.

Annika laughs. 'Santi's and Blair's birthday is tomorrow and they told everyone to block out Friday and Saturday for a get-together. Not even Bebe is brave enough to face the wrath of Blair.'

I don't know anyone who would face it willingly, I think to myself.

'How's my make-up?' Jolie asks, and I squint. It's dark in the taxi, but she looks good to me.

'Perfect,' I reply with a smile.

'Okay, ready, girls?' Annika asks.

I'm not ready. This isn't my scene at all. I wish I was at home painting, or curled up in my bed tackling my to-be-read pile, but this is my last year of college and I promised myself that I'd try to be more sociable. I don't want to look back and have any regrets. I look down at my hands and notice there are still specks of red paint on them from a new piece I was working on earlier. I scratch at them and paint floats down onto my lap.

I step out of the car and pull down my short skirt. Before summer, I wouldn't have been able to fit into it, and I'm still not used to wearing clothes this revealing. Annika and Jolie follow behind me, dressed in equally short-fitting clothes, and Jolie ruffles her brown pixie cut so it looks spikier, adding height to her tiny stature.

'Don't tell, but I feel like I'm going to be sick,' Jolie whispers, her face looking paler than usual.

11

I don't feel too hot either. There's something about being around popular kids that makes me feel weird. I look back at the taxi wistfully but it drives off, as if the driver knows I want to get back into it.

Annika links arms with us. She's wearing a tight dress that fits her like a second skin. She hops from high-heeled foot to high-heeled foot. 'Come on, I'm freezing my tits off.'

We walk towards the front door and I can hear Drake asking Kiki if she loves him. The music is so loud that the base vibrates through my body, but I can still feel my heart beating nervously. What if Bebe's changed her mind and decided she only wants Annika at her party? I wouldn't be able to show my face in college again.

Annika rings the bell, and for a moment I think no one will even hear us over the music, but then the door opens and Bebe's standing there with a glass full of red liquid, flicking her long, black curls over her shoulder with her other hand. She looks gorgeous in an off-the-shoulder gold dress that complements her light brown skin. Her waist looks tiny and her lips look extra plumped. Everyone knows she gets fillers even though she swears she just overlines them. She looks at the three of us, her gaze lingering a little longer on me, but then she smiles, an actual genuine one, and my heart calms down.

'Welcome, girls!' She hugs Annika. 'Come in, come in. You're letting the heat out.'

Jolie squeals beside me and hurries inside. I walk in slowly and catch my breath. Everyone is dancing, talking, taking selfies. I can smell the sweat and hormones from the crowd. Who *are* all these people?

'Wow, good turn-out,' Annika says. 'Especially for a Wednesday.'

'Yeah. I told everyone to bring a friend and get themselves in the Christmas spirit.' Bebe takes a sip of her drink and her eyes pause on my bare legs. They're double the size of hers. She catches my eye and smiles, but this time it doesn't reach her eyes. I tug at my skirt, hoping it will cover me, but of course it doesn't.

A girl I vaguely recognize from college comes over and pulls Bebe towards the dance floor. 'Drinks and food are in the kitchen,' she manages to call over her shoulder as she walks away.

'Drink?' Annika asks, and Jolie nods.

I don't like alcohol – it makes me feel tired – but I don't want to be that girl who's a bore at the party.

'Lead the way,' I say.

We push through the crowd and I notice that, despite the room being full, everyone is still in their cliques. Bebe is downing shots on the dance floor with the popular kids from college, like Yarah Mectah and her boyfriend, James West. They're usually glued beside Trey Anderson, Boogs and the Bailey twins, although I can't see them anywhere tonight. I spot a few people I'm friendly with at college and wave. Annika says hi to more people than Jolie and me. She's one of those girls that can float from social group to social group and still act herself.

Annika and I have been friends since we were little kids and she's always had my back, especially when people have teased me about my weight. Her high cheekbones, long legs and smile that lights up her whole face haven't changed much since I first knew her. We met Jolie in secondary school. I thought with a name like Jolie Love-Jones, her symmetrical face and doe-like brown eyes with the longest lashes I've ever seen in real life, she was destined to be popular, but Jolie clicked with us straight away. She's the only person I know who agrees that *Twilight* is the greatest love story of all time. Hello, Bella became a vampire for love! The three of us have stuck together ever since.

Annika pours us drinks just as a cheer comes from the living room, where everyone is dancing. From where I'm standing, I can see Trey, Boogs and Santi as they walk into the party, waving at everyone.

'Trey looks good,' Annika says, handing me a drink and eyeing me closely. 'What do you think, Ariel?'

I roll my eyes as Jolie laughs. I had a crush on Trey the first time I saw him at college. Actually, I had a crush on Trey *and* Boogs. Most of the girls did. Boogs is light and slender, while Trey is dark-skinned and lean, but muscular like a hundred-metre athlete. Then Trey started dating Blair, and, well, if you've met Blair, anyone liking her would put you off. Which is weird because her twin, Santi, is nice to everyone. And Boogs is pretty cool. We bonded over art before he dropped out of class.

'Basic,' I respond, and Annika throws back her head and laughs.

Sometimes I think I'm the only one at college who's not obsessed with Trey, Boogs and the Bailey twins. The more they've grown in popularity, the more they've drawn people to their foursome. But after my crush died down, I've barely noticed them. We don't often cross paths in college because we're not on the same timetable, but sometimes when I'm grabbing lunch, I see them in the canteen, surrounded by people.

I take a sip of my drink and almost choke. 'What the hell?'

Annika laughs. 'Too strong?'

'I can't.' I hand the glass to her and watch with wide eyes as she downs it in one. I pray she doesn't get too wasted – I don't want to have to watch her all night.

I turn back to the living room and old-skool 90s hip-hop is blaring from the speakers. I love 90s music and I love to dance, so I drag Annika and Jolie to the dance floor and we form our own little space. Whatever insecurities I have always disappear when I'm dancing or painting.

'I love this song,' Jolie says, closing her eyes and swaying her hips. A cute mixed-raced boy begins to dance behind her. He whispers something in her ear and she turns round and dances with him.

I feel strong hands on my waist and, unlike Jolie, I don't appreciate it. I spin round, ready to cuss out whoever is behind me.

'Lil' Mermaid, you can move,' Boogs says, mimicking my dance moves, except he has that Boogs swag that no one can copy.

Boogs used to call me Ariel in a pretty-much-perfect Jamaican accent like Sebastian the crab, but when I walked into art with red hair one day he laughed out loud and said, 'Now you're asking for it!' He's called me Lil' Mermaid ever since.

I laugh. 'I swear I'm going to dye my hair black just so you stop calling me that.' I look round for Santi and catch her dancing with Trey. His shoulders are drooped and he's looking at the floor more than he is at Santi. I guess he's missing Blair.

Boogs leans in close and says, 'I saw your art piece in the courtyard. So sick.'

I blush at his compliment. Boogs might have a girlfriend, but, damn, he looks even more fine this close up. 'Thank you.'

A few weeks ago, Eden, the head of art, asked me to paint something 'uplifting' in the college courtyard, something that showed the beauty of nature, so I created a rainbow meadow with colourful flowers and butterflies. I could tell it was a hit when I saw some girls taking selfies in front of it for Instagram. There was this big unveiling and I was even in the local newspaper. Mum framed the article and now it hangs proudly in our living room.

Boogs takes out his phone and passes it to me. There's a picture on his Instagram of him and Santi posing in front of my art. They're a stunning couple and my backdrop complements them. I snort when I see the hashtag: *#ArielInSebastianVoice*.

'Any excuse,' I say.

Boogs laughs and pockets his phone. 'You love it really.'

We dance to song after song and end up creating a circle

16

with Jolie, Annika and a couple of guys. I don't know who they are, but they can dance and they're not trying to hit on us, so I'm fine with it. I'm pulling down my skirt for the millionth time just as Santi joins us and waves at me. She's wearing a floral-print, ruffled-hem dress that on any other girl would look meh, but on her it looks like it could be Balmain. Most girls would be pissed or possessive if you were dancing with their man, but not Santi. She's the type of secure I want to be.

'Where's Trey?' Boogs shouts over the music.

'I think he went to the bathroom,' Santi says. 'He's in such a mood. What's up with him?'

Boogs shrugs.

Someone pushes me to the side and I stumble, but I manage to catch myself, unlike Jolie who literally falls into the arms of a tall, broad guy.

'Oh, thank you,' she says with a hand on her chest. He grins and helps her upright, like a perfect scene from a romcom, before he looks up and stares across the room. Jolie frowns and follows his gaze.

'What's going on? I can't see,' Jolie says, her face flustered.

Annika laughs and nudges me. 'You've got to see this.'

I turn round and realize everyone is looking at the door, and that's when I spot Blair Bailey walk in, parting the crowd like she's the Queen of England. It's not a costume party, but she's wearing a sexy Santa outfit that consists of a cropped red-velvet top with white furry trim, a tiny matching skirt and red stilettos. She and Santi are both rocking the same long twist braids, but Blair's are piled on top of her head in a bun with red ribbon weaved through it.

'Blair Bailey,' I say, and Jolie tiptoes to see for herself.

I don't dislike Blair. To be honest, I don't know her that well. But on the rare occasions I've spoken to her she's always been so dismissive, and I have no clue why. It doesn't help that everyone fawns over her and treats her like she's Beyoncé. If anyone rules Corden College, it's her.

'I'm shocked she came,' Annika says. 'She was pissed at Bebe for having a party during her birthday week.'

That explains the Santa costume. I find Bebe in the crowd and she's smiling at Blair, but it's the type of smile she gave me – forced.

Blair waves someone over and Trey squeezes through the crowd. As soon as he's in arm's reach, she pulls him towards her by his shirt and kisses him passionately right in front of everyone. My mouth drops.

Annika laughs. 'Blair one, Bebe zero.'

THREE

Trey's playlist: 'This Christmas' by Mustard ft Ella Mai

Blair's cold hands are round my neck and I gently pull them off. I'm not in the mood for this. Why did I even come to Bebe's party? My mind is stuck on Wonderland. The idea of losing it is making me feel like someone has hit me hard in the gut. Maybe this is karma for all the times I've wished we didn't have the bookshop so I wouldn't have the pressure of taking it over. Blair searches my face, her thick eyelashes framing her cat-shaped eyes, as she tries to figure out what's wrong, but I don't want to embarrass her, especially with everyone watching.

We're 'that couple' at college, and whenever we've broken up we've always got back together again a few weeks later. Everyone thinks we're going to be with each other for ever, and maybe we are, but thinking that far ahead scares me a little.

At seventeen, how would I even know if she's the love of my life? I force my mouth to move so I can smile at her, gently stroking the side of her face. Blair closes her eyes and leans into my chest and I can hear people saying 'Awww'.

We walk hand in hand to the nearest sofa. My palm feels clammy but Blair doesn't seem to mind. I look up and it's like the entire party has followed us with their eyes. Usually I don't care, but I could do without the spotlight on me tonight. I sink into the soft cushions with my arms stretched out, trying to look like I'm relaxed. I've never told anyone this, but sometimes it feels like I'm playing a part. Blair waves at everyone as she sits down, perfect for the role, and then squeals when Santi and Boogs join us, as if she hasn't seen them in weeks.

Bebe is standing by us, her eyes never leaving Blair. She looks like she ate something sour. I catch her eye and her face instantly changes to a smile. I guess I'm not the only one pretending.

'I'll get us a drink,' I say in Blair's ear before I stand up.

I'm stopped multiple times as I head towards the kitchen. I try to keep moving, motioning that I'm getting a drink, which helps to get people to back off for a second. The kitchen is pretty empty when I get there and I feel like I can finally breathe. There's only one person by the drinks, a thick, red-haired Black girl in a short skirt and fitted, sparkly top. I can't remember her name, but I think she painted the artwork in the courtyard. I linger a second longer on her legs. Nice.

I don't know how the next bit happens, but I go to reach for a glass at the same time she turns, and her drink ends up down my fresh white top. I jump back and she covers her mouth, her black-framed glasses hanging at the edge of her nose.

'Oh! I'm so sorry!' She starts looking around the kitchen for a cloth or something.

What is it with today? I touch the wet patch and it's sticky and smells like Coke.

'Here.' She starts to rub my T-shirt with a bundle of tissues, making the stickiness touch my skin.

'It's fine.' I grab the tissues from her, much harsher than I meant to, and she looks at me, surprised.

She pushes up her glasses and says with a frown, 'It was an accident.'

'Whatever.' I turn on my heel. I'm over this stupid party.

I walk quickly through the crowd, keeping my head down so I can avoid everyone, especially Blair, who I know will beg me to stay. I grab my coat from the closet and leave.

As soon as I get outside, I zip up my coat, lift my head to the clear, black sky and take a deep breath, filling my lungs with the cold, sharp air. It's freezing out here and I wonder if it's going to snow this year. It never seems to snow around Christmastime. It's always some random month, like February. On the last snow day, Boogs and I helped Reon create a superhero snowman – the kid is obsessed with superheroes. Thank God for Boogs, because between him and Reon's artistic eye they actually made an Instagram-worthy snowman that managed to stay intact for three days.

'Trey?'

The sound of music fills the air for a moment but it's silenced once Boogs shuts the door. He's only in a T-shirt and jeans, but he's been working up a sweat from dancing so I'm sure he can't even feel the cold.

'You good?' he asks.

I open up my coat so he can see the huge, brown stain on my white T-shirt. Boogs puts his fist to his mouth.

'Oh shit, what happened?'

'Some girl spilled her drink on me.' I re-zip my coat. 'That was the last straw. I'm going home.'

'What else happened? You've been in a mood all night,' Boogs replies concerned.

I scuff my trainer on the ground. 'Mum said Wonderland's in trouble.'

Boogs' mouth drops open. 'Swear down?'

I fill him in and he only interrupts once, to say, 'Sell? You can't *sell* Wonderland!'

I shrug. 'I know, but unless things change I dunno what our options are. I wish there was something I could do to help ... but what?'

'Sorry, bro, that's rough. Don't worry though – you'll think of something. Wonderland isn't going anywhere.' Boogs gives a reassuring smile.

That's easy for him to say, but I don't see how we can keep the bookshop if we're in debt. We need money quickly, and there's only so many customers a day.

'So ... Blair's outfit?' Boogs raises his eyebrows and I laugh. He always knows the right time to lighten the mood.

'You know that was just to piss off Bebe, right?' I say with a smirk.

'Blair is the definition of petty.' Boogs wraps his arms round his body. 'Damn, it's cold. Look, don't go, man. Hang out – it will make you feel better.'

'Nah, I'm really not in the mood.' I glance back at the house. 'I'll message Blair. You go have fun.'

We dap and Boogs walks back to the house. I hover for a moment, unsure whether to order a taxi, but it seems wasteful now I know about Wonderland's money issues. Instead, I put my hands into my coat pockets and start the walk up towards Highbury station so I can catch a bus home.

I open the front door and instantly hear a film playing loudly in the living room. Mum and Dad are cuddled up on the sofa under the twinkling fairy lights of the Christmas tree. Mum pauses the film when she sees me.

'You're home early,' she says, confused.

'Yeah, I wasn't feeling it. What are you watching?' I ask, quickly changing the subject.

'*Love Actually*,' Mum says, and Dad shakes his head. I stifle a laugh. Mum loves that film, but Dad hates it. 'There's some dinner left for you if you're hungry, baby.'

As soon as Mum mentions dinner, I realize how hungry I am, but first I need to take off this sticky top and shower. I'm praying the stain comes out. I go upstairs and peer into Reon's room, immediately spotting the torchlight under his duvet.

'I can see you,' I sing, and the torchlight instantly goes out.

I switch on the main light and pull down the duvet, and my ten-year-old brother frowns at me. While I clearly took my dad's genes, Reon's a miniature version of Mum, even down to the same one dimple in his cheek.

'Hey!' Reon says.

'You're meant to be asleep,' I say firmly.

Reon groans. 'Can I have five more minutes? I want to see what happens next with Shuri.'

I gave Reon access to my old Marvel comics last week, and he's spent all his free time since then reading them. He's a really good artist and his room is covered in his drawings of Thor, Spider-Man and Black Panther, which suddenly gives me an idea.

'You can have ten more minutes if you design me a birthday card for Blair before you go to school tomorrow. Maybe draw her in a manga style?'

'You know there are different types of manga, right? There's Shōjo, Josei ... which one do you want?' Reon asks.

God knows. 'You decide,' I say quickly.

He shrugs. 'Okay, but I want *fifteen* minutes, *and* you have to take me and Noah to the cinema.'

'Who's Noah?'

'My best friend from my Saturday art class. He's really good. His sister sometimes teaches us,' Reon replies.

I sigh and Reon grins. He knows he's won.

'Fine, but fifteen minutes and it's lights out.'

'Thanks, Trey.' Reon disappears back under his duvet with his torch and comic book and I smile. The kid just played me.

FOUR

Ariel's playlist: 'Every Year, Every Christmas'
by Luther Vandross

What the hell is Trey's problem? Honestly, like I meant to spill my drink on him? I don't even know why I'm surprised: he has to be a diva if he's dating Blair. I watch him as he walks out of the front door without saying a word to anyone.

I throw the used tissues in the bin and wash the sticky Coke off my hands before I grab another drink and head to the living room. I can feel the change in the party's atmosphere as soon as I step back in. Everyone is gathered around the popular kids, and the others are scattered about, unsure what to do with themselves. There's now only a small huddle on the dance floor. Jolie is still dancing with the same boy from earlier, but Annika's nowhere to be seen. It's funny how one person in a Santa outfit can change the whole dynamic.

My shoes are digging into my feet as I continue walking, and I'm convinced the pain is making me hobble. I don't usually wear heels so I purposefully bought a pair with a solid heel that the sales assistant promised would be pain-free. So not true! I search for somewhere to sit and eventually find a spot on the stairs outside the living room. Thank you, God!

I sigh as I sit, taking off one of my shoes and leaning forward so I can massage out the pain. I'm already dreading having to put it back on.

The music's now in the 2000s era and Ja Rule is blasting through the speakers. From where I'm sitting, I can see Jolie talking animatedly with the guy she's dancing with. She's so short she only comes up to the guy's torso.

I close my eyes briefly as I massage into my heel.

'Don't tell me you're done dancing? Come on, let's go for it,' a deep voice says.

I open my eyes and Boogs is leaning on the banister. I sit up quickly, aware that my top has a deep neckline and I don't want him sneaking a peek. I shake my head. 'I don't have your stamina.'

Boogs flexes his muscles. 'That's what Santi says.'

'Spare me, please!' I laugh. 'Besides, you try all your moves in these heels and see how long *you* last.' I hesitate before continuing. 'Trey okay?' Boogs raises an eyebrow at me. 'I mean, I spilled my drink on him and then he left.'

'Oh, so you're the culprit!'

'It was an accident,' I say quickly.

26

Boogs shakes his head. 'Trust me, Trey's got bigger issues than a spilled drink.'

I want to ask him what he means, but I stop myself. I don't want him thinking I'm being nosy. Boogs looks back at the party and starts bopping his head in time to the music. I can tell he's itching to dance and I can't help but smile. I swear the house could be on fire and Boogs would be dancing out of the door.

'Where's your crew?' he asks, snapping me back into the moment.

I point. 'Jolie's over there, but I can't find Annika.'

Boogs walks into the living room and looks left and right. He returns a few seconds later. 'She's with Bebe.'

I'll leave her to it, I think to myself. The last thing I want to deal with is Bebe looking me up and down, making me feel like a weirdo for trying to talk to my best friend. It's already half ten, which I know is still early for a party, but I told myself I wouldn't leave late and I can't see myself getting back in the mood now. I'm ready to take off this make-up, put on my pyjamas and watch re-runs of *Sister, Sister* on Netflix.

'Wild Thoughts' plays over the speakers and Boogs breaks into a perfect Salsa step. I put on my shoe, grimacing as I stand up. My feet are practically begging me to be released from the prison I've put them in.

'I'm going to call it a night,' I say.

'But the party's just getting started,' Boogs replies with a frown.

I raise my eyebrows. We obviously have two very different definitions of a good party. In the living room, Blair stands up

27

from the sofa and starts looking around. It's clear who she's searching for and Boogs notices too.

He groans. 'Trey said he would tell her. There's no way I'm going to.'

'Why?' I ask curiously.

'So she can have one of her freak-outs? Then she'll want to leave – Santi too, and I'll have to go as well. This music's a bit of me.'

I laugh. Boogs is literally in his own dance world. 'I'm out of here,' I tell him and lean over, and Boogs stops moving long enough to give me a hug. 'See you at college.'

'Bye, Lil' Mermaid.' He smiles and wanders back over to the dance floor.

I walk up to Jolie, who's still talking to the same guy. They both have a drink in their hands.

'I'm gonna go,' I say.

Jolie's face drops. 'No, stay! Dance with us?'

The guy smiles awkwardly at me.

'No, I'm tired. I'll see you tomorrow, okay?' I point at the drink in her hand. 'How many have you had?'

Jolie laughs. 'A few. Don't worry – I feel fine.'

'Hmm, text me when you get home?'

'Will do,' she promises.

We hug and I wave to the guy, who holds up his drink to me. I try to wave to get Annika's attention, but she's busy talking to Bebe and doesn't see me. I'll text her later. I just want to get out of here.

*

When I get home, I see Mum asleep in the living room with the TV on in the background. I gently nudge her until her eyes flicker and focus on me.

'Hi, darling. What time is it?'

'Just gone eleven. I texted you when I was in the taxi,' I reply.

Mum yawns and stretches. 'Sorry, I was waiting up and didn't even realize I was falling asleep. How was it?'

'It was okay. Bebe's house is gorgeous.' I pull off my heels and sigh loudly, making Mum laugh. 'Why isn't it perfectly acceptable to go to parties in trainers? I feel like I've walked the whole of Hackney.'

Mum tuts. 'You're so dramatic. When I was your age, I practically lived in heels. I couldn't keep the boys away!'

I roll my eyes as I sit down. 'Well, a guy will have to take me in my old Converse with paint all over my jeans and be satisfied with that.'

Mum pats my leg. 'I'm glad you went out,' she says. 'I know you love nothing more than staying in and painting, but you're only seventeen once.'

I gasp. 'Are you actually encouraging me to go out to parties on a school night? Work hard, play hard?'

'Well, maybe not too hard,' Mum says, and I laugh and snuggle into her. 'It's been rough, hasn't it?' For a moment my body tenses. 'But as long as we stick together, we'll be all right.'

I glance up at her, expecting to see her eyes watery like they often are whenever she talks about Dad, but for once she seems okay. 'Rough' doesn't even compare to how I feel. It's more like 'broken'. We went from a family of four to three in the space of a few hours, and ever since then there's been this giant piece missing from our lives. It took months before we could go a whole day without one of us breaking down in tears, and even longer for the house to be filled with laughter again. I had to step up and help Mum look after my little brother, Noah. I had to make sense of all the bills that Dad would have paid. And, sometimes, I had to parent Mum when she couldn't get out of bed. It's been almost a year since Dad passed now, and somehow we've got through it.

'We'll always stick together,' I say before I kiss Mum's cheek.

FIVE

Trey's playlist: 'Someday at Christmas' by Mario

Sixteen days till Christmas

I wake up to the sound of my phone buzzing on the bookshelf next to my bed. There's no way it's time for college already.

'Hello?' I answer, my eyes still closed.

'Are you serious, Trey?' Blair shouts down the phone. 'You just leave me at a party without so much as a text? You didn't even comment on my outfit. I wore it for you!'

That's a lie.

'What?' I say dumbly, and Blair takes in a deep breath.

'You better have bought me an amazing present,' she hisses before the line goes dead.

Great. Now I have a headache. I knead my forehead with my fingers. If I don't manage to wow Blair, today is going to go from bad to worse. I jump out of bed and head to Reon's room. His voice carries upstairs as he tells Dad about some art project he's doing. On his bed is the birthday card for Blair, and it looks just like her, even down to the pink bag she takes everywhere. It's perfect.

I shower and get dressed before I write in the card, head downstairs to the kitchen and thank Reon, then grab a piece of toast. Mum is sitting at the table with her laptop and I say bye as I head for the door.

'Wait – isn't it Blair's birthday today? What did you get her?' she asks before I leave.

I show her the birthday card and Mum glares at me. 'A birthday card made by Reon? Trey, that isn't enough when you've been dating for almost two years.'

I grimace. 'I know, I know . . . but I forgot. Any advice?'

Mums takes off her glasses. 'Girls like to be romanced. Do something that's from the heart.'

'Thanks, I will,' I say, even though I've got nothing.

I close the front door behind me and Boogs is already waiting outside so we can walk to college together. He's holding a dozen red roses and has a cheesy grin on his face.

'What the hell, man?' Is he just trying to make me look shit? Santi's really changed him. Boogs didn't even pay for dates before. 'Why didn't you tell me you were doing flowers?'

'Hey, don't be mad that I'm on point.' He gestures to my hand. 'Is that Blair's card?'

'Yeah.' I show it to him and he nods in approval, but I know what Blair's going to think when Boogs gives Santi her presents. She'll feel like crap. And guess whose fault that will be.

'How are you feeling after yesterday?' Boogs asks as we start to walk.

I sigh. 'The same. I just wish there was something I could do to help.'

We continue in silence and I can't help but window shop as we turn onto the high street. I'm hoping I'll see something last minute that screams romance but is also cheap.

'Yo, I've got an idea.' Boogs grabs my arm and I stop. 'You know how the twins are doing that pizza and chill at their house?'

'Yeah, so?' Blair was so annoyed that they couldn't throw a proper birthday party, but then their parents are taking them to the Bahamas for New Year, so I don't feel too bad for them.

'We should scrap it and throw them a surprise birthday party instead. Blair would especially love it.'

'Erm ...' I begin, but Boogs waves his hands in my face, cutting me off.

'Hear me out. This could help the bookshop too!' he says excitedly. 'We organize the party for tomorrow, invite some people from college, but we charge a tenner a head.'

I scoff. 'Who's going to pay that?'

Boogs stares at me. 'Are you kidding? A party thrown by us will be packed out.' I hesitate. He's not wrong. People would turn up. 'We can get that girl – what's her name ... ?' He clicks his fingers as he tries to remember. 'Bev Smith. She can make the cake. She works at the bakery, right? And we'd need a theme, cause girls love that, so how about ... a pink party! To get in, people have to pay and wear pink.'

I pinch the bridge of my nose, my head suddenly pounding even more. 'That sounds like a lot to organize in one day. And where exactly are we meant to host this party?'

Boogs slaps my arm. 'At the bookshop!'

I laugh out loud, expecting Boogs to join in, but he's dead serious. 'You think my parents will let me throw a party at work?'

'Just say you're doing a stocktake,' he replies, deadpan.

I roll my eyes. 'By myself?'

'Say I'm helping you to check stock for the January sales or something. Who cares, Trey? This is genius. Any money we make from the party goes straight to the bookshop.'

On the surface, it sounds good, but I can think of a million things that could go wrong, and Wonderland doesn't need any more shit to deal with. 'I don't know, man.'

'Come on, Trey! The bookshop can fit how many people?' Boogs asks.

'Seventy, maybe?'

Boogs is practically jumping with excitement now. 'Bro, that's seven hundred pounds.'

That gets my attention. 'You really think we can pull it off? We'd have to get everything done today.'

'Hell yeah! Look, I can pay for the cake, some balloons and drinks—'

'No drinks!' I interrupt. 'I can't have spills on the floor or the books.'

'Bro, we can't have an eighteenth birthday party without alcohol! We'll move the books on the display tables to the

34

basement. And maybe we can get some sheets or something to cover the bookshelves? Don't worry – I'll be on it, and I'll make sure there are no spills.'

It's a mad idea, but a brilliant one, and at this point any money for Wonderland is a good thing.

'Okay, I'm in.' We dap and I take the opportunity to steal one of Boogs' roses before breaking into a run.

'Hey!' he yells after me.

'Sorry, I need it!' I shout over my shoulder. Mum said *romance*. I can do romance.

Corden College is a five-storey building that they modernized a few years ago. It has massive glass windows, so from the outside you can see students walking up and down the stairs and the lift going from floor to floor. I run into college and I can see Blair and Santi at our usual place in the small lounge, sitting on the wooden tables and surrounded by our friends. My hands are starting to sweat, but I need to do this for Blair. *Come on, Trey.* I stop and straighten out my clothes. *For Blair.*

I take a deep breath, close my eyes and start to sing the chorus of 'The Most Beautiful Girl In The World' by Prince. I quickly open my eyes to check I've got Blair's attention and I see everyone looking at me. I shut them again and keep singing. When I finally reach the end of the chorus, everyone in the lounge breaks into a round of applause. I exhale and give a mock bow, and, when I straighten up, I see Blair with her hand over her mouth in shock. Santi claps her hands to her chest looking like she's about to cry. I reach Blair and hand her the birthday card and the rose. 'Happy birthday, babe.' My heart is going crazy, but it's over. I did it.

'Trey! That was epic!' Blair tiptoes and kisses me, leaving strawberry lip gloss on my mouth. 'Best present ever!'

'That was so romantic,' Santi sighs.

'Oh, I wish my man would do that.' Yarah elbows James. 'Why don't you do romantic shit for me?' James splutters as he tries to respond.

I lean in close so my lips brush Blair's ear. 'And I meant every word.'

'Baby!' Blair squeezes me tight.

'That was not cool.' Boogs' voice breaks me and Blair apart. He's sweating in his winter jacket and some of the roses look like they've fallen on the floor and got trampled on. He glares at me. 'You think you're slick?'

Thankfully, I'm saved by Santi, who gasps when she sees the flowers in his hand. 'These are so beautiful!' She skips over to Boogs and squeals as she hugs him. He's still giving me a killer look over Santi's shoulder, but thankfully Blair misses it as she's too busy smelling the rose in her hand.

'Babe, you missed Trey singing to Blair,' Santi says, holding the flowers.

'Oh, a song?' Boogs raises his eyebrows. 'When did you plan that?'

I shrug. 'It's been up my sleeve for a few weeks now.'

'Trey is very romantic,' Blair says knowingly. 'I knew he wouldn't let me down.'

'Yep, Trey is so thoughtful,' Boogs says with an edge to his voice.

I plead with my eyes for him to shut the hell up. Before the twins can pick up on his tone, I gesture for them to sit down.

'Now, I know you wanted to do something low-key for your birthday—'

'Santi wanted to,' Blair interrupts me.

Santi tuts. 'We're going to the Bahamas! Pizza and chill is fine, and people can stay over if they want. It will be fun.'

Blair rolls her eyes.

'Well, Boogs and I have something really special planned.' I grin.

'What is it?' they ask at the same time.

I used to be fascinated when I first met them and they did their twin thing.

'It's a surprise, but it's going to be amazing!' I reply. *Or it will be if we can pull it off.*

SIX

Ariel's playlist: 'Silent Night' by The Temptations

This is it! I pick up the bulky letter from the floor and hold it close to my chest. I've been waiting ages for the Artists' Studio to send me an application form. I had to submit a portfolio with my best work to even get to this stage. It's where all the top-tier artists study.

I hurry past the kitchen where Mum is sorting out breakfast and go to the living room, sinking into the sofa and ripping open the letter. Ever since I was a kid I've wanted to go to the Artists' Studio. Dad attended and he always used to tell me stories about his time there. After he passed, I decided it was time to follow in his footsteps, and I know he'd be so proud of me if he was still here today. For a moment, my chest feels tight, like it always does when I remember that Dad isn't with us any more. I close my eyes, taking in deep breaths until I feel normal again. Dad would be happy for me and I need to focus on that.

I scan the letter to double check if they still take their students for a week to Art Basel in Switzerland ... *Yes, they do!* I gasp as I continue reading and have to lift my glasses and wipe my eyes to double check I've read the next sentence correctly. One student will have their work displayed in the National Gallery in Trafalgar Square for the weekend. This is basically all my dreams come true!

My high doesn't last long once I see the price I'll have to pay if I get accepted on the course. Who can even afford to go to this place? There's one scholarship, but there's bound to be tough competition for it. I know Mum will do her best to help pay for it – she wants me to attend just as much as I do – but she doesn't make much money at her supermarket job.

There must be a way I can contribute to the fees. Maybe if I find a job I can start saving the money to pay towards the tuition. I glance back down at the letter and scan through the questions on the form ... *'How has your art made a change to your local community?'*

I tap my fingers on the armrest. How has my art made a change? The only artwork I've done in a community space was in the courtyard at college, which I doubt is enough to get me on the course. I need something epic, something that screams *I'm Ariel Spencer and you need me at the Artists' Studio!*

But I've got nothing.

'Ariel! Noah! Breakfast is ready,' Mum calls.

I take the letter and application form with me and sit at the kitchen table next to an already-waiting Noah. Mum glances at it. She's in her supermarket uniform with her hair braided back into a bun.

'What's that, darling?'

'The application for the Artists' Studio came. Mum, it sounds so perfect, and there's an open day soon. But the deadline to submit the form is the thirty-first of January and the deposit needs to be paid as soon as they confirm whether I have a place on the course.'

'That's brilliant! When will you know?' Mum asks.

'It says mid-February.'

'Let me have a read.' Mum sits down and I hand the letter over.

I'm already anticipating her reaction when she sees the fees and, true enough, her face doesn't disappoint. She drops the letter like it's on fire and it hits the table with a *boom*, making Noah jump and spill his bowl of cereal.

'Are they joking?' Mum asks. 'This is way more than I thought they charged.'

I grab a cloth and wipe up the milk. 'I know, and there's not even a payment plan, but I was thinking I could get a part-time job. There must be loads of Christmas temp positions flying around.'

'I don't know, honey.' Mum gets to her feet as the toast pops up from the toaster. It's slightly burnt, just how I like it. She hands one to Noah too. 'You've already got a lot on your plate at college,' she says, 'and don't forget you're going to be working at The Grotto in a couple of weeks selling your cards.'

When I don't respond, Mum stares at me. 'You are still doing it this year, right?'

'It feels weird without Dad . . .' I mumble.

'Oh, darling.' Mum puts an arm round me. 'Dad would want you to do it.'

'Maybe.' I walk to the counter and grab the butter and jam. 'But it doesn't earn me anywhere near enough money. Let me at least look around and see if I can get a job so I can save more towards the deposit.'

'Will you buy me some new paints?' Noah interrupts with his mouth full of toast. Noah recently got into art and Mum enrolled him in a local art class. He gets to go for free because I sometimes volunteer there. I would so love to have a job there, but it's a small organization and I know they don't have any vacancies.

'Don't talk with your mouth full, Noah. And, Ariel, I don't want your college work suffering—'

'It won't,' I protest.

Mum eyeballs me, but eventually sighs. 'Fine.'

I blow her a kiss and bite into my toast. Now all that's left to do is find a Christmas job.

I arrive at college with two minutes to spare, weaving in and out of the crowds while holding a massive poster in my arms and hoping nobody bumps into me.

'Ariel!'

I turn round and Annika hurries over. She's in a skin-tight black jumper dress, leather boots and a bomber jacket, making me wish I'd made more of an effort than just the faded ill-fitting jeans and checked shirt under my coat. I always dress a bit meh when I'm painting, so, yeah, that's most days. Annika's holding my favourite gingerbread latte for me in a red cup.

'Sorry, I should have told you I was running late.' I look down at my full arms.

'I'll walk you to art with your coffee,' she says, flashing a smile. 'Everything okay?'

'The Artists' Studio finally sent me an application form, which is great. But if I'm accepted onto the course, I have to pay a pretty big deposit, so I need to find a Christmas job ASAP. Do you know of any going?' I ask.

'Okay, first of all, that's amazing, girl!' Annika says, gently nudging me. 'Christmas temp roles in retail are usually gone by now, but check in the foyer. There are always job ads up on the noticeboard.'

'Thanks, Annika,' I reply with a smile.

'You missed the most romantic display this morning,' Annika says, changing the subject.

I raise my eyebrows. 'Romance? At Corden College?'

'I know, right? Trey literally serenaded Blair with a song and a rose. Where can I get a guy like that?'

I sigh. I doubt a guy would ever do anything that nice for me.

Annika walks with me into the art room and sits down while the class waits for our teacher, Eden. I take off my coat and green scarf before laying out the poster on the table.

Annika gasps. 'Girl, this is gorgeous!'

'You think?' I watch as she takes in the poster and my

heart starts racing. I always get so nervous when someone is looking at my art. It's like baring my soul in paint. 'I wanted to see what my courtyard display would look like as pop art. I'm trying to channel Warhol.'

'I mean, these colours are wow!'

Just then, Eden walks in, wearing her usual black attire, her curly hair big and bouncy. Annika stands up and hands me my drink.

'See you at lunch,' she says, and I wave as she walks off.

Eden's my favourite teacher. She's only thirty, so she feels more like a friend. And despite us being in Hackney, she's one of the few Black teachers at college. She's so pretty and all the boys love her – I'm convinced that's the real reason Boogs took art in the first place.

Eden doesn't waste any time and lets us get back to working on our portfolios. I gather some paints and take them to my table, and I see Eden standing there, inspecting my pop art. Whenever she's reviewing any of the class's pieces, she keeps her face completely blank for a few seconds before she breaks into a smile or a frown. Today I get a smile with teeth.

'Wow, Ariel! I love this.'

'Thanks, Eden. I was planning on adding a bit more red over here.' I point to the section and she nods.

'Yep, that will really bring it together.'

'So, guess what? This morning I heard back from the Artists' Studio,' I say, and Eden claps her hands together, drawing attention from everyone in the room.

'Sorry, guys, ignore me,' she calls out, and everyone goes

back to their own worlds. 'Ariel, that's incredible! You must be so excited.'

'Yeah, I am. The thing is, though, it's really expensive,' I reply quietly.

'What about the scholarship?' Eden asks.

I shrug. 'I'll try for it, but I don't want to put all my hopes on getting it, you know?'

'With your talent, you'll get in regardless. Plus, I'll write you a killer recommendation letter.' Eden smiles at me and I know with her support my application will be even stronger.

'Thank you. That would be great. One of the questions on the form is how has my art made a change to my local community. Does the courtyard count?'

Eden frowns and her tiny nose scrunches up. 'You have to think bigger than that. Ask yourself how your art can make Stoke Newington better. What can you create that will make people feel how you and I feel when we look at art? It needs to be something that will make people stop.'

I sigh. I have no clue. Creating artwork for college was tough enough, as I constantly worried what other students would think, but impressing the whole of Hackney is an even harder job. On the one hand, the community appreciates the iconic Hackney Peace Carnival mural in Dalston, but then on the other, Hackney Council painted over a Banksy! They eventually restored it, but only after major intervention ... some ten years later! And I've seen countless other pieces of amazing street art that have been spray-painted over. Just thinking about it makes me feel nauseous.

Eden pats my shoulder and says, 'It will come to you, Ariel. I'm sure whatever you create will be magical.'

I really hope she's right.

SEVEN

Trey's playlist: 'Rudolph the Red-Nosed Reindeer' by DMX

I'm in English when everyone's phones go off at the same time. I look up just as Mr Johnson does too from marking papers. He stands up, showing off his trousers that are way too short for him, and puts his hands on his waist.

'Phones off. You all know the rules.'

I take out my phone and switch it to silent mode. But as I do I see that Boogs has added me as well as what looks like the whole of college to a WhatsApp group called 'Surprise Party at Wonderland'. I skim the message and grin when I get to the final line: 'TELL THE TWINS AND YOUR INVITE IS CANCELLED'. But there are so many people in the group and there's no way the bookshop can fit everyone ... I start tapping my pen nervously on my workbook.

'Trey!' Mr Johnson barks.

'Oh, sorry, sir.' I immediately stop.

By the time I look at my phone again it's lunchtime, and I have over one hundred notifications from the group chat. People are buzzing about the party, which is sick, but I really hope everyone doesn't turn up.

I walk into the canteen and spot Boogs and James at our usual table. James always looks like he's just rolled out of bed, with his rumpled, baggy clothes and uncombed, mousy-brown hair.

'Am I great or what?' Boogs says.

'Yeah, but you've invited way too many people!' I reply.

'That's what's genius about it – everyone will be fighting to get in! But don't worry – I'll make sure the shop's not over capacity. You better not let me down with the venue after all this work.'

'I won't, I won't,' I mumble.

'Pink? Really?' James says. 'I don't have to pay, right?'

'Everyone's paying,' Boogs replies very seriously.

Bebe and Yarah join us and our table quickly fills up. The twins arrive last, wearing plastic tiaras and badges that read: 'It's my birthday, bitch!'

'I'm having the best day! I wish it was my birthday every day,' Blair says, sitting next to me. She turns and waves. 'Annika! Come sit with us.'

I look up and Annika is standing with a girl whose name I don't remember, but she's the red-head that spilled the drink on me at Bebe's party last night. I feel kind of bad that I was rude to her.

'Why is Annika bringing *her*?' Blair says under her breath as Annika walks over with her friend.

'Happy birthday, twins!' Annika says and grins. 'You know my girl, Ariel? You mind if she sits?'

'Of course.' Santi taps the chair next to her and the girl sits, but Blair purses her lips.

'What's good, Annika?' I say. I like Annika. She's herself around everyone, and it's rare to meet people like that.

'Trey!' She places her hands on her heart. 'Your singing voice is to die for. I swear I'll be first in line when you headline Wembley.'

I look at the table and feel my cheeks flush. 'Thanks.'

Blair leans over and kisses my cheek. 'My baby is so talented.'

'Lil' Mermaid!' Boogs suddenly yells, and the girl with the red hair rolls her eyes and smiles. *Ariel – that's her name ...* but how does Boogs know her?

The question must show on my face because Ariel says, 'We used to do art together.' At the same time she reaches for her drink and it wobbles.

I reach out to steady it. 'We don't want another spill,' I say under my breath. I'm not sure if she hears me, but she looks away.

'I only dropped art so she could stand out,' Boogs says, making everyone laugh. 'Now she's all famous and shit for the painting in the courtyard.'

'So, tell me, what presents have you got?' Annika asks the twins.

48

Blair stretches out her arm showing off a gold bracelet that pops against her dark skin. 'Mum and Dad got us one of these each, but Santi doesn't like it.'

'It's not that I don't like it,' Santi says. 'It's just not very me. Boogs bought me the new Estee Mase, which is more my vibe.'

I glance at Boogs and he winks at me, but I mouth 'Traitor', and he jerks his head back like I've slapped him. Did he think I'd forget that he didn't buy the book from Wonderland?

Blair scoffs. 'It's beyond sad that you're happy with a book for your eighteenth.'

'Says the girl who's dating a bookseller!' Santi glares at her.

'Hey! Keep me out of this mess,' I say, and everyone around the table chuckles. 'But for the record, I love a book for my birthday.'

'Me too,' Ariel says in a small voice.

'You see! Someone with taste. What do you like?' Santi asks Ariel.

Blair tuts and turns away to talk to Yarah. She doesn't like book talk.

'I'll admit, I do like Estee Mase,' Ariel says and Santi claps her hands. 'To be honest, I devour anything YA.'

We used to have a YA book club at Wonderland that was pretty popular for a while, but Dad didn't like hosting the events after hours so it stopped.

'Just don't get her started on *Twilight*,' Annika says. 'Her and Jolie drive me wild when they talk about it.'

'*Twilight*?' I say, surprised.

'I actually hate the librarian for recommending it to her and putting me through this torture,' Annika continues, and Ariel playfully nudges her.

I remember the bookshop being flooded with customers wanting to buy a copy. That summer my parents took me to Disneyland, so, yeah, I guess I owe it to Edward and Bella's weird relationship for one of the best summers of my life.

'It's an amazing love story!' Ariel argues.

I don't know if it's because I'm around books every day, but I swear I'm programmed to have an opinion on any form of literature.

'I have to disagree,' I say, and Ariel gasps. 'I read it once to see what all the fuss was about, and that book is weird as hell. Edward is literally telling Bella that they can't be together cause he'll kill her, and Bella's just like, okay, sure, can we have sex now?'

Annika and Santi laugh. Ariel's staring at me with a look on her face that I can't read. I wasn't trying to be forceful with my opinion, but come on, *Twilight* is not a great love story. It's weird as fuck.

'I think you're wrong,' Ariel says forcefully. 'I look at it more like Bella's so madly in love that she'd do anything to be with Edward. She would literally die for him. How many relationships are like that?'

She plays with her chicken and limp salad, and I stare at the specks of paint on her hands. I never really thought about the book like that. Maybe Edward Cullen has more game than I thought. I can't even get my girlfriend to read a book I love, let alone turn into a vampire for me.

EIGHT

Ariel's playlist: 'A Child Is Born' by Rihanna

I'm waiting for Trey to argue back, so I'm surprised when he says:

'Maybe I should re-read it then.'

I look up at him, trying to gauge if he's taking the piss, but he seems genuine.

'Did Ariel just school a bookseller on a book?' Santi says.

Trey laughs and his whole face comes alive.

Okay, so sitting with the cool kids isn't as awkward as I thought it would be. When Annika first told me she'd agreed to eat lunch with this lot, I'd tried to think of any excuse to get out of it, especially because Jolie's not at college today. She texted us this morning to say she had the hangover of all hangovers.

I look around the table and notice Blair and Bebe whispering about something. I don't get them. Didn't Blair completely outshine Bebe at her own party last night? They sneak a glance at me and their eyes flicker down to my hands before they laugh quietly to themselves. I suddenly get a sinking feeling in my stomach. Annika was in such a rush to get the peri-peri chicken that's on the menu today that I didn't get a chance to wash my hands properly after art. I quickly hide them under the table.

'You can tell a lot about a girl when she can't even look after her hands,' Bebe loudly whispers, staring right at me.

My heart starts to race. Annika's talking to Santi and completely misses it. She would have cussed Bebe and Blair out if she'd heard. I want to stick up for myself for once so they leave me alone, but what do I say?

Trey clears his throat. 'I think it's so cool that some people are naturally artistic. My little brother is constantly drawing and painting and his hands are always covered in paint, but that's the sign of a true artist, right?'

I'm surprised that Trey is coming to my rescue, but I thank him with my eyes and he nods, acknowledging it.

Blair runs her hand up his neck. 'Trey *loves* what I do with *my* hands.'

'Blair, please,' Santi says, pulling a face as everyone laughs. Trey shakes his head, smiling at the same time.

I force myself to join in with the laughter. But now that we're not talking about books, I go back to wondering what I'm even doing here.

'Trey, have you got any vacancies at the bookshop?' Annika suddenly asks. 'Ariel's looking for a job.'

'Oh, you are?' Trey asks, his perfectly arched eyebrows raising. I wonder if he plucks them.

I swallow my lukewarm chicken. 'Yeah. Where's your bookshop?'

'Wonderland on Stokey High Street.'

'No way! I've been there a few times but I've never seen you around,' I reply, surprised.

'Guess we must have missed each other. We don't have any vacancies at the moment, but you could come down and talk to my mum. If anything, she might know someone who's looking to hire.' Trey smiles at me and I'm not expecting to feel the jolt that goes through my body. My crush on him disappeared ages ago . . . or so I thought.

Blair has her arm resting on his shoulders and her perfect hands are casually hanging down over his chest, making it very clear who Trey belongs to. Bebe leans forward and instantly my guard comes up. She looks at me for a few seconds, squinting her eyes as if she can't see me properly.

'Has your hair always been that colour?'

My hair is red like Rihanna on the 'Loud' album. It took me a while to get the right shade and I love it, but the way Bebe is staring at me now is making me wish I still had my natural black hair.

I touch it self-consciously. 'For a while now.'

'It's very "Look at me!",' Bebe says. 'It's not like we can miss you.' She laughs and Blair snorts and covers her mouth.

Instantly, I'm reminded of the times when I was a kid and

I got bullied for being bigger than the other girls. I used to go home and eat whatever I could find in the fridge and cupboards until I felt like I was going to burst, just so I could momentarily forget about what had happened. Thankfully, I've overcome the need to binge eat now, but I still don't feel like I'll ever be enough.

'Don't,' Trey says sharply.

'What?' Blair replies, feigning innocence.

'It takes a bold girl to pull off red hair. Lil' Mermaid definitely can,' Boogs says, but a voice in my head says he's just being kind.

'Bebe, your hair hasn't looked good for at least six months. That wig is tired,' Annika says, standing up, and Blair, who clearly has no loyalty to anyone, bursts out laughing. 'Come on, Ariel.' Annika starts walking away.

I scrape back my chair, leaving my plate on the table, and without saying a word I follow her out of the canteen.

'I'm sorry about Bebe,' Annika says once we're in the hallway.

'It's fine.' It's not really, but I can't blame Annika for her bitch of a cousin who clearly dislikes me.

'No, it's not.' Annika stops and stares at me. 'No one should talk to you like that. You've got to stand up for yourself and learn how to read.' Annika clicks her fingers.

'The only thing I can read is a book!'

Annika laughs, but I'm not joking. I've never been good at cussing people to their faces or throwing shade. My great comebacks only ever seem to come to mind hours later.

I link arms with Annika. 'I've finished for the day so I'm going to head to Trey's bookshop. Wanna come?'

Annika groans. 'I wish, but I've got editing to do for my film project. Trey's parents are really nice, but if his dad's there make sure you don't hover around. He shouted at me once for doing that.'

'Right. No hanging about. Gotcha.'

'Call me later.' She hugs me before heading to the media suite.

I take a deep breath. Time to find me a job.

When I arrive at Wonderland I see a Black woman with glasses at the till, which has white tinsel wrapped round it. A man that looks like an older version of Trey is carrying an armful of books. I assume they're Trey's parents.

The bookshop is covered in pretty fairy lights and a Christmas tree is twinkling in the corner. I look around, taking note that they mainly sell children's, YA and adult fiction, with a few non-fiction books here and there. There are only a handful of people milling around, which surprises me as I thought it would be busier, especially getting near Christmas, but maybe it picks up later in the day. I hover by a bookshelf, waiting for the two people in the queue to pay, and then I remember Annika telling me *not* to hover, so I pick up the first book I see and stand in line.

If I'm being honest, there isn't much wonder at Wonderland, even with all the decorations. It's outdated and it needs something to make it pop, like a cool artwork piece or installation. If that wall was painted white, it would make the whole room look brighter. Ooh and that wall could have some author quotes—

'Hello!'

I didn't even realize that the customer in front of me had finished paying.

Trey's mum smiles at me as I shuffle forward. 'Welcome to Wonderland. Would you like that gift-wrapped?'

I look down at the book I'm holding. I don't even have the money to buy it.

'Oh . . . erm.' I put the book on the counter. 'I was actually wondering if you had any jobs going or if you knew of anywhere hiring at the moment? Your son Trey said you might be able to help?'

'You go to college with him?' Mrs Anderson asks.

'Yeah, I'm Ariel.' I smile.

Mrs Anderson smiles apologetically. 'Nice to meet you, Ariel. But I'm afraid we don't have any vacancies.'

'Oh, have you already hired your Christmas temps?' I say, swallowing my disappointment.

Mrs Anderson hesitates and I frown. Did I say something wrong? Her eyes wander past my shoulder and I turn my head. Mr Anderson is up on a ladder, putting books on the top shelf.

'Clive, be careful!' Mrs Anderson shouts. She rolls her eyes. 'He's so impatient. I've told him twice today that Trey will put those books away later. Anyway, sorry, Ariel. Maybe try the florist next door—'

56

A sudden crash makes us jump and Mrs Anderson's eyes widen as she runs round the till and across the room. The few people in the bookshop stop what they're doing and hurry to Mr Anderson, who is on the floor, books scattered around him. His left leg is twisted at a weird angle, making me suck in my breath. He groans loudly.

I quickly rush over and take out my phone. 'Shall I call an ambulance?'

Mrs Anderson nods and holds her husband's hand while I dial 999.

Luckily, the ambulance arrives fifteen minutes later and I move out of the way as the paramedics place a stretcher on the floor. It's like everyone's frozen as they watch them attend to Mr Anderson, and I'm instantly transported to earlier in the year, when Dad collapsed and the ambulance came to our house. The familiar tightness that always comes when I think about Dad grips my chest and I will myself to calm down. By way of distraction, I pick up the books from the floor and take them over to the till. Slowly the tightness eases up and I sigh with relief.

'Ariel . . .' Mrs Anderson walks towards me as I'm placing the books down. 'I'm going to go to the hospital with Clive. Trey won't be here for another twenty minutes. Is there any chance you could stay and mind the shop?'

'Of course,' I say, surprised they're not closing early.

'Trey can manage everything when he gets here.'

'I'm happy to stay and help with the customers even after Trey arrives,' I say quickly. 'I'm a fast learner and I can do a free trial run. If I do a good job then maybe I could work a few hours each week?'

I know I'm pushing it, and the timing obviously isn't great, but I really need a job. My fingers are crossed tight behind my back and Mrs Anderson looks at the customers and then back at me.

'You're friends with Trey? You've worked in a bookshop before?'

I nod. I know we're not *friends* friends, but we did have lunch together today, and how hard can it be to talk about books?

'Okay,' she says after a pause, and I have to stop myself from screaming. 'I'll call Trey to let him know what's happened. Tell the customers the till will be fixed in twenty minutes, and if you need to access any books on the really high shelves, please wait for Trey. The office is in the back if you want to put your stuff down.'

'Thank you, and I really hope Mr Anderson gets better soon.' Mr Anderson groans as if responding back to me, and Mrs Anderson flashes me a quick smile before she hurries over to him.

I take off my coat and scarf and survey the bookshop. Everyone is slowly going back to looking at the books.

I can do this.

NINE

Trey's playlist: 'Loneliest Time of Year' by Mabel

I run to the bookshop as soon as I get off the phone with Mum, sweating through my many layers of clothes. I wish she'd let me go to the hospital, but she says we can't afford to close up early. Man, this is so annoying! Who cares about Wonderland when Dad's injured? And I can't believe she left Ariel in the shop by herself. How could she even ask for a trial knowing the situation my family are in? Who does that?

I race inside Wonderland out of breath, and the door heater blows air on me, making me feel even hotter than I already am. There are a stack of books on the till and Ariel is behind it serving a customer. What does she think she's doing? Mum told me that Ariel would just be watching over the shop until I arrived. I see her take cash from the customer and her hand reaches behind the till. Is she stealing? She waves goodbye to the man before writing something down on a piece of paper. I march over to her.

'Hey.'

She looks up and smiles. 'Hi, Trey.' Then her face falls. 'I'm sorry about your dad. Has there been an update?'

'Not yet,' I reply bluntly.

I walk round the till and spot a container filled with notes and coins.

'Sorry, some of the customers wanted to pay in cash. I think they felt bad about what happened. I don't have a float, but they were fine about not getting change.' She laughs nervously.

I glance at the piece of paper she was scribbling on. It has the name of the book, author, ISBN and price. I peer closer at the paper to make sure I'm reading it right.

'You sold six books already?' *And a few of them are really hard ones to sell*, I think to myself.

Ariel nods and a lock of red hair falls from her messy bun. 'It hasn't been that busy, but I persuaded a few customers to buy another book.'

I know I should say thank you to her for selling books and helping my parents, but instead I snap, 'So my dad's hurt and you try to secure yourself a job?'

Ariel's mouth drops. 'No! Wait ... it wasn't like—'

I don't even let her finish. I walk to the office and sit down on the swivel chair with my head leaned back, eyes closed and my mind buzzing. Mum said Dad's leg didn't look right and now I have this mental image of it all twisted up. What if they can't fix it and it's damaged for ever? Mum hasn't texted me since we spoke on the phone, but she said Aunt Latrice was going to pick Reon up from school. If they're not back by tonight, what am I supposed to tell Reon when I collect him later?

There's a gentle knock on the door and my eyes snap open. Ariel's standing in the doorway, looking at the floor and drumming her fingers on her thigh.

'Sorry, Trey, but there's a man here to see your parents.'

I follow her to the shop floor and as soon as I see the white guy in the expensive suit, I immediately have a hunch about who he is. He's my height with cropped, black hair, small eyes and a neat goatee, probably in his late thirties. I notice he's carrying a black Tom Ford briefcase and when we catch eyes he grins at me. I don't return it.

'Can I help you?' I ask, sharper than I mean it to sound.

The grin doesn't leave the guy's face, and he extends his hand out to me. 'David Raymond from Raymond and Raymond Properties.'

I shake his hand. Hard. 'My parents aren't here. What can I do for you?'

'We've been trying to talk to them about the property.' He looks around the shop as if to emphasize his point. 'Can I give you my card?' He takes one out of his breast pocket before I say anything and hands it to me. The card is thick and smooth with gold foil that catches the light, and I twirl it in my fingers. 'I look forward to hearing from them,' he adds, then he nods at me and at Ariel, who's standing behind me.

Once he's out of the door, I scrunch up the business card

until it's a tiny ball in my hand and throw it in the bin behind the front desk. Ariel follows me with her eyes, but she doesn't say anything.

I type in the PIN code for the till and it pings open. The money looks okay, but if we want to keep this place, we need more sales – and soon. I glance at Ariel, who's now brushing imaginary dust off the counter. Even though this is her only day working here, I need her to secure some more sales like she did earlier. Somehow she's getting the customers to spend.

'Do you think you can sell two books per customer now that the till is open?'

Ariel hesitates, but then she nods.

I hate myself for the lie already forming on my tongue. 'If you want this job then I'm going to need that from you.'

Ariel frowns. 'Oh, your mum didn't mention—'

'I call the shots when she's not here. Is that a problem?' I say coldly.

Ariel's face darkens. 'No.'

I glance at the time and sigh. Two more hours until we close up. It will be a miracle if the customers don't clock how tense and awkward the atmosphere is today.

TEN

Ariel's playlist: 'My Gift to You' by Alexander O'Neal

I want to tell Trey that he can shove the job up his arse. I know it looks bad that I asked for a trial when his dad was being bundled into an ambulance, but at least I've made the bookshop some money. Trey's had a face on him throughout the whole shift, and he's literally said about two words to me. I know I should rise above it because I actually need this job, but I end up responding back to him in the same sharp tone. This is not how I imagined my first day at work.

I approach every single customer in the shop, giving them my friendliest smile. It's weird that I sometimes don't know what to say around the popular kids at college, but talking to random strangers is pretty easy. Although it's not like there's many of them. I keep waiting for it to pick up, but it's really slow.

I can feel Trey watching me as I engage in conversation and help customers take their books to the till. Good. He should be paying attention to how great I am at this job.

'Thanks,' he says when I place three books on the counter for an elderly woman.

I scoff and walk away. I can't wait for this shift to be over and done with.

The hours drag on, and I'm grateful when the last customer leaves. Trey is too busy counting today's takings, so I don't know what to do with myself. I start putting books away and fixing the fairy lights that have dropped on one side. Only when I grab the dustpan and brush does Trey look up.

'You don't have to do that,' he says.

'It's fine,' I reply quickly.

I look up and his shoulders are slumped. I'd actually forgotten about what happened to his dad earlier and I instantly feel bad. I could barely function when my dad was in hospital.

'Any update?'

Trey leans forward and rests his elbows on the counter with his hands clasped. 'My mum just messaged me and said they'll be home soon, so that's good news, I guess.'

'That is.' I bite my lip. It's not the best time to ask, but I need to know if he'll at least tell his mum that I did well today. Maybe then she'll hire me. 'How were the sales?'

'Oh.' Trey glances at the till. 'Yeah, great ... thank you. You're good at this.'

I smile. 'So, you think I have a shot at a job here?' I see him hesitate and I don't understand why. He practically just told me I'm a natural.

'My mum will call you,' he eventually replies before closing the till and walking towards the office.

What the hell is his problem?

I stand holding the dustpan and brush, waiting for him to come back out. I don't know if he's avoiding me or busy doing something else, but he doesn't return. I sweep up anyway and throw the contents in the bin before heading to the office and knocking on the door.

'Is it cool if I go?' I ask.

Trey's packing his bag, but he looks up and nods.

I grab my things without another word and leave. It's dark and freezing outside and I walk quickly to keep warm. Clearly Trey's still pissed with me. I was so excited to tell Mum that I'd found a job, and now I don't even know if I have.

The bus stop is empty when I arrive and the next bus isn't due for five minutes, so I take out my phone and headphones. Annika think's it's cheesy that I make playlists for every mood. I have one for creating art, one for when I'm making dinner and, of course, I have one for Christmas that I update every year, even though nothing beats the classics. 'My Gift to You' by Alexander O'Neal croons through the headphones. It was one of my dad's favourite songs and I hum under my breath, which instantly calms me down.

A bus comes and it's so packed that I can't even get on. It was cold earlier, but now it's practically freezing. I go to tighten my scarf and that's when I realize I don't have it.

Damn! My heart starts racing. That green scarf is the last present my dad gave me before he died. It's the most precious thing I own and not having it feels like losing a part of him. Did I leave it at college? Did I even wear it today? I take a deep breath.

Calm down, Ariel.

I close my eyes, trying to retrace my steps. Yes, it was with me in art and then at lunch. Did I have it when I arrived at Wonderland? I frown. I can't remember! Oh, where is it? My eyes start to water, but then in my mind I see Mr and Mrs Anderson leaving the bookshop with the ambulance, and I remember taking off my scarf and leaving it in the office. I was in such a rush to get out onto the shop floor that it must have slipped off the chair I hung it over.

I quickly turn and walk back towards Wonderland, hoping that Trey is still there. But as soon as I turn onto the road I see the bookshop is dark. I press my face against the glass, my breath leaving mist on it, but, just as I thought, everything is still inside. Damn it. I have no choice but to talk to Trey tomorrow. That's exactly what I'd been hoping to avoid.

ELEVEN

Trey's playlist: 'The Little Drummer Boy' by
The Jackson 5

'Hey, baby.' Aunt Latrice, my mum's younger sister, steps aside so I can come into her house and out of the cold.

If she's wondering why I have a bright green scarf around my neck, she doesn't say. Ariel left it at the bookshop and it made sense to wear it when it's freezing outside. I'll give it to her at college tomorrow ... Actually, I'll give it to Annika instead. I don't really want to face Ariel after how awkward it was today.

Reon and our cousin, Cayan, are shouting at something from the living room and I turn towards the noise.

'They're just finishing a game. You want something to eat?' Aunt Latrice asks and I shake my head. I follow her into the kitchen anyway, taking off my coat and scarf as I go. She presses some buttons on the microwave and it comes to life. Then she turns back to me and smiles sadly, and a dimple appears in her right cheek, just like Mum's.

'You doing okay?'

I nod as I pull out a chair and sit down. 'Has Mum called you?'

'She texted me not long ago saying they'll be home soon. What I want to know is why Clive was up that ladder in the first place.'

'Exactly! He knows I would have done it,' I say, frustration creeping into my voice. Dad rarely climbs the ladder, so I don't get what made him go up it today. We really don't need this extra level of stress on top of all our debts.

The microwave pings and Aunt Latrice hands me a steaming plate of rice and peas with fried chicken. She passes me a fork and smiles knowingly. 'You always say you don't want nothing, and then you eat me out of all my food.'

'Thank you.' I chuckle and then my stomach rumbles loudly, making her laugh so hard that she flashes one of her gold teeth.

I eat the food quickly, closing my eyes and savouring the taste. I always forget how good Aunt Latrice's cooking is. Reon and Cayan run into the kitchen when I'm almost done, and Reon leans into me with his arm resting on my shoulder. I gently nudge my head against his as a way of saying 'Hi', with my mouth full of food.

'Can we have some cake?' Cayan asks breathlessly, even though he only ran in from the room next door.

Aunt Latrice eyeballs him. 'Bedtime.'

'Ah, man,' Cayan moans, and he stomps out without even saying hello to me.

'Are we going home?' Reon asks. I nod.

'You sure you don't want to wait here until they get back?' Aunt Latrice asks.

'Nah, we're okay. I need to get Reon ready for bed anyway.' I walk over and kiss her on the cheek and she pats my arm. 'Thank you,' I say. 'I'll message you when they're back.'

'Okay. Give me some love, gorgeous,' she says, holding her arms out to Reon, who grins and runs to her and she spins him round. 'You're getting too big. Can you stop growing?'

'That's impossible,' Reon says seriously when she puts him down. 'Did you know that kids grow about six centimetres a year?'

'Oh, is that right?' Aunt Latrice looks at me over his head and mouths, 'Really?'

This is the thing about Reon. Sometimes he comes out with the most random information. I don't know if he picks it up from school or a book, but usually I act like I really care about the new facts I've just learned. At the end of the day, I want Reon to enjoy being knowledgeable.

'Wow, that's amazing, little man,' I say, and Reon smiles at me.

We say goodbye once again and I brace myself for the cold. I hold Reon's hand tight as we cross the road.

'Are Mum and Dad home now?' he asks.

'I don't think so.' I glance at him. 'Do you know what happened?'

'Aunt Latrice said Dad fell and hurt his leg.' Reon falls silent.

'You okay?' I ask softly.

'Yeah. I was just thinking about whether Dad would get superpowers now.'

I laugh. 'What? Why?'

'Well, Spider-Man was bitten by a spider and then he became Spider-Man. So maybe Dad will get something cool?' Reon says, looking up at me with so much hope that I take my time answering. I wish my brain would take me to where Reon's is. If thinking Dad will become a superhero helps him to deal with what's happened, I'm definitely not going to burst his bubble.

'You know Wakanda's real, right?' I say and Reon nods. 'Maybe they'll put some Vibranium in Dad like they did to Bucky.'

Reon gasps and vigorously nods his head. 'They definitely will.'

The house is dark and empty when we return and I send Reon up to bed, promising to check in on him soon. He's so hyped about superhero Dad that I'm sure he'll be drawing him by torchlight under his duvet. I take off my coat and Ariel's scarf, sit on the sofa and sigh. I just want my parents to come home.

My phone pings and I rush to look at it, but it's Boogs saying he'll be at the bookshop tomorrow at seven when I close to set up for the party. I haven't thought about the twins' surprise party for hours, let alone told my parents my cover story. I had to mute the notifications in the WhatsApp group because it was all getting too much. If it wasn't for the money, I'd cancel it right now.

I glance at Ariel's scarf. Maybe I should let her know that I have it? I don't have her number so I find her on Instagram. Wow, she's talented. The courtyard painting is dope, but this stuff is even better. It's so vibrant and bold. Her last picture is a selfie of her in front of a colourful canvas looking over her shoulder at the camera and smiling. I don't know why but it makes me smile back at her, so I press like on the photo just as the front door opens.

'Mum? Dad?' I rush to the door and Mum walks in with Dad behind her. He's walking slowly, with crutches under his armpits and a cast on his leg.

'Hi, baby.' Mum kisses me on the cheek. She rubs her tired eyes. 'Is Reon in bed?'

'Yeah, but I need to check on him.'

'Don't worry – I'll go. Can you keep an eye on your dad?' she says before heading upstairs.

Dad slowly makes his way to the living room.

'Is your leg hurting?' I ask.

'A bit,' Dad says, but his face is scrunched up and it looks like he's holding in the pain.

Dropping his crutches, he balances on one leg and puts both his hands on my shoulders as I help him to the sofa. He breathes heavily and I gently pick up his feet so they rest on the seat. I take off his shoe and place a pillow under his neck.

71

He smiles. 'Thank you, son.'

I look around, wondering what else I can do for him. 'You need water or anything?'

'No, I'm okay. I'm not going to be able to work for the next six weeks though.'

'For real?' I sit down opposite him.

'I know it's a lot, with Christmas round the corner, but I need you to be there for Mum, okay? Anything you can do to ease the pressure off her, please do.'

I nod. What with Raymond & Raymond sniffing around and now Dad's broken leg, Mum must be going out of her mind. Dad's eyelids are fluttering, so I quietly stand up and leave the room to let him rest. I go upstairs and Mum is gently closing the door to Reon's room. She sees me and nods towards my bedroom.

Mum sits at my desk with her head in her hands, and I don't know what to do with myself so I put a hand on her shoulder. It's weird seeing Mum look so defeated and it makes me nervous. Mum's usually so strong and put together – the back-bone of our family. What will we do if she breaks? She holds my hand and smiles sadly at me.

'I'm here to help with whatever you need,' I say.

'Thank you. I spoke to Latrice a few minutes ago and she's happy to help with Dad. It's going to be tough, but we've got to keep the bookshop open. How was Ariel?'

'Yeah, she was really good. She made some strong sales. But I don't like the timing of her asking for a job.'

'I actually appreciated that she stepped in. It made me feel better knowing you weren't alone.' Mum gives me a look. 'I hope you were welcoming?'

'Yeah, yeah, of course,' I mumble, annoyed that she doesn't agree with me. What is it about Ariel that makes me get so heated? First the spilt drink, then my opinions about her book choices . . . and now this.

'You've got her number? Tell her to come by on Saturday and I can sort out her contract and hours. We need all the help we can get now your dad is going to be out of action.'

'I don't have it, but I can catch her at college.'

Mum frowns at me. 'I thought you were friends? That's what she said.'

Friends?

I hesitate. 'We're . . . cool. Look, can we even afford her?'

Mum shrugs. 'We don't have a choice, Trey. I don't want you trying to work all the hours under the sun when you have college. Latrice will help with Dad this weekend, but I need someone with him tomorrow.'

'Don't worry – I can work tomorrow and half a day Saturday.' At least that gives me enough time to clean up any mess from the party before the customers come in.

Mum raises her eyebrows. 'You sure? I'll do the afternoon shift on Saturday. Maybe see if Ariel doesn't mind working this weekend?'

'I'll sort it.'

Mum stands up and her eyes look red and tired. She heads downstairs as my phone pings with a notification from Instagram. I have a new like from Ariel on a selfie I took a few days ago. Maybe she's forgiven me? I guess this is my chance to show her that I'm not being a dick . . . well, not on purpose. I press follow and send her a DM:

TreyAnderson: Hey. Dad's home and is on bed rest. Thanks for today and for working so hard. You have the job. Mum wants to know if you can work this weekend? She'll give you a contract to sign. It does mean you'll be stuck with me for a bit though 😊 Also, I have your scarf. I don't have college tomorrow so I'll be at Wonderland all day, but you can pick it up when you come to the surprise party.

I add a kiss but delete it before I press send, then I head downstairs. Dad's fast asleep while Mum is watching something on TV.

'You okay?' I sit next to her.

She pats my knee and smiles. 'I'm okay.'

Dad snores really loudly as if to say he's okay too and it makes us laugh, which instantly lightens the mood.

'Let's watch an episode of *Housewives*. Do you want anything from the kitchen?' Mum says as she pushes herself up from the sofa. Yes, *The Real Housewives* is my secret pleasure. Dad thinks it's weird, but I find it hilarious, and Mum loves that she has someone to watch it with.

'A lot of chocolate!' I reply.

Mum winks at me and heads to the kitchen. I check my phone and Ariel has seen my DM but hasn't responded. I guess she's still pissed at me after all. A WhatsApp pops up from Blair and it's a picture of black lacy lingerie on her bed. I instantly cover my phone even though my parents can't see it.

> Is that for me?

I can see her typing back.

> Maybe? Come over and see for yourself ;)

I groan. Why today? Now I have a mental picture of Blair wearing lingerie and I can feel myself getting hot. But I can't leave Mum tonight. That wouldn't be fair.

> Can't. Fam stuff. Tomorrow after the surprise?

> Everything okay? x

> Yeah, will tell you later . . . So tomorrow night?

> Tomorrow's good. If you were here right now, I'd walk over to you slowly—

'Trey,' Mum says and I quickly close my phone, leaving Blair and her dirty talk as far away from Mum as possible. She hands me two bars of chocolate. 'So is it Atlanta or Potomac tonight?'

'Whatever you want,' I reply, grateful for the change of topic.

Mum grabs the remote and starts to surf Sky. I wish I was with Blair and whatever film she wanted to play out with me.

TWELVE

***Ariel's playlist: 'Christmas Time to Me'
by Jordin Sparks***

Fifteen days till Christmas

One of the things I do when I'm stressed, sad or happy is paint ... so that's pretty much most days. I can paint on anything: paper, canvas, a wall, clothes – it doesn't matter where just as long as I'm able to be creative. The only time I couldn't paint was when Dad died.

I'm back in the art studio during my free period and I'm working on something completely separate from my portfolio. I'm using blacks and greys and creating a storm with bolts of yellow and white. Anyone who looked at it would think I'm angry, but I'm not. I'm confused, and it's all Trey's fault.

He was so cold to me yesterday at Wonderland, but then he liked one of my Instagram posts that evening. And it wasn't just a random picture – it was a selfie of me, which must mean he likes how I looked in it. I liked his selfie for that reason. I thought I was over my crush on Trey, but the way I got excited when that notification popped up got me thinking maybe there's still something there. Then if that wasn't enough, he followed me! Trey has over ten thousand followers and only follows about a hundred accounts, who are mainly musicians and sports stars, but now I'm one of them. He mentioned something about a party in his message. I have no idea what party he's talking about, but at least my scarf is safe.

I still haven't responded to him though. And I don't know why, but I feel nervous about it. I splat more black onto the canvas. I want the job. I need the job. But working with someone whose mood is so up and down is not my idea of fun.

My phone rings, cutting off my thoughts, and I groan. My hands are splattered with paint so I look around for somewhere to wipe them. As I can't find anything, I smear the paint on my ripped jeans ... Maybe people will think it's a look.

'Hello?' I say.

'I just got off the phone to Jolie and she'll be at college later today,' Annika says (she always dives straight into the conversation). 'You're coming to the party tonight, right?'

I press the phone between my ear and shoulder so I can keep painting. 'Party?'

'Girl! Where have you been?' Annika asks, and I can practically feel her rolling her eyes down the phone. 'It's all everyone's been talking about ... well, via WhatsApp, cause it's a surprise.'

I huff. 'I deleted WhatsApp cause I ran out of storage space, remember?'

Annika tuts. 'Come to mine after college with Jolie and we can all go together. The theme is pink, okay? Oh, and do not tell the twins or Trey and Boogs will lose it.'

I pause. 'Trey?'

'Yeah, him and Boogs are organizing it. They're charging everyone to get in – God knows why. I've got you covered though … Okay, one sec … Ariel, I've gotta go, but later, okay?'

'Hello?' I say, but the phone is already dead. Annika must have got the details mixed up. Trey's dad literally had an accident yesterday, so why would he be organizing a party for tonight?

I add more grey to my painting before taking a step back and studying it, but all I can think about is Wonderland. Mum was so pleased last night when I told her that I got the job, and I just wish yesterday had gone differently so I could feel happy too. I sigh and put down my paints, wiping my hands on my jeans again. I pick up my phone, my finger hovering over Trey's profile and the follow back button glaring at me. I press it and type a response to his DM.

ArielArt: Glad your dad's okay. I'm sorry about the timing of me asking for a job. Looking forward to coming back to Wonderland, and, yep, I can work on Sat. I'm at college all day today but will get my scarf at the party. Thanks x

I stare at the kiss. Is it weird to add it when we're not exactly close? Plus, there wasn't one at the end of his message. I quickly delete it and send the DM before going back to my painting.

It's a full day of sociology and English lit and by the end of the afternoon I'm tired out. Luckily my last session is back in the art studio and I've been busy working on my portfolio. There are only a few more minutes until the bell signals home time and I'm washing my paintbrushes at the sink when Ezekiel Rada joins me, gushing about the party tonight, his huge Afro moving as he talks. No disrespect to Ezekiel, but he definitely doesn't hang out with the cool kids. I don't remember Boogs talking to him once when he was in art, yet somehow even *he* got an invite!

'I think the whole of college is going. Apparently if you don't wear pink you can't get in, so I went and bought a pink shirt.'

'Is it just a Christmas party?' I ask, half listening.

'No, it's a surprise birthday party for the twins.' Ezekiel gives me a look. 'Aren't you in the WhatsApp group?'

Ah, the famous WhatsApp group.

'Why do we have to pay?' I ask, ignoring his question.

Ezekiel shrugs. 'Yeah, it's a bit weird, and I don't know why it's in a bookshop. It's not really where you expect to have a party.'

I drop the brushes I've just cleaned into the colourful water in the sink. What did he say? 'Bookshop?'

'Yeah, Wonderland. You know – Trey's family's shop?' Ezekiel fishes out my paintbrushes from the sink. 'His parents are clearly cooler than mine.'

I bet his parents don't know, I almost say, but I bite down on my lip instead.

THIRTEEN

Trey's playlist: 'I Still Have You' by Charlie Wilson

The bookshop is quiet once again and I tap my fingers on the till. Despite me reshuffling the books in the window and hanging a wreath on the front door in the hope of attracting customers, the shop still isn't any busier. I bet Books! Books! Books! is rammed.

I glance towards the door as Boogs walks in with giant pink '18' balloons and several bags. I gesture to the office.

'I feel kind of bad that you've taken on all the work by yourself,' I say, grabbing a couple of bags from him and setting them down.

Boogs collapses on the chair, taking off his beanie hat. 'It's cool, bro. You're providing the venue. Besides, you've got a lot on.' He sighs. 'Six weeks?'

'Yeah, six weeks of rest. Luckily Ariel's gonna help out round here while Dad's off.'

Boogs nods. 'I like Ariel. She's cool.'

'Yeah, man.' I think back to seeing Ariel's response to my DM flash up on my phone. At least now it won't be awkward working together.

'What time are the twins meeting you?' Boogs asks.

'I've told them to be outside Whole Foods at eight p.m. Hopefully everyone will have arrived by half seven, not Black people time. Are you gonna be okay handling things?'

I don't want to sound ungrateful, but there are so many people coming tonight. Names keep being added into the group. I'd put my phone away when I helped a customer earlier and when I looked back there were over a thousand notifications in the chat.

'Yeah, I'm good,' Boogs says, clearly much more chilled than I am.

'Do you think everyone will come?' I question a little nervously.

'Nah, not everyone will want to pay, but it will be a sick turnout.' Boogs rubs his hands together. 'Wonderland's gonna make bank.'

I snort. 'You know I haven't even worked out how I'm going to explain all the money in the till to my parents.'

Boogs shrugs. 'Just tell them the truth.'

My eyes bulge. 'Are you mad?'

'You really think they're going to be pissed when you bring in all that money? Look, if you need to, blame the party on me.' He puts his beanie back on. 'Cake's coming in a few hours, yeah? I'll be back in a bit.'

Boogs exits and I go back to the front desk, spotting a few new customers milling about the shop floor. I need to be more positive about tonight. It's going to be rammed, but that means I'll make enough money to help the bookshop, and that's what's important.

An older woman comes over to me with an armful of children's books. She smiles as she places them down. 'Grandkids,' she explains. On the counter next to her pile is a small display of colourful Christmas sticker books that I'd told Dad to buy for the till even though he was reluctant. The woman peers at them, and I pick up a copy and open it so she can see the reindeers and Father Christmas.

'All the kids love these books,' I tell her.

'Really?' She takes one and looks at the price before she hands it to me. 'It's Christmas! Let's get one for every grandchild.'

I grin. 'Perfect.'

I finally get a chance to reply to the messages on my phone at lunchtime and see Blair's been texting me all day asking for clues about the surprise. I can't believe no one's blown the secret yet. I fire off a quick message.

Just look hot x

Blair responds instantly.

I roll my eyes and laugh. Last Christmas we stumbled upon this place called Backyard Cinema and, when we walked in, it literally felt like we'd stepped into Narnia or something. We thought they were going to be showing Christmas films, but they were playing *Legally Blonde* on the big screen. Blair had squealed so loud. She's obsessed with that film. I'm pretty sure it's why she carries around a pink bag.

Just before closing, Boogs reappears holding a cake and wearing a slim-fit pink suit with a crisp white shirt. My mouth drops open. Boogs does a perfect turn and grins.

'Sick, right? My cousin Jermaine let me borrow it.'

I swear only Boogs could pull off wearing a pink suit. Dressed like that, it's hard to imagine that he used to be in a gang.

'You look like a 70s pimp,' I say, and Boogs screw-faces me.

'Hater. You wish you looked this good.'

To be honest, I wish I'd made more of an effort. My shirt is more light purple than pink, but it's the best I could do on short notice.

'Let me see the cake,' I ask eagerly.

Boogs puts it gently on the office table and opens the box. It's a pretty baby-pink cake, half covered in pink roses and macarons and half with strawberries dunked in white chocolate and a little hot-pink heeled shoe. The topper reads HAPPY 18TH B & S. It's not easy finding a cake that both the twins like because they have different tastes, but this one's perfect.

'Half is vanilla for Santi and the other side is chocolate for Blair. It's also egg and dairy free cause I'm not dealing with one of Santi's lectures.'

'Nice!' The detail on the cake is crazy. It must have cost a fortune. 'How much?'

'You know Bev Smith's always had a thing for your boy! It was practically free.' Boogs flashes me a smile.

I laugh and go to put the cake in the fridge before turning the OPEN sign on the door to CLOSED. We immediately cover the windows with bin bags so no one can peep in, then we start blowing up the rest of the balloons and hanging them around the shop. We thankfully don't have to do too much to make the room look nice because the bookshop is already decorated for Christmas.

We carry some of the books from the small tables down to the basement and place them next to a box of books on the floor. Then we push the rest of the empty tables that are upstairs to the side and fill some bowls with crisps, sweets and, randomly, mince pies. I gesture at them.

'What?' Boogs says when he sees my confused face. 'It's Christmas! Besides, it was two for one.'

I open up one of the bags Boogs brought over earlier and shake my head when I see what's inside.

'And what about this?' The bag contains several bunches of green plants, each tied with a red ribbon. I hold one up.

'Mistletoe. Mrs Avard next door was selling a load of it for cheap. Maybe we can hang them up or something?' Boogs suggests.

I scoff. 'Like anyone at college needs a reason to kiss at parties. I don't want anything taped to the walls in case it pulls off the paint. We can just leave them on the table.'

Boogs rolls his eyes. He starts to add bottles of alcohol and cups to the table and I reach for the vodka.

'Boogs, I don't know—'

'We can't have a birthday with no alcohol! Don't worry, I got you – the books will be fine.'

'Weren't you going to bring sheets to cover them?' I ask.

Boogs averts his eyes sheepishly. 'Ah, I forgot. My bad.'

I sigh and put the bottle down. 'I'm going to get changed. Be back in a sec.'

I trundle downstairs and quickly shove on my 'pink' shirt. The lighting in the basement isn't great, but with the torch on my phone I study myself in the mirror, liking what I see.

'It's going to go great, stop stressing,' I say to my reflection.

Back upstairs, I look around the bookshop, admiring the set-up. But then I spot some candles scattered about the room and my face drops.

'Boogs!' I go up to each one and blow it out. I don't even know how he found Mum's emergency box in the office.

'Why did you do that? It's sexy when the lights are down.'

I punch his arm and he automatically holds it. 'Paper plus fire,' I say. 'You see the problem?'

Boogs huffs. 'How many times ... ? The books will be *fine*!'

'No candles.' I pick them up and take them back to the office before sending a quick text to Mum reminding her that I'll be home late and not to wait up. She thinks I'm reorganizing the books in the stockroom and basement, helping out while Dad's off. I don't know what she's going to say when she sees that I haven't done any of those things ...

Nicki Minaj is playing through Marcus's speakers. Boogs' cousin is a local DJ and he's the only person we're letting in for free tonight given that he's providing the music. He keeps glaring at me because I told him to keep the volume low, but I don't need the neighbours snitching on me after all this effort.

Everyone has been instructed to come through the delivery entrance at the back, and when I peek outside there's a crazy long queue of teenagers in pink. I keep pulling the neck of my shirt in and out, trying to cool myself down. It's not even hot in here. I'm legit just stressed. There are too many people waiting to come in – I should have never let Boogs be in charge of invites.

I go out to greet everyone and Boogs is at the door taking cash and putting it in a black waist bag.

'This looks amazing, Trey,' Yarah says, hugging me. She's wearing the tightest pink latex dress that doesn't leave anything to the imagination.

James scowls at me. 'Ten pounds, bro?'

I laugh and shrug. 'You can negotiate with Boogs if you want.'

'Ignore him,' Yarah says. 'The twins are going to love this!'

The party fills up quick, and before I know it, it's rammed and everyone's dancing and drinking. My eyes are trying to track every drink to make sure no one spills anything on the books. *What if Mum comes to see how I'm doing with the stocktake?* I think to myself. I check for the millionth time and there's nothing there from her.

'Here.' Boogs presses a drink into my hand.

'Aren't you meant to be minding the door?' I ask.

'Bro, I can see you eyeballing everyone. Can you, like, chill?' He raises his eyebrows and I reluctantly nod. 'Drink up, man, and don't forget to greet people, yeah?'

He walks off and I down the drink in one, pulling a face as I swallow the bitter alcohol. *Relax, Trey, just relax.*

It doesn't take long for the alcohol to kick in and suddenly I don't even know what I was stressing about. Everyone is being respectful of the books and the shop. This is exactly what I needed: a cool party and a chance to loosen up. It feels like everything has been so full on recently and now I can breathe.

I look towards Boogs, who's gesturing at me to get a move on. It's almost eight p.m. and I need to meet the twins. I grab my coat and walk over to Marcus.

'Remember to cut the music when we're back.'

Marcus gives me a thumbs up. I head out of the delivery door and Boogs is back out here dealing with the final people in the queue. We're definitely over capacity. Maybe I should tell him not to let any more people in? But then I think about the money ... I hurry off before I change my mind. I really hope this is all worth it.

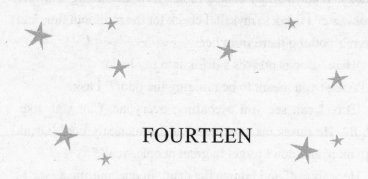

FOURTEEN

Ariel's playlist: 'Christmas Love' by Ashanti

It's very unlike me to go to a party, let alone twice in a week, but that's exactly what I'm doing. I'm outside Annika's house in a pink summer dress, even though it's freezing out here. It's the only pink thing I own and it clashes ridiculously with my red hair. I look down and inspect my hands. Luckily, I've managed to scrub all the paint off them this time. I don't need stupid girls making fun of me again.

Annika and Jolie come out of the house and we hug in greeting. Annika's wearing a pink crop top with a pink fitted skirt. Jolie's gone all out with pink hair colouring and a neon-pink jumpsuit. She says she still doesn't feel one hundred per cent recovered from Bebe's party and has vowed not to touch a drop of alcohol tonight. *Yeah, right!*

We get on the bus and I lean over Jolie to talk to Annika. 'Is the party really being held in Wonderland?'

Annika nods. 'I was surprised too, but I figured, how else would they have found a venue this last-minute?' She opens her bag and applies pink lipstick to her full lips. 'I know the twins were planning on having a chilled pizza night, but a surprise party is way better.'

Jolie sighs. 'I'm so jealous that they have such amazing boyfriends!'

'But why are we paying?' I ask.

Just like Ezekiel, Annika shrugs. 'Maybe to cover the cost of everything? They must be making a small fortune cause everyone's going.'

'I heard people from Felts College are coming too,' Jolie adds.

I look out of the window as we zoom by. Something isn't adding up. Trey walked out of Bebe's party because of 'bigger issues' than me spilling my drink on him. Now his dad's injured, and he's hosting a party that everyone has to pay to get into ... Maybe the bookshop's in trouble? But, that can't be right – they just hired me.

We pull up outside Wonderland and the windows are covered in some sort of black material. I can't hear any music and, for a second, I think Annika must have been wrong after all. But then she starts walking down the side alleyway towards the back entrance. I hesitate and stop. A big part of me is nervous to even step foot in the bookshop after hours. I only got the job yesterday and I don't want to get in trouble for being at the party if Trey hasn't asked his parents.

'Come on, Ariel,' Jolie says, gently pushing me forward.

We walk towards the back door and no one else is around but Boogs, dressed in a pink suit. He gestures for us to hurry up. I mean, we are nearly half an hour late. From here, I can hear the pulse of the music.

'Look at you,' Annika says, checking him out as she hands him a few notes.

'You know how I do.' Boogs grins, popping his collar.

'Are they here?' Annika asks.

'Not yet, but there'll be here in a few. Trey just went to meet them.'

Boogs stamps our hands, leaving a black circle on them. He opens the door and I'm immediately hit with the smell of alcohol and sweat, the sound of loud music and a sea of pink. There's barely any space to move. Drinks are resting on bookshelves and some of the books are even being used as coasters. This is not good.

Boogs follows us inside and heads towards the DJ. A moment later, the music abruptly stops. Boogs is holding a microphone and he starts speaking into it. 'The twins are coming. Everyone – quiet.'

An excited chatter travels round the room before a shushing sound takes over. Everyone finally falls silent and I can hear muttered conversation outside the shop.

'What are we doing here?' Blair's distinct voice rings out, and a few people laugh. Boogs shoots everyone death stares.

A deeper voice responds, but I can't hear it properly. I know it must be Trey. Suddenly the door opens and everyone screams 'Surprise!' The music blares with Stevie Wonder's 'Happy Birthday', and I join in clapping my hands to the beat. Blair has her hand over her mouth, Santi is waving at everyone and Trey is surveying the crowd. He's smiling but there's something else behind his eyes – is he nervous? Maybe it's because of my red hair, but his eyes quickly land on me. I tentatively wave and he nods.

'Move out the way,' a voice yells.

I have flashbacks to Bebe's party as I'm pushed to the side, but this time it's because Boogs is walking slowly through the crowd, holding a gorgeous pink cake covered in candles. Everyone takes their phones out to record the twins making a wish. I find myself looking around at all the people gathered in Wonderland and I literally don't know half of them. Maybe Jolie's right and people from other colleges are here.

'Thank you, everyone. This is so beautiful,' Blair says into the mic. She looks stunning in a baby-pink dress. 'We're honestly so lucky to have these guys. I love you, Trey.'

He bends down to kiss her and everyone cheers . . . everyone except me. I look up at the pink balloons instead, because watching them kiss makes me feel weird. What is wrong with me?

All my favourite songs have been playing and I've been trying to dance for over an hour, but there's too many people here and I can barely move. I keep getting bumped into and it's really starting to piss me off.

'I'm going to the toilet,' I shout over the music, and Annika gives me a thumbs up.

The toilet is in the basement and it takes me ages to get through the crowd and downstairs. I walk slowly in my heels, careful not to trip and fall. In the corner, there are stacks of boxes and bestsellers piled on the floor. I can't help but think Trey should have covered the books to protect them from the drunk guests who are stumbling to the toilet.

The music is really muffled down here and it's peaceful. I gently touch one of the books before picking it up and running my thumb across the pages, inhaling that book smell.

'Hey.' Trey is standing on the steps. I watch as he walks down them. 'You okay?'

'Yeah, sorry. I was just going to the toilet,' I reply with a smile as I place the book down.

Trey stands beside me. 'You look nice.'

I look down at my dress as if seeing it for the first time and feel my cheeks flush. 'Oh, thanks. It's the only pink thing I own.' I squint at his top. 'Is that pink?'

Trey laughs. 'Nah, I didn't have anything.'

'So why are you hosting a pink party?' I grin.

'It was Boogs' idea. Everything was really.' Trey sighs. 'Wonderland isn't doing too good at the moment so we figured out a way to make some quick cash for the bookshop.'

My smile drops. 'Oh, I had no idea. I'm really sorry, Trey.'

'It's not really public knowledge,' he says, looking down at his shoes.

'So that's why you're charging. And your parents—'

'They don't know,' Trey interjects. 'I'm doing the early shift tomorrow, so I'm planning on cleaning up then. I'll definitely breathe easier once everyone's gone tonight though.' He looks at me nervously. 'Please don't tell my mum. I literally won't survive.'

I grimace. 'Just promise me if you get caught out, I was never here.'

'Deal.' He holds out his hand and I shake it. His palm is warm and I feel a jolt go through me again. I quickly withdraw my hand and Trey frowns at me, but we're interrupted by Boogs coming down the stairs.

'Don't get mad but a few books—'

Trey doesn't even let him finish. He's already taking the stairs two at a time. 'Boogs! I told you this shit would happen.'

'Do you need any help?' I call after him.

He stops and looks back at me. 'Don't worry – it'll be okay. Enjoy the party, Ariel.'

Trey and Boogs disappear and I walk to the toilet. Only then do I remember that I didn't ask him about my scarf.

FIFTEEN

Trey's playlist: 'Santa Claus Goes Straight to the Ghetto' by Snoop Dogg ft Nate Dogg, Daz Dillinger, Tray Deee and Bad Azz

I knew it! I fucking knew serving alcohol was a stupid idea. Look at the mess everywhere! There are books on the floor, books being used as coasters ... I cry out loud when I see a book on the counter, ripped to pieces.

'It's okay, it's okay,' Boogs says quickly. 'It's just one book.'

'Just one book! We're meant to be making money, not losing it,' I practically shout back.

This was such a bad idea. Why did I even agree to it? Mum is going to kill me.

'Trey,' Blair sings, walking towards me. 'You looking forward to later on, baby?'

She puts her arms round me and I jerk my head back. She

stinks of alcohol. Great. Sex definitely isn't on the cards any more. I should have kept a better eye on her – she can only handle two drinks max. Boogs takes the ripped book to the office, leaving me standing with a drunk Blair.

'Having a good time?' I ask, forcing a smile on my face.

'This –' she opens her arms wide – 'is the best party ever.' She stumbles in her heels and I grip her waist tightly. Her hand is on my chest and she's looking at me with big, brown eyes outlined with black eyeliner. 'Dance with me?'

My mind is still on the books, so I hesitate for literally a second, and Blair pulls away from me.

'You never want to spend any time with me!' Her voice is super high, almost screechy, and loud enough for some people to hear, even over the music. They look at us.

I've lost count of the number of times Blair's got drunk at a party and taken me on an emotional roller coaster.

'Babe, that's not true,' I say gently, pulling her towards me. She tuts.

'You don't care any more.'

'No, I—' Out of the corner of my eye, I catch sight of this guy who I don't even know using one of our Christmas bestsellers as a telephone. He's shouting, 'Hello? Hello?' into it and then slamming it against the bookshelf before repeating the whole process again and again.

What the hell?

'Yo!' I yell, and he looks at me. 'That's a book, bro.'

The guy looks at it dumbly and then laughs before he throws the book on the floor. I leap for it and pick it up, wiping it down with my top. Blair's face scrunches up, like I'm a bad smell. She looks me up and down and then she walks away.

'Blair!' I shout after her, but she ignores me. I'm not going to lie, there's a small part of me that's relieved that I don't have to deal with her drunken behaviour. She doesn't turn back and I end up losing her in the crowd of pink.

I try to enjoy the rest of the party and be 'on', like the Trey everyone loves, but my heart's not in it. The party's going to end at midnight and then I'll see what damage has been done. Blair is nowhere to be seen. Every time I think I spot her, it's actually Santi. I find myself leaning on the counter with a glass of vodka and Coke, noticing Ariel in my eyeline. She stands out with her bright red hair and, damn, the girl can *dance*! She gives Boogs a run for his money. This is the first time I've ever seen her loosen up. She always seems kind of nervous or really serious, so to see her laughing and moving and flicking her hair is pretty refreshing. She must feel eyes on her because she looks up, straight at me, and waves shyly. I hold my drink up to her.

A heavy hand lands on my shoulder and then my drink is snatched away.

I turn. 'Hey!'

Boogs downs it in one go. I don't know where his pink blazer has gone, but his shirt is rolled up and some of the buttons are undone. 'Why aren't you dancing? This party is actually sick.'

'I was having a drink.' I scan the crowd. 'You seen Blair?'

Boogs raises an eyebrow at me. 'She's dancing with some random guy. You two fighting?'

Even Boogs knows how Blair carries on when she's angry. I shrug. Usually I'd march over to wherever she is and go nose to nose with the guy, and then Blair would tell everyone I'm a hero, as if she was forced to dance, but tonight I can't be bothered.

'Well, I've got news that's gonna blow your mind,' Boogs says, grinning. 'We made just over a grand.'

My eyes bulge. 'Swear?'

'Swear! So can you actually loosen up? We did it, man. We pulled this shit off.' Boogs shakes me until I start laughing. 'This is good news, bro!'

'I know, I know. I owe you, man.' Thank you, God – the party was worth it.

Boogs puts an arm round me. 'Why you doubt me, I'll never know. Now there's this sexy girl here who's been asking me to tell you to dance with her.'

I shoot him a look. 'At Blair's birthday party?'

Boogs shrugs. 'You can blame it on the alcohol,' he says, and I grin. 'Look, we have about an hour left, so can you own this shit? You threw one of the best parties this year and got these cheap-ass people to pay for it.'

Boogs is right. We made money for the bookshop and this party will go down as one of the best parties of college. Period. I clap Boogs on the shoulder.

'Let's go party.'

*

99

The room is slightly spinning and I have a vague memory of Blair shouting at me, but I don't know why or where she is now. The party is easing out and people keep stopping to tell me they had the best time. Even people I don't recognize wish me a Merry Christmas, which makes me start singing 'We Wish You a Merry Christmas' at the top of my lungs. Boogs is in the corner holding mistletoe over Santi as he kisses her. This random girl waves goodbye before kissing me on the cheek. She disappears somewhere, but I'm still dancing by myself, and I'm the happiest I've been for a while. My parents won't believe it when they see all the money.

The music starts to slow down and Usher's smooth voice fills the room. I feel like I'm on stage with a mic and there's a sea of people watching me, cheering my name. I start to sing.

'Get it, Trey,' someone yells, and I wink in their direction.

I'm spinning and sliding like I'm in a full 90s music video. All I'm missing is a torn white vest top and rainfall. I spot Ariel watching me with a smile on her face, and I walk slowly towards her. The closer I get, the more uncertain her smile becomes. I reach out my hand and she backs away, shaking her head.

'Go on,' one of her friends says, pushing her forward into my arms, and I grab her before she can topple over.

She's soft and sexy and she smells so damn good. I start singing in her ear, forgetting about everyone else in the room.

'You're so drunk.' She laughs, but I notice that she doesn't push me away. Instead she's side-stepping with me. 'I think you need some water.'

'Just vibe with me, girl.' I wrap my arms round her waist.

'You have a really good singing voice,' she says, and I smile.

It feels like Marcus plays the entire 'Confessions' album, or maybe it's just me singing it out loud. Now that there aren't so many people, everyone is paired up and dancing. Blair walks up to me with a smile on her face, which is weird because Blair doesn't like me dancing with other girls. Ariel pulls away, but I hold onto her hand. She looks down at it and then at me. I don't know why, but I don't want her to go yet.

'Trey, I'm going to head out.' It's not Blair, it's Santi. This time, Ariel manages to pull her hand out of mine before giving Santi an awkward hug.

'Happy birthday again.' Ariel looks back at me. 'I'll grab you a glass of water. We have work tomorrow, remember?'

Santi and I watch her walk off. Santi raises her eyebrow at me, and I grin and shrug.

'She's a good dancer,' I say.

She shakes her head. 'You're lucky you're drunk and Blair went home.'

'Blair went home?' I question innocently.

Santi rolls her eyes. 'You need to sober up.' She kisses me on the cheek. 'Thanks for a great party, and don't worry, I won't tell her you were serenading girls with that voice of yours.'

'Shall we just say I was crying in the corner cause she left me?'

'Good shout.' Boogs walks over to us and Santi nods towards me. 'Sober your boy up, babe.' She kisses him before she walks away.

'Okay, let's get you some . . . ah, Lil' Mermaid, you're a star.' Boogs takes the water off Ariel.

'I thought she was a *mermaid*?' I say, and it's literally the most hilarious thing I've ever come out with.

Boogs and Ariel share a look, but they're clearly jealous they're not as funny as me.

'Drink it. We've got to start tidying up,' Boogs says as he hands me the water. I drink it down in one go. It's cool and refreshing.

'Got any more?' I ask.

'I'll grab some,' Boogs says. 'Maybe you should sit down for a bit?'

Ariel looks around the bookshop. 'Do you guys need help tidying up?'

'Nah, we're cool. Once this lightweight sobers up, we'll be able to sort everything.'

Ariel touches my arm and I grin at her stupidly.

'I'll see you tomorrow,' she says slowly. 'I'm gonna grab my scarf from the office before I head out with Annika and Jolie.'

'Okay, Ariel,' I sing back to her. A lock of her red hair is hanging on her cheek, and before I can stop myself, I gently push it aside. My finger leaves a soft trail on her face. She jerks back in surprise.

'Trey!' Boogs slaps my arm away and shakes his head at me.

I shrug and dance to the music. Ah, I love this song . . . !

SIXTEEN

***Ariel's playlist: 'Christmas (Baby, Please Come Home)'
by Jennifer Hudson***

Annika and Jolie spend the bus ride home talking about how good the party was. I'm nodding along to the conversation, but I'm barely listening because my mind's on Trey and him dancing with me. I'm sure it meant nothing. He was drunk and he's in a relationship – well, he might not be after the way he acted with Blair. But why did he seek me out? And then stroke my face . . . ?

'Earth to Ariel?' Jolie waves her hand in front of me and I blink.

'Huh?'

Annika and Jolie laugh.

'I've literally called your name twice,' Annika says. She raises a pencilled eyebrow. 'Are you drunk?'

'No, I was just thinking about my shift tomorrow,' I lie. 'Do you think Trey and Boogs will finish cleaning up in time?'

Jolie snorts. 'I wouldn't want to be Trey if they don't.'

Jolie's right – dealing with Mrs Anderson if the bookshop's a mess would be a nightmare. Whatever happens, I hope I still have a job tomorrow.

I get off the bus first and wave to the girls as it drives off. The house is quiet and dark when I get in, and I walk up the stairs soundlessly, past Mum's and Noah's closed bedroom doors. Once my make-up is off, pyjamas are on and glasses are resting on my side table, I jump into bed and pull the duvet tight round me. The heating must have gone off ages ago because there's a chill in the air.

I close my eyes and I'm suddenly back in Wonderland, but this time it's just me and Trey, dancing to Usher with Trey's arms round my waist.

I can't help but smile. I know I can't have Trey in real life, but in my dreams he's all mine.

SEVENTEEN

Trey's playlist: 'Wonderful Christmas Time' by
Kelly Rowland

Fourteen days till Christmas

I wake up in a brightly lit room. Shielding my eyes with my hand, I slowly sit up and take in my surroundings – a black wardrobe, white curtains, basketball posters on the wall. Why am I in Boogs' bedroom? There's a glass of water on the side and some paracetamol. I don't know who it's for, but my throat is so dry and my head hurts, so I pop the pills and down the water.

The bedroom door opens and Boogs in blue pyjama bottoms walks in holding a cup of something steaming hot. He looks at me and laughs.

'Yo, I swear you had one drink and was out of it.'

'I was?' I croak. Damn, what's wrong with my voice? I

cough, trying to clear my vocals. 'Did the bookshop look okay when we left?'

'I mean, it looked all right. It didn't help that you were refusing to clear up with me. You kept spinning that stupid mop around the dance floor. I couldn't let you go home smashed, you know? But, don't worry – I told your Mum you're here. The way you just collapsed on my bed, bro, I had to sleep on my own damn couch. You know James was asleep in the corner of Wonderland? God knows for how long. I don't even know where Yarah went.' Boogs takes a sip of his drink and I'm grateful for the silence. He's talking way too much and my head is pounding.

I look around the bedroom and find my phone by the side. At first I think it's dead, but then it powers to life. I rub my sleepy eyes. My phone buzzes with back-to-back notifications. There are a few messages from Blair and a crazy amount from a number I don't have saved. I frown as I see missed calls from the same number, as well as from Mum.

It feels like someone just poured a bucket of ice-cold water over me. Something has gone wrong. I can feel it.

I open the text from the unknown number.

Got your number from Annika. Where are you? Problem at bookshop. Your mum's here.
Ariel

'Shit!' I jump out of bed and grab my clothes from last night. I have an hour until we open, but what problem is Ariel talking about? And why is Mum at the bookshop? 'Did anything get broken last night?' I ask Boogs.

He hesitates for a second. 'Well, yeah.'

I freeze, and my heart starts racing like crazy. 'What? You didn't say! What's broken?'

'Some books got mashed up. A bookshelf broke—'

'Shit, shit, shit! Damn, Boogs, you couldn't fix it?' I ask, not even trying to hide the panic in my voice.

Boogs glares at me. 'You for real? I had you acting a fool, James refusing to wake the hell up, but *I'm* meant to Bob the Builder everything?'

I hold my head in my hands wishing I could go back and never have agreed to this stupid party. What am I going to say to Mum?

'Here.' Boogs hands me an envelope. I open it and there are hundreds of notes inside.

'Thanks, man,' I say sheepishly, and Boogs shrugs but I can tell he's pissed with me. I'm pissed with me! Why did I drink so much and not clean up the bookshop last night? I put the envelope in my back pocket with my phone. I don't even know where my coat is. Boogs hands me one from his wardrobe without a word. I really don't deserve him.

I run all the way to Wonderland and the cold air wakes me up and clears my head. I arrive at the bookshop breathless, and Mum and Ariel are standing in the middle of it. Ariel sees me first and her eyes go wide. Mum spins round and gives me the look. It's the look reserved for when me and Reon do something completely stupid. Her eyes become slits and her nostrils flare, and even though she's only five foot two I feel her towering over me and I shrink.

'What the hell happened here, Trey?' she shouts.

I survey the damage. The shelf on one of the bookcases is clearly broken, the fairy lights are a tangled heap, mistletoe has been trampled on the floor, and a few pink balloons and red cups are scattered around. It's bad, but it's surprisingly better than I'd imagined. Maybe I don't look as sorry as I should because Mum suddenly pokes me hard in the chest and I wince.

'You think it's okay to lie to me and throw a party at the bookshop? And flood the basement!'

'W-what?' I look from her to Ariel and Ariel looks down at the floor. 'The basement?'

'Some genius left the taps running in the bathroom. All of the stock there is damaged. That's thousands of pounds gone down the drain. Now I have to buy dehumidifiers with money I don't have to dry out a basement that shouldn't be flooded in the first place.' Mum puts her hands on her hips. 'How could you be so stupid? You know the problems we're having and you throw a party here for your whole college?'

'I'm really sorry,' I mumble, shame creeping over my face.

'Were you here?' Mum asks Ariel, who blinks furiously in response.

'No, she wasn't,' I say quickly and they both turn back to me.

'Thank you,' Ariel mouths.

Mum takes out her phone and clicks on the bookshop's Instagram. I know she spies on my account through

Wonderland's, and I so wish I'd thought to block it. One time she commented on my topless selfie. She doesn't really get the emoji thing so she used a bunch of smiley faces and heart eyes ... I almost died. Mum clicks on my story and a video pops up of Wonderland, packed out and with music blaring.

'Listen, I know it looks bad, Mum ... But I did this for us! Here.' I hand her the envelope.

Mum opens it and catches her breath. 'What is this?'

'I wanted to help raise the money to keep Wonderland open, so I threw a party for the twins' birthday and charged everyone to get in. I wanted to surprise you and Dad.'

'Oh, Trey.' Mum sighs and looks up to the ceiling.

My eyebrows furrow. How did I turn a shit situation into an even shittier one? 'I'm so sorry,' I say pathetically. 'I promise I didn't mean to make things worse. I'll fix everything.'

'But what about the stock we've lost?' Mum waves the money at me. 'This won't fix that.' Her face is pained, and for a second I think she's going to cry. 'I'm going to sort out the basement.' She walks off, leaving me feeling like the worst son in the world.

EIGHTEEN

Ariel's playlist: 'O Holy Night' by Mariah Carey

'I'm sorry – I tried to stall her to give you more time,' I explain.

'It's okay.' Trey picks up the nearest pink balloon. 'It's my fault anyway.'

He sighs deeply and looks around Wonderland. I feel so bad for him. He's in last night's clothes and I'm curious to know where he slept. There's no way it could have been at Blair's after what happened at the party.

Ever since last night when Trey danced with me, held my hand and stroked my cheek, he's been on my mind. I even dreamed about him. But I have to keep reminding myself that he was drunk and that he has a girlfriend. It was only the other day that he was being all moody with me, so who really knows how he feels? But I can't stop myself from thinking that maybe last night meant something to him too.

'If we lose Wonderland cause of me, I'll never forgive myself,' Trey says, and I can hear the concern in his voice.

'Hey, think positive – you won't lose the shop. Look, let's clear this mess up and hopefully there are books that can be salvaged from the basement. Your parents have insurance, right?'

'I think so,' he mumbles.

'Then the damage should be covered.' I give him a small smile.

'I guess ... You like coffee?'

Ten minutes later, we're back on the shop floor with steaming cups in our hands. Trey is already on his second coffee, but I've only half-drunk mine. I was worried that Mrs Anderson would see us hanging about and be mad, but Trey shrugged off my concern.

'Did you have fun last night?' he asks.

I nod. 'It was good. What about you? Was it worth all of this?'

Trey smiles. 'We made more than I thought we would and, not gonna lie, it felt good to chill out and forget everything, even if it only lasted a few hours.'

'I have a question. Why was I hired if Wonderland's in trouble?'

'Dad's out until his leg's healed and we need the help,' Trey says. 'Plus, you're good.'

I grin, and he reaches out for my now-empty cup.

'Let me wash up the evidence before Mum cusses me again.'

We get to work and Trey picks up the damaged shelf before inspecting it. He goes to the office, then returns with a toolbox. I pick up the balloons and cups scattered around the floor.

Mrs Anderson comes up the stairs with a bundle of books in her hands. I'm so thankful she didn't see us loitering.

'You need any help?' Trey asks, but she ignores him. She goes into the office and places the books down before coming out again.

'I can help you,' I quickly say, and Mrs Anderson nods at me.

'Thank you, Ariel. I need to move all the books downstairs up here.' She shoots a look at Trey before disappearing.

I follow her down and try not to gasp when I see the damage in the basement. 'Do you want me to help dry the floors too?' I ask, and Mrs Anderson smiles sadly.

'It's okay, darling. Just grab those books there please and leave them in the office.'

When I come back upstairs holding an armful of books, Trey immediately stops working on the bookshelf. 'Is it bad?'

I nod and he groans.

I go into the office and then start to organize the shelves on the shop floor where loads of books have been knocked over. It's really quiet and I'm used to working with music playing. I want to put some on, but Trey is focusing so hard that I don't want to disturb him.

Noah was asking me this morning when we were going to watch *Home Alone* and I couldn't bring myself to tell him that, without Dad, it feels weird to watch our family Christmas film.

Now all I can think about is the *Home Alone* soundtrack and I start singing 'Rockin' Around the Christmas Tree' softly as Trey starts hammering the shelf. I get to the bridge and Trey joins in singing over me.

I burst out laughing. 'You like that song?'

'Oh, yeah.' Trey pauses his work, swinging the hammer in his hand. 'It's a classic. It's on my second go-to Christmas playlist.'

My eyes widen. 'I have a Christmas playlist too! I actually create playlists for everything.'

Trey laughs. 'Me too. I can spend hours making them.'

Finally someone who speaks my language!

'Let's see what songs we have in common,' I suggest, interested to know what Trey's taste in music is.

He grins. 'Go for it.'

'What about "All I Want For Christmas Is You"?'

Trey waves his hand dismissively. 'Give me a challenge, woman.'

I giggle. 'Okay ... "I Saw Mommy Kissing Santa Claus"?'

'Of course! I said *a challenge*. Let me give you one. "O Holy Night"?'

I scoff – call that a challenge? – but Trey is looking at me with a smile on his face.

'But you have to name the version.'

'Ooh, you're sneaky, Trey Anderson!'

'O Holy Night' has been covered by so many artists. I have a few versions on my playlist because I think the song is gorgeous, but which one would Trey have? I think back to

Trey singing the Usher album last night. This is definitely a guy who loves a good riff.

I hesitate for a moment longer. 'I think it's Whitney or Mariah.'

Trey crosses his arms. 'Interesting, but the question still remains: which one?'

He watches me intently, and for some reason it feels really important that I get this right. I love Whitney Houston, but in my opinion Mariah Carey is the queen of riffs and crazy impossible high notes. Plus, her version is my favourite one.

'Mariah?' I say uncertainly.

Trey's blank expression doesn't give anything away, but then he suddenly opens his mouth and sings Mariah's version of the song. It's so pure and beautiful and pitch perfect that my mouth literally drops open. He stops.

'You're meant to join me.'

'Oh, no.' I shake my head. 'I can't sing like that.'

'It doesn't matter. There's no one here but me.' His mouth turns up in an encouraging smile.

Like that's meant to comfort me.

'You wanna know a secret?' Trey says. 'I'm way more comfortable singing to one person than a crowd.'

I frown. 'Isn't that more intimate?'

Trey places the hammer on the floor and walks towards me, and I suddenly have another flashback to last night, which makes me feel hot all over.

He stops in front of me and shrugs. 'Maybe that's why I like it. There's a connection between me and that other person. It's

114

way less intimidating than having to impress a bunch of people all at once.' He starts singing again, adding in all the diva riffs. 'Come on, join in, Ariel!'

I look up to the ceiling, then give in and start to sing. And even though I don't sound great and Trey legit sounds like a recording artist, it's fun and freeing, and he doesn't take his eyes off me once, which is so sexy. Although I guess that's kind of weird when we're singing about Jesus being born!

'Trey, turn off that damn music and come help me!' Mrs Anderson yells from the basement. I jump and Trey bursts out laughing.

'Coming!' Trey shouts back. He rolls his eyes at me. 'I've been summoned.'

'I'll keep tidying up here.'

Trey nods, but he doesn't move. He's standing so close to me that if I took a step forward I'd be standing on his feet. Damn, he's so fine. He looks at me with his eyes half closed, and suddenly there's this weird energy between us. Are we having a moment? For a split second I think we're going to kiss, and it makes me nervous – but the good, excited kind.

'You have a pretty voice,' Trey says, breaking my thoughts.

I feel so dumb. Of course he's thinking about singing.

'Oh,' I say in a flat voice, and Trey cocks his head to the side, clearly trying to understand why my tone's changed.

'Trey!' Mrs Anderson yells, and this time Trey moves.

'Don't touch that bookshelf,' he shouts over his shoulder before he runs downs the stairs.

NINETEEN

Trey's playlist: 'Christmas in Hollis' by Run-D.M.C.

I take the stairs two at a time but my mind is on Ariel. It felt like we just had some sort of connection, almost as if the air was buzzing around us. Did she feel it too? She seemed mad when I mentioned her voice though. Maybe she thought I was taking the piss?

My phone vibrates in my pocket, but I ignore it when I see Mum glaring at me. There's water on the floor, at the bottom of the boxes and the loose books are soaking wet.

'I'm glad you're having fun upstairs while I'm here fixing your mess,' Mum says bitterly.

'But you told me to fix the book—'

'I'm going to run down the street to buy some sheets or something to help soak up the water,' Mum speaks over me.

'Then I need to find a shop that sells dehumidifiers. I've taken pictures for the insurance, so we'll see what they say.'

'Do you think they'll help?' I ask, and Mum shrugs.

'Go through the boxes and salvage what you can, then take the dry books to the upstairs stockroom. There are too many in the office now.' Mum pushes up her glasses and holds the bridge of her nose. 'Trey, I can't believe how irresponsible you've been.'

'I'm so sorry, Mum.' The water squelches under my trainers and I wish I knew who left the taps on so I could kill them. 'I really am.'

'Sorry doesn't pay the bills. It doesn't fix all of this. What am I supposed to tell your dad, huh?' she continues angrily.

There's nothing I can say to make the situation better so I stay quiet.

'I'm going to open up before I go. Ariel can be on the shop floor, but I need you to check in on her. Did you fix the bookshelf?'

'Almost,' I mumble.

Mum gives me the look again before she heads up, leaving me to fix the basement.

I lose track of time salvaging books, running up and down the stairs, trying to get rid of the water and ringing through purchases because Ariel isn't till-trained yet. I'm sweating alcohol and my headache is back, but I don't dare complain. I wish I could be on the shop floor hanging out with Ariel, but I barely have time to talk to her.

Mum pops in and out with cleaning equipment and

dehumidifiers, and she helps Ariel on the shop floor. It takes me until lunch to get the basement in a reasonable state and I call Mum down to inspect. My muscles are aching, and I'm tired and starving, but all I want is for her to stop being angry with me. She looks around and I hold my breath.

'It looks good,' she eventually says, and I breathe. 'I bought lunch for you. It's in the office.'

'Thanks,' I reply, glad to be somewhat out of her bad books.

My phone buzzes in my pocket. It's been going off all day and I'm sure it's just photos and videos being sent to me from the party. I go to the office and Ariel is there eating a sandwich.

'Your mum told me to take one,' she says, holding it up so I can see.

'What filling?' I sit down opposite her.

'Chicken and sweetcorn. She said you love the chicken and avocado ones.'

I hate avocado and Mum knows it.

'So, how are you finding your official first day?' I ask her as I peel the avocado out of my sandwich.

'It's been fun. Christmas time always puts me in a good mood.' Ariel pauses. 'You not gonna eat those?' She points at the avocado.

'Nah, help yourself.' She smiles and takes them from the top of my sandwich wrapper. 'I'm cool with Christmas; I just usually hate how busy the shops get. But this year, everything's different. I need Wonderland to be busy.'

I take a bite of my sandwich, focusing on it real hard because I can feel Ariel looking at me. What I can't take right now is pity. My phone buzzes again and I sigh as I take it out. The WhatsApp group is active with everyone talking about the party. I scroll through the notifications and can't help but smile. That really was some party.

I also see a shitload of missed calls from Blair. I hesitate. I'm really not in the mood for a fight, and I vaguely remember her shouting at me last night but I don't know why.

'Hey, do you know why Blair was angry with me yesterday?' I ask Ariel, who shuffles uncomfortably in her seat. 'Please, I need to know what I'm apologizing for.'

She brushes her red hair away from her face and I have a sudden flashback of me doing the same thing to her last night.

'You haven't apologized?' she says, and I feel my stomach drop. 'How can you not remember?'

'Put me out of my misery, please,' I beg.

'There was a girl that was hanging around you a lot, and at one point the two of you were talking. Blair saw and was giving the girl shit, but you started defending her. I dunno, I guess Blair thought the girl wanted to do more than talk to you.'

I groan and squint my eyes, bracing myself for more. 'And?'

'Blair obviously went crazy that you were hanging out with this girl and then she said you'd ruined her party and . . .' Ariel looks away.

I gulp. 'Oh, it's bad?'

Ariel nods. 'Well, you told Blair that she'd been dancing with a guy all night, so what was the problem? And then you started dancing with the girl in front of Blair.'

I hold the side of my head. '*Nooooo*, you're lying? I don't remember any of that.'

'Blair looked like she was gonna cry and then she walked out,' Ariel finishes.

I am officially a dick.

'Santi didn't say anything?' I ask, trying to piece memories together.

'She was on the other side of the party. I just happened to be walking by during your conversation with Blair.' Ariel looks at me with serious eyes. 'I can't believe you haven't apologized yet.'

I hold up my phone, showing all the missed calls from Blair. 'I'm going to step out for a sec to call her.'

I close the door behind me and stand in the small corridor, where I can see Mum at the till. I turn my back on her and dial Blair, but I have to ring several times before she finally picks up. Before she can speak, I'm in there telling her how sorry I am.

'I was drunk, babe, but that's no excuse. I didn't mean to ruin your party.'

She doesn't say anything, but I can hear her breathing.

'There's nothing between me and that girl. You know me. I don't go around dancing with random girls.' Unlike her, who dances with any and every guy when she's mad at me.

'You really hurt my feelings, Trey. Everyone saw the way you acted.'

'I know and I'm so sorry. Let me make it up to you. I'll take you somewhere romantic,' I suggest, hoping she'll say yes.

'Tonight?' Blair asks, sounding more forgiving than she did earlier.

I rub my forehead. 'No, I can't do tonight. Mum's on the warpath. Someone left the taps on in the basement and the bookshop—'

'Oh, for fuck's sake, all you care about is the bookshop!' Blair screeches, making me pull the phone away from my ear. 'You have no time for me any more. I'm basically in a relationship with myself.'

'Are you serious?' I hiss into the phone. How can she be so selfish? 'I threw a party for you.'

'That you ignored me at,' Blair counters. 'You're always prioritizing work over our relationship.'

'This is my family's bookshop, Blair. How can you even think it wouldn't be a priority for me?' I ask, anger bubbling in my chest.

Blair barks out a laugh. 'Are you kidding me? This is the same bookshop you used to cuss out for being forced to work there. It's only recently that you've become even remotely interested in it. So what's changed, huh?'

Blair's not wrong, but her reaction still hurts. It's on the tip of my tongue to tell her about what's been happening at the bookshop but, for the first time in our relationship, I don't feel comfortable sharing my business with her.

'I've got to go back to work,' I say bluntly.

'Of course you do,' she replies, her voice dripping with sarcasm. Then the phone goes dead.

TWENTY

Ariel's playlist: 'Sleigh Ride' by TLC

I can tell by Trey's face that the call with Blair didn't go well. He sits back down in the office and leans his arms on his thighs, staring at the floor. I continue eating my sandwich silently, not knowing what to say. Mrs Anderson opens the door and looks from me to Trey.

'You okay?' She gently taps his shoulder, and Trey looks up and gives her a small smile.

'I'm cool. You off?' he answers.

'In about ten minutes, so I'll wait until you finish lunch and can return to the shop floor. I'm picking up Reon from his art class on the way home. What time are you going to the cinema tomorrow?' Mrs Anderson asks.

I glance at Trey, who frowns.

'Reon said you promised him?' Mrs Anderson presses. 'He said it was something to do with Blair?'

Trey throws back his head and lets out a loud groan. Mrs Anderson looks at me and pulls a face, and I try not to laugh so I don't betray Trey.

'Ariel, I'm sorry today has been so hectic,' Mrs Anderson says, 'but I hope you've found it okay?'

I nod. 'It's been good, thank you.'

'Can you do a half-day tomorrow in the morning with Trey? He has to cover his Dad's shift and I'll be at church.'

'No problem,' I say at the same time as Trey pipes up with 'What?' He throws up his hands. 'I have to work *and* take Reon to the cinema?'

Mrs Anderson ignores him and takes out a brown envelope from her bag. 'Here's your contract. Have a read, and if it's all okay, bring it back tomorrow.'

'Thanks, Mrs Anderson.' I take the envelope from her and she smiles at me. A deep dimple appears on one side of her mouth, but it disappears as soon as she looks at Trey. 'I'll see you at dinner. Remember, you're taking Reon *and* his friend tomorrow. Oh, and I expect you to pay for them both.'

Mrs Anderson leaves and Trey rubs his face. 'Is this actually my life?'

He looks so defeated that I genuinely feel sorry for him, and even though I don't like Blair, and Trey and I had a moment earlier, I have an idea that could help him. I ignore my heart that's telling me to keep my mouth shut and say, 'There's this place called The Grotto in Shoreditch. It's a pop-up Christmas fair.' Trey looks at me. 'There's live singing, really cool stands, and you can even toast different-flavoured marshmallows on an open fire. Anyway, it's pretty romantic.' I shrug. 'Maybe you could take Blair?'

There's a part of me that hopes Trey will laugh off my suggestion, but he sits up and his eyes go wide. 'Yeah? Is it expensive? As you can tell, I'm low for cash.'

I smile. 'It's free to get into, so you just need money if you want to buy something there. I'm not sure if it's really Blair's scene. She seems like an up-West kind of girl, and this is a bit more hipster, artsy vibes, but it's fun and really festive.'

Trey scoffs. 'You're right about that. Her favourite film is *Legally Blonde*. But this place sounds cool. You said artsy? Do you do stuff there?'

'My dad and I used to sell Christmas cards with his friend Matty. But I'll be selling them on my own this year. It's a good way to earn some money.'

'How come your dad doesn't want to sell any more?'

It's an innocent question, but any time I have to mention that Dad is no longer around it feels like someone is squeezing my heart, making my chest physically hurt. Every time I say it aloud, it makes it even more real. And I honestly don't know how I'll manage The Grotto without him. I take a deep breath.

'Cancer. He died at the beginning of the year.' I shrug, like it's no big deal, but my eyes betray me because they well up and I have to blink loads until the tears disappear.

Trey leans over and takes my hand. 'I'm so sorry, Ariel.'

'Thank you. It's weird – sometimes it doesn't feel real, you know?'

Trey squeezes my hand. 'Your dad must have been proud of you though, with all your beautiful artwork.'

My heart flutters the way it always does when someone compliments my art, but this time it's an even stronger sensation and I know it's because the words have come from Trey's mouth.

'Art was our thing. My dad went to the Artists' Studio in West London, and I've wanted to go there ever since he told me about it. They have the best art teachers, who I'm hoping can take me to the next level. Maybe then I could be an artist for a living and sell my work in galleries. I'm writing my application form now. It's actually the reason I asked for this job – I need the money to afford the tuition.'

Whenever Dad used to describe the Artists' Studio to me, he made it sound like one of the best times of his life. He said it was where he became the artist he always dreamed of being, and it's how he met Nigel Harley, the eccentric gallery owner of Attic in the Barbican, where Dad's pieces were on display for years. I used to love nothing more than going with him to see his new pieces, and I always went home and tried my best to recreate them.

'Christmas was a special time for us cause every year we sold our cards at The Grotto. It's gonna be strange without him.' I push up my glasses and wipe my eyes with my spare hand.

Trey's rubbing his thumb in a circle along my hand, and there's something so comforting about the small gesture.

'I'll buy a bunch of cards from you,' Trey says, shooting me a smile.

I don't really talk about my dad, especially with people I'm not close with. I suddenly get this weird feeling where I feel super exposed, almost like Trey's just seen me naked. I stand up abruptly, forcing our hands apart, and he looks at me, concern etching his face.

'We better get back to the shop floor so your Mum can go.'

'Oh, yeah, right,' Trey says. 'You sure you're okay?'

I nod and lead the way out.

For the rest of the shift, Trey and I talk to anyone that comes in, both of us trying to make as many sales as possible. But it stays pretty quiet all afternoon. Some customers buy more than one book, and I think we've done okay, but when Trey counts the money at the end of the day I see his shoulders sag.

'Not great,' he says when he notices me looking at him.

'We'll do better tomorrow,' I reply enthusiastically, but all Trey does is shrug.

Before clocking off, I place a few more discarded books on the correct shelves. I keep glancing to the side of the bookshop where the ground is raised, making it look like a stage. That would be a perfect place to have a sick backdrop. Then in the corner there could be a children's area, so parents can sit with their kids and read books. I look at the YA section. There's room there for a small sofa and a coffee table. Maybe Wonderland could try a weekly book club to get the community involved. The bookshop's cool but dated. It needs to be brighter, lighter and more current, which would be pretty easy to make happen. If they switched it up, it could be one of the coolest bookshops in London.

I'm only home for a few seconds before Noah runs up to me. I ruffle his thick Afro hair. He really needs to go to the barber's.

'Look what I did at art!' He hands me a Christmas card.

'Wow!' It's Mary and Joseph in the stables, holding baby Jesus. His detail and shading are brilliant – much better than I was at his age.

'Can you sell it at The Grotto?' he asks.

'Of course,' I say, and Noah grins. 'Can you make more? I'm sure these will fly off the shelves.'

He wraps his arms round my waist. 'Thanks, Ariel!' Then he takes the card back and runs up the stairs.

Mum peeks her head out of the kitchen door. 'Noah! You better calm down with all that running!'

'Sorry, Ma!' Noah shouts down.

Mum tuts and smiles when she sees me. 'How was your day, darling?'

I join her in the kitchen and breathe in the delicious smell of stew chicken. 'It was good. I'm working tomorrow morning as well – is that okay?'

'Sure. I'm off tomorrow, but I'm dropping Noah at the cinema. He's going with one of his friends from art.'

'Nice.' My eyes linger on the packet of biscuits on the counter, but instead I pick up a pear and bite into it, catching the juices that race down my chin. 'How long until dinner?'

'About a half-hour,' she answers.

'Okay, cool. I'm going to sketch some Christmas card ideas for The Grotto.'

Mum looks at me, her eyes softening. 'I'm really glad you're doing it, Ariel. Dad would be so proud.'

I swallow hard, a lump forming in my throat. 'I'll be down in a bit,' I say, turning towards the kitchen door.

I dump my bag, coat and scarf on my bed, ignoring the Artists' Studio application form that's sitting on my desk waiting for me to fill it in. I still don't know what I'm going to do to make me stand out.

I grab a piece of card and fold it in half. I know exactly what I want it to look like so I draw quickly. The large window that frames the whole card is misty and has frost on it. Inside the window, there are bookshelves and a table, and a young couple are leaning in, smiling at each other and holding hands. When I'm done, I study the card, frowning as I spot some issues with it. I need more snow . . . and the details of the bookshop could be stronger. But the biggest problem is that the couple in the centre look just like me and Trey.

TWENTY-ONE

Trey's playlist: 'What You Want for Christmas' by Quad City DJ's, The 69 Boyz and K-Nock

I collapse on the couch opposite Dad, who looks up from studying something with Reon.

'Where were you last night?'

'Boogs', I say. I don't know if Mum told Dad what happened, so I wait to find out, but he just nods and I breathe a sigh of relief. Dad would have lost it a lot worse than Mum.

'What's that?' I ask, pointing at what they're reading.

'Go show him.' Dad gently pushes Reon's back and he runs over, thrusting a comic strip into my hand.

'It's Super Dad, but I need a better name.'

Reon's drawn Dad falling on the floor, but rising up with bulging muscles and half a body that looks like steel, which I know is meant to be Vibranium. It's brilliant.

'We gotta get this copyrighted so Marvel don't steal it.' I ruffle Reon's hair. 'This is so good, little man.' He beams at me.

Mum walks in with a tray of food for Dad, and me and Reon go to sit at the table. Since Dad's fall, we've been eating together in the living room rather than in the dining room. I love it because it means we get to watch TV at the same time.

Mum serves up fried chicken, corn on the cob, rice and a bean salad – my favourite.

'Thanks, Mum.' I smile at her, but she doesn't return it. Okay, maybe I haven't been totally forgiven yet.

There's a game show on TV that I'm barely following. I just want to eat, shower and sleep, but I have coursework to finish for business studies. (Dad's idea, not mine. He said it would be wise to prepare me for taking over Wonderland). I'm way too tired though, so it will have to wait until tomorrow night.

I glance at Mum, who's being strangely quiet. Usually when we watch game shows, she's the first person to shout out what she thinks are the right answers, but instead she sits in silence, her plate untouched.

'You okay, Mum?' I ask.

'Huh?' She looks up at me. 'Yes, of course . . .' She shakes her head. 'Actually, no, there's something I need to speak to you all about.' She reaches for the remote and pauses it. We all stare at her. Mum takes a deep breath and now I'm worried. 'I met with David Raymond today from Raymond and Raymond.'

'You did what?' Dad throws his cutlery on his plate. It clatters noisily before falling to the floor.

Reon frowns. 'Who's that?'

'They're property developers, and they contacted me to ask for a meeting,' Mum explains. 'The bookshop's in trouble and it's not getting any better. There was a flood today in the basement.'

'A flood? What flood?' Dad looks from me to Mum, and a wave of guilt washes over me.

'Well, it's—' I start.

'I'm not sure where the water came from,' Mum says over me, avoiding my eyes. 'It's one of those things. But we lost a lot of money because some of the stock was destroyed. And we're just not hitting the numbers like we used to.' Mum stands up and sits on the armrest so she's next to Dad. She puts a hand on his shoulder. 'Baby, we're sinking, and we need to get out while we can.'

'I'm not selling,' Dad says firmly, crossing his arms.

I'm sure if he could stand up right now, he would have already walked out of the room.

'I don't want to sell Wonderland either, but Raymond and Raymond are offering to pay above value. We can start something new if we—'

'No,' Dad says, and Mum gets to her feet.

'I gave up my career to help you with the bookshop,' she says through gritted teeth. 'Now, Clive, we've tried – okay? But if things don't turn around, then we have no choice but to sell the shop after Christmas.' With that, Mum storms out of the living room.

Dad huffs. 'Someone come take this food.'

Reon jumps up to grab it and takes it into the kitchen. I put my head in my hands. This is all my fault. Because of me, we've lost even more money, and now we're going to lose the bookshop.

'Trey—' Dad's voice makes me look up. He looks pained, and at first I think it's because of his leg, but it's not. Dad thumps his chest. 'Wonderland is my family's bookshop. We can't lose it. Please go talk to your mother. Please try to convince her—'

'Hey, hey, it's okay, Dad.' I kneel beside him and Dad hangs his head. 'Everything is going to be all right. We'll think of something.'

Dad nods and I put my arm round him. I *have* to save Wonderland. I just don't know how.

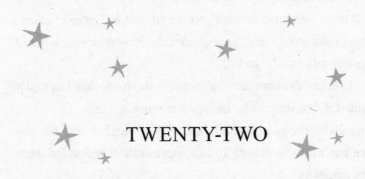

TWENTY-TWO

Ariel's playlist: 'Oh Santa!' by Mariah Carey

Thirteen days till Christmas

I'm outside the bookshop holding two gingerbread lattes. Trey waves as he gets closer and I hold up the drinks.

'You're a lifesaver,' he says, taking one off me and using his other hand to open up the bookshop. He goes to the back to turn off the alarm, and I switch on the lights, smiling as the fairy lights twinkle in greeting. I walk to the office to dump my belongings and Trey joins me a few minutes later, reaching over the table to grab some sugar.

'I like it extra sweet,' he says when he sees me looking, but my mind is on my Christmas card.

'Did you bring it?' Trey asks.

'Huh?' My heart stops.

How does he know?

'The contract.'

'Oh ... yeah, of course.' Relieved that he wasn't talking about the card, I stand up and grab the brown envelope out of my bag and hand it to him.

He takes the contract out, I guess to check that I actually signed it, but instead he looks up at me solemnly.

'I know you're only a temp, but I feel like I should tell you that my mum is definitely looking to sell Wonderland after Christmas.'

'Oh, no!' I gasp. 'Is it cause of the flood?'

'It didn't help. My dad doesn't want to sell though. The bookshop has been in his family for generations.' Trey rubs his hand over his hair. 'I feel like this is all my fault, you know?'

'You didn't leave the taps running,' I say, trying to reassure him.

'But I didn't check they were off.' Trey drums his fingers on the table. 'I just ... I need to save Wonderland.'

I want Wonderland to be saved too. I know I've only been at the bookshop a short while, but I love working here, especially with Trey. It's weird the difference a few days can make. 'I have an idea.'

I tell Trey my ideas about what could be done to the space to make it cooler, and he listens quietly.

'You know, I had a similar idea,' he says when I'm done. 'But Dad wouldn't agree to it. Wonderland has barely changed since my great-grandad ran it.'

'Why don't you suggest it again? There are only two weeks left until Christmas. It's worth us trying, right?'

Trey leans back in his chair and smiles. 'Us?'

'I need the job,' I say quickly.

Trey laughs. 'Fair play. So where should we start?'

'We could try the book club idea? It'll encourage the community to come to the shop and support a local business.'

'The resurrection of Wonderland Book Club.' Trey must see my confused face because he adds, 'Oh, we had one years ago, but Dad stopped it. I'm up for bringing it back.'

'Okay, great, and what about a Christmas showcase or something?' I ask.

Trey's eyes light up. 'Hey, that's not a bad idea. Every year at church we always do a Christmas guest service, with singing, dancing, acting. It's always really cool. Maybe something like that?'

'Yes, that's brilliant! We can give out mince pies and maybe mulled wine and ask for donations.'

I'm already lost in my fantasy of a packed-out crowd, watching in awe as Trey sings Christmas carols onstage in front of an amazing mural of Black writers. I gasp. That's what I can use for the Artists' Studio application form! That's definitely something that would inspire the community – a painting by local talent, Ariel Spencer, in a Black-owned bookshop that the community needs to save.

'I can paint a mural!' I announce, just as Trey takes a sip of his latte, which he immediately coughs up.

'What?' he chokes.

'Come, let me show you.'

He follows me to the other side of the bookshop where I point at the current blank wall behind the raised stage.

'Just imagine a vibrant mural right there to really bring the bookshop to life. Name me some of your favourite Black writers.'

'Toni Morrison, Estee Mase – wait, you can draw them?'

I nod enthusiastically. 'And if you or your parents hate it, I can paint over it.'

Trey scoffs. 'Like I could hate anything that you create.'

My cheeks flush. He has no idea how that offhand comment has literally made my whole day.

'I need to run all this by Mum first, but don't you think we're going to need help if we're organizing a whole showcase?'

Trey's right. There's so much to do and we'll need a team to help us. Then it hits me!

'Don't worry – I know exactly who to ask.'

We're two hours into opening when Annika and Jolie arrive. Annika has a Strawberries and Cream Frappuccino in her hand, even though it's about zero degrees outside. I'm serving a customer and Trey's on the tills, but I can see them looking around the bookshop. Like me, they've come in a few times but not enough to know the layout of the shop. To be honest, we're all Amazon next-day-delivery girls, but after seeing how hard the Andersons work to keep their independent bookshop running I'm definitely going to shop more locally.

In the summer, Jolie and I helped Annika with a film project for her media coursework. Annika's a visionary and she knew exactly how everything should look. I was in charge of bringing the set to life and Jolie was the practical one. Everything artistic Annika and I wanted to do, Jolie would bring us back down to earth and made us question how we were going to do it. At the time, we really hated that Jolie wasn't allowing us to be creative, but she was spot-on about everything, and Annika got top marks in her class for that project.

I catch Annika looking at everything with an appraising eye, while Jolie actually has a notepad in her hand. The customer I'm talking to goes back to browsing and Trey finishes up on the till, so we both walk over to them.

'I know what the problem is,' Annika announces. 'There are too many books.'

Trey looks at her like she just sprouted two heads. 'It's a bookshop.'

Annika cups his face. 'Trey, thank God you're cute.'

Trey swats her hand away. 'Your hands are freezing.'

To be honest, I can see what Annika means. There's no breathing space on the shop floor, everything just feels cluttered. At the party, there was just more room to move – well, once you'd ignored the ridiculous number of people that were here.

'If we move that and that, I think it could make a big difference.' I point at the rows of books, ignoring Trey's alarmed eyes.

'Exactly,' Annika says, sipping her drink.

'Do you have any chairs that people can sit on?' Jolie asks Trey.

'Erm . . . no.'

'Hmm.' Jolie writes *CHAIRS* in capital letters on her

notepad before turning to Annika. 'I'm thinking we can fit seating for about forty people for the showcase.'

'Sounds good. We need a cool hashtag too,' Annika says. 'We trend this shit, get the whole community excited for the showcase and willing to donate, and then Wonderland will be in the clear. What about hashtag WonderlandBlackOwned or hashtag SaveWonderland?'

'Yes, I love that.' Jolie writes them down. 'They're easy to remember and highlighting that the bookshop is Black-owned is key.' She looks at Trey and holds out her hand. 'Phone, please.'

'W-what?' Trey stutters, but he takes his phone out of his pocket and hands it to her.

'Password?' Jolie holds his phone and he types it in. 'Okay, let's see here.'

Trey leans forward, and without looking up Jolie says, 'I won't look at your nudes.'

'I don't have any nudes!' Trey says, but he doesn't sound super convincing. He turns to me, as if he's read my mind, and adds, 'I don't!'

'I didn't say anything!' I stifle a laugh. I definitely wouldn't mind seeing a topless selfie.

Jolie goes straight to Trey's Instagram and looks at his followers.

'You have ten thousand followers and all you post is yourself. Why don't you use your platform to spread the word about the bookshop?' Jolie asks.

Trey shrugs. 'Wonderland has its own account.'

'Yeah, but it only has four hundred followers.' Jolie presses something else on the screen. 'Boogs has eleven thousand. You both have a ridiculous amount of girls that follow you just cause you're hot. Boogs posts videos of him dancing and they always get loads of likes, so maybe you could post a video of you singing and then talking about the bookshop?'

Trey shakes his head. 'To share with my followers? I don't know—'

'Maybe not singing,' I say, and Trey looks at me gratefully. 'But Jolie has a point. Think about how many of your followers would come down to support you if you asked them.'

'You think?' Trey says, looking deep in thought as he takes back his phone. Has he forgotten that he managed to get a whole bunch of people to pay to party in a bookshop?

'Right, so a Christmas Eve showcase at Wonderland around four p.m.?' Annika says.

'How about midday in case people have to travel out of London to see family?' Jolie responds.

'Good thinking.' Annika raises her Frappuccino at Jolie.

Trey looks back and forth between the two of them.

'Now we just need a rough running order, so, Trey, can you sort that?' Annika says, and we all look at Trey, who gulps.

'Erm . . . yeah, I guess.'

'Great! Girl, I've got to go, but call me later?' Annika leans over and we hug.

'Thank you, guys.' I hug Jolie next. 'I'll talk to you about the book club idea later too.'

'Defo! Let us know.' They wave as they leave.

'I didn't know Jolie was so ... forceful,' Trey says once they're out of earshot.

'She's not usually, but give her a task and she's on it. So, what do you think? Wonderland at Christmas Eve, saving the Black-owned bookshop?'

Trey rubs his jaw. 'You really think this will work?'

I nod. 'Especially if you use your platform to get people talking about Wonderland. Who knows, maybe other bookshops and authors will back it. And maybe think about singing at the show?'

'I'm not going to sing,' Trey says, sounding final.

'Okay, well Boogs can dance, and there must be lots of talent around here.' I wait for Trey to say something, but instead he's staring at me with an expression on his face that I can't read. 'What?'

He shakes his head. 'Sorry, I was just thinking about how much you've helped me since I've got to know you. Thank you, Ariel. I really do appreciate it ... I appreciate you.'

My stomach does a somersault. I'm about to say the same back to him when he adds, 'Even though you lied about us being friends to get a job at Wonderland.'

'Shut up, Trey.' I playfully hit him.

'You know what I was thinking? Are you up for a bit of spying by any chance?' He raises an eyebrow at me and I match it.

'What's the mission?'

Trey grins. 'Books! Books! Books!'

*

I leave Wonderland and walk to Books! Books! Books! It's busy on the high street and everyone is in a rush, carrying shopping bags. If only they could rush into Wonderland and make us some money.

Books! Books! Books! is rammed when I arrive, and I'm glad Trey isn't here because seeing this definitely would have made him feel crap. It's a two-floor bookshop with assistants in blue T-shirts running back and forth. The shop is packed with books and signs that scream *HALF PRICE!*, *3 BOOKS FOR £5!*, *6 CHILDREN'S BOOKS for a TENNER!* I take out my phone and jot down some notes. Unlike Wonderland, they have books on everything, from gardening to fiction to craft books. I take a picture of a stack of the new Estee Mase book that's ten per cent cheaper than at Wonderland. How can Wonderland even compete with them? We'll have to offer discounts too.

I spy a group of people in the middle of the shop, bending down into what looks like a tube. One of the sales people walks by me.

'Excuse me?' I ask.

Rachel, according to her name tag, backs up and smiles at me. I point at the tube. 'What's that?'

She follows my finger. 'Oh, that's the bargain bucket. Every day we throw in slow-selling books for a pound. It's a massive hit.'

One pound? I don't know if Mrs Anderson will go for it, but if she agrees, we'd be able to bring in a few more sales each day.

Trey greets me with an eager smile when I arrive back.

'I have notes.' I hand him my phone and slowly his smile starts to fade.

'These prices! I'll speak to Mum. Maybe we can get a better discount from the wholesalers, but I dunno . . .'

'Why don't we ask the publishers directly?' I say. 'I'm sure they'd love to help an indie bookshop. We should give it a shot. What's the worst that can happen?'

TWENTY-THREE

Trey's playlist: 'The Mistletoe and Me' by Isaac Hayes

'Ariel!'

It's the afternoon and I look up from the book I'm reading at the till at the sound of my brother's voice. Reon runs into the bookshop with Mum behind him, but he goes right into Ariel's arms, who giggles as she hugs him. How do they know each other?

After I greet Mum, I walk over to them, pointing at them both. 'Is someone going to explain?'

'Ariel's my art teacher,' Reon says, hugging me. 'She's Noah's sister. You know, Noah my best friend from art? The one that's coming to the cinema with us.'

'Wait, you're his art teacher?' I ask, and Ariel glances at me with the same look of surprise.

'And you're taking my brother to the cinema?' she replies.

'Can you come with us?' Reon asks, looking excitedly at Ariel and then back at me.

Ariel's eyes find mine and I realize I actually do want her to come. I shrug like it's no big deal, but my heart starts to race.

'If you haven't got plans after work, you should,' I say nonchalantly.

Ariel puts her finger on her chin and looks up at the ceiling as though she's really thinking about it.

'Please?' Reon begs with his hands clasped.

'Oh, go on then,' Ariel says.

'Yay!' Reon jumps up and down and I have to suck in my cheeks to stop the cheesy grin that's trying to spread over my face. To be honest, I think I'm more excited than he is.

Mum takes over on the shop floor so Ariel and I can leave, and I head downstairs to the toilet, brushing my waves in the mirror.

'Trey, you down here?' Mum calls.

'Yeah,' I shout back.

A moment later, Mum leans on the door. She peers at me over her glasses.

'Hey, I forgot to say that I sent Ariel to do some spying at Books! Books! Books! and the discounts are crazy. Can we offer some here and see how they do? Maybe even go direct to the publishers for a better discount? They might be more generous if they know that an indie is at risk of closing.'

'That's a good idea,' Mum says, looking impressed. 'I can definitely ask.'

I grin at her in the mirror. 'I've got some other ideas too. Can I run them by you later?'

'Sure.' She smiles. 'So, Ariel's going to the cinema with you ...?'

'Yeah. Did you know she's Reon's teacher? Small world!'

'Trey,' Mum says in such a serious tone that I suddenly freeze, expecting more bad news. 'Do you think it's a good idea bringing her?'

I frown. What's the big deal? It's not like it's a date or anything.

'Does Blair know that Ariel is going with you?' Mum asks when I don't respond.

I turn to face her and she has her arms crossed over her chest. What has Blair got to do with this? I know Mum likes her, and, to give Blair the credit she deserves, she's always polite and gifts Mum a present every birthday and Christmas, but it's not like I'm cheating on her.

But you really wanted Ariel to come, a voice in my head says.

'Me and Blair aren't great right now,' I confess, and Mum's eyes widen. 'But I'm taking her out next week ... once I get her to talk to me. Ariel and I are just friends. You're reading this all wrong.' I look back at the mirror.

'Hmm,' Mum says suspiciously. 'I've never seen you brush your hair when you're going to meet any of your other friends.'

And before I can respond, she's gone. I like Ariel, but I don't like like her. Do I? I mean, yeah, she's pretty, smart,

talented and really caring, but we're friends. Just friends ...
And anyway, I have a girlfriend.

A plus-sized, dark-skinned woman with her hair in a bun is
waiting outside the cinema with a young boy with an Afro.
They wave at us as we approach.

'Ariel!' The little boy, who I assume is Noah, runs up to her.
'What are you doing here?'

'I work with Reon's older brother, Trey, so I'm joining you
guys.' Ariel nods her head in my direction. 'You gonna say hi?'

'Hi.' Noah waves shyly at me before he high-fives my
brother, and they excitedly start to discuss all the cool sweets
they think I'm going to buy them.

I greet Ariel's mum with a handshake.

'Nice to meet you, Trey.' She reaches into her purse.

'Don't worry, Mrs Spencer, I've got this,' I say. 'Everything's
on me today.'

'A gentleman,' Mrs Spencer says, nodding at me
approvingly. But Mum's in my head and now I'm wondering
if she thinks we're on a date.

'Reon asked Ariel to join us,' I say quickly, feeling the need
to explain myself. 'I only found out today that Ariel teaches
the art class he goes to.'

'Oh, you didn't know? The children love her.' Mrs Spencer
looks proudly at Ariel, and she rolls her eyes but she's smiling.
'Well, have fun, kids. Noah, give me a kiss and be good for
your sister and Trey, okay?'

We head inside and it's not too busy so there's only a short queue. Christmas music is playing over the speakers and I notice that Ariel keeps tapping her foot and playing with her hair, like she's nervous. Is she nervous being here with me? I haven't got vibes from her before that she's into me like that. I look at the boys and they have their faces pressed up against the ice-cream counter, their breaths creating mist on the glass.

I wish Marvel did Christmas films, because our only options are a *Star Wars* spin off (too long) or a holiday romance film (too grown). But, to be honest, I'd take either over the film Reon and Noah choose, which is about animals trying to save Christmas. I'm already falling asleep thinking about it.

'Ninety minutes we'll never got back,' Ariel whispers to me, as if she read my mind.

'At least we have each other,' I respond, and she blushes. 'I mean, so we're not suffering alone.' *Stop talking, Trey.*

It's our turn in the queue now and Reon and Noah run over.

'Four tickets to *The Unexpected Christmas Helpers*, please,' I ask the woman behind the desk.

'Can we get ice cream?' Reon asks, and Noah nods enthusiastically.

'It's ice cream *or* popcorn,' I explain.

'Ooh, popcorn,' Noah says, but Reon's deep in thought.

'Popcorn is one of the most common choking hazards. Plus, it's dry, which means I'll drink more and have to go to the toilet during the film, so I think ice cream is the better choice.'

The ticket woman stares at him agog, making me laugh.

'Okay, how about we get four ice creams and a large popcorn to share.'

'No ice cream for me, thanks,' Ariel says, shaking her head. 'I'll just have the popcorn.'

We get our tickets and food and head to the screen. I'm thinking about where I should sit as we walk into the room, but the decision is made for me. Noah sits on the seat by the wall and Reon plonks down next to him. I'm secretly pleased but kind of nervous, because that leaves me and Ariel next to each other for the whole film. I sit down with the popcorn resting on my lap.

Noah insisted on getting a cone and it's stacked up. He leans forward and says to Ariel, 'Try it! It's so good.'

Ariel wavers and eventually gestures for us to pass it down, going from Noah to Reon, then me to Ariel.

'Ah, shoot.'

I look over and see a bit of ice cream on her chest. I quickly look away, hoping she didn't see me, but out of the corner of my eye I notice her scooping it up with her finger and placing it in her mouth. I suddenly feel very hot and reach over for Reon's water.

'Dry popcorn?' Reon asks, looking at me knowingly.

'Yeah, you were right,' I say with a smile.

Thankfully, Ariel is done, Noah has his ice cream back and I'm able to look at the screen. The lights go down and the trailers start. I put my hand in the popcorn at the same time Ariel does, but we're going for the same piece, because for a brief second my finger wraps around hers.

'Sorry,' I say, withdrawing my hand.

What is going on? I feel so aware of her. Her arm is resting against mine on the armrest, which usually annoys me – I love an armrest – but her bare skin is touching mine and it feels nice. Her leg occasionally brushes against mine too and it sends a shiver up my body every time. And her tits ... I squeeze my eyes tight. Do NOT think about her tits. I glance over at her, and she's engrossed in the film. I take in her full lips that are painted red like her hair, her large brown eyes behind her black-framed glasses, the beauty spot by her ear. And for the second time today, I ask myself, do I like Ariel?

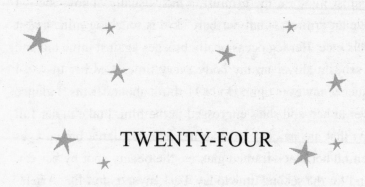

TWENTY-FOUR

Ariel's playlist: 'Hallelujah' by Fantasia

I can feel Trey watching me, so I deliberately keep my focus on the screen. Is he checking me out? *Oh God, please let him be checking me out.* The film starts and I try to get into it, but it's hard when he's sat right next to me. I sneak a glance at him. He has the most chiselled face I have seen in real life, and how is his skin so perfectly clear? His arms look even bigger from this angle and I can see the outline of his muscles through his shirt.

Focus on the film, Ariel!

Trey leans over to me and his lips brush my ear. It takes everything in me not to collapse to the floor. 'Out of ten, how bad is this film?'

'Ten,' I say, and Trey laughs.

'Shh!' Reon glares at us and Trey presses his lips together to stop himself from laughing.

I avert my eyes back to the screen, but I can't even tell what's happening. Reon and Noah are pissing themselves laughing though.

Eventually, the end credits roll and I brush my tongue over my teeth, praying there's no popcorn stuck in them. The lights come on and I stand up, putting on my coat and scarf.

'There might be a bonus scene,' Reon protests.

'That's Marvel, little man,' Trey says.

'We won't know unless we stay,' Reon responds.

Trey rolls his eyes and I sit back down. But I don't mind – this way we get a little bit more time.

'Favourite part of the film?' I ask, and Trey scoffs.

'You think I was watching that? I can't wait to get home and sleep.' Trey groans. 'Damn! I've just remembered I've got an essay to finish.'

I laugh. 'Are you going to talk to your parents about the ideas we came up with, like the Christmas showcase?'

Trey nods. 'Mum seems cool about the discounts. Hopefully her and Dad will let us try anything.'

Us!

He continues. 'I've been thinking about this social media stuff, and, you're right – I'll get on it. Any tips?'

'Hmm, I think just be yourself and be super clear about what you want to achieve. Maybe an Instagram post on your actual page, rather than just your story, and then hopefully people will share it,' I say.

Trey raises his eyebrow. 'Topless or not topless?'

'Topless, for sure,' I say in a sultry voice that I didn't even know I had. Trey slowly looks down from my eyes to my lips, and I honestly feel like I can't breathe.

'There's no bonus scene!' Noah moans loudly, breaking whatever that was between me and Trey.

I look around and realize the cinema has completely cleared out. It's just us and a black screen now.

'Coats on, boys,' I say, standing up.

Trey hands them the rest of the popcorn to finish and they laugh as they throw pieces at each other as we walk out. We get to the foyer and Trey and the boys go to the toilet. I'm looking at the upcoming film posters when I hear my name being called.

I turn to see Bebe and Kyle Torano from college, hand in hand. At first glance, Bebe looks like a Kardashian imitator, with her long black hair, fake lips and tight dress under a fur coat.

'Oh, hey,' I say, surprised.

'What are you doing here?' she asks.

I can't help but flinch. There's something in the way she says 'you' like she doesn't understand how I could possibly be at the cinema.

'I just came out of a film,' I reply. *Because why else would I be here?*

'I told them I'd meet them outside— Bebe? Hey, Kyle.' Trey comes over and greets Kyle first.

Bebe frowns as she looks from me to Trey, and then her eyes lock with mine and a slow smiles creeps onto her face. It reminds me of when the villain in a film realizes how to take down the hero.

'Hi, Trey.' Bebe hugs him, keeping her eyes on me. When they let go, she says, 'So, you two are here together?'

'Yeah,' Trey says easily. How can he not see that Bebe is practically salivating? He and Kyle start talking about something, but Bebe is watching me intently with a smirk still on her face.

'We're here with our little brothers,' I add. 'They're best friends.'

Bebe leans forward and looks from left to right. 'Oh? I can't see them.'

'They're in the—'

'Babe, we're gonna miss the film,' Bebe says over me, tugging on Kyle's arm.

'Cool. See you tomorrow, T.' He and Trey do that handshake into a hug that guys always do, and then Kyle waves at me.

I watch them walk away. Bebe looks unsteady in her leather thigh-high heeled boots and I hope she falls over. The boys run over to us once she's out of sight – just my luck. They're talking animatedly, still buzzing about the film, and Trey is doing a good job of pretending to be interested, but I have this weird feeling in my gut that stops me from joining in.

Why do I feel like Bebe is up to something?

TWENTY-FIVE

Trey's playlist: '3 Kings' by Yo Gotti, Fabolous
and DJ Khaled

We get home in time for dinner. Reon immediately runs into the living room to tell Dad – lucky guy – all about the film. I find Mum in the kitchen cooking up something that smells delicious.

'How was it?' Mum asks as she stirs a big pot of fried rice.

'Boring, but Reon and Noah had fun.'

'And Ariel enjoyed it?' Mum asks with an edge to her voice.

'Yes, my *friend*, Ariel, had fun,' I respond, overemphasizing the word friend. Mum shakes her head but doesn't respond. I don't know why she's giving me shit for taking Ariel to the cinema. She knows I wouldn't cheat on Blair.

'Look, can we be friends now?' I walk over to her with my arms open.

'I'm cooking,' Mum says, but I don't listen as I wrap my arms round her, hugging her tightly. She taps me lightly on my arm. 'No more mess-ups, Trey.'

'Yes, ma'am.' I give an army salute. 'After dinner, I want to run those ideas about the bookshop by you and Dad.'

'Baby, I was thinking about what you said, and I'm fine with discounting some books, but I don't want to get carried away when the margins might not work for us.' She looks at me with a sad smile before continuing. 'The insurance finally got back to me today and they said, because the taps were left on, it's our fault. It would have been different if we had had a leak or something. They're not paying up.'

'For real?' Damn. Now this hashtag SaveWonderland idea really does need to work. 'I'm so sorry, Mum.'

Mum waves her hand at me as if to say *Forget about it*. 'Dinner will be ready in a bit. Help me set up.'

We eat dinner, with Reon giving a play-by-play of the film. I'm glad my parents can hear how much I suffered today.

'How was closing?' I ask when Reon finally takes a breath.

'Quiet,' Mum says. 'I walked by Books! Books! Books! on the way home and it was packed. If we had even a quarter of their customers it would make such a difference.'

Dad kisses his teeth in response.

I put down my fork. 'I've been thinking really hard about ways to help Wonderland. Do you remember when I was a kid and you ran that YA book club? What if we brought it back, but bigger and better? We can do an Estee Mase night and offer two-for-one on her books.'

'A book club *now*? I think it's a bit too close to Christmas,' Mum says.

'I'll organize it all,' I jump in with my most convincing voice. 'And Ariel and her friends Annika and Jolie are down to help.'

Mum doesn't look convinced, but she nods.

'Plus, Ariel said she can create a mural of Black writers to help modernize the shop.' I glance at Dad, waiting for him to object, but surprisingly he nods his head. Encouraged, I continue: 'I was also thinking we could do a Christmas showcase to raise money for Wonderland. Let's get the word out that a Black-owned indie bookshop that's been on the high street for years is suffering and we need help.'

'Charity?' Dad glares at me. 'We're not asking for no charity.'

'We're not! It's an opportunity to celebrate Christmas and get the whole community behind us. We'll just encourage everyone to give what they can. Look, I saw when the Black Lives Matter movement was in full force and the public showed how much they wanted to help people like us. It was one of the few times Black businesses asked for help and received it. I really think we should try.'

Mum reaches over and grabs my hand. 'I love that you want to fight for Wonderland, baby, but I don't think we'll earn enough money from a showcase. It's a good idea to celebrate Christmas with the community, though. One last hurrah before we close up?'

'What about a GoFundMe?' Reon says, and we all look at

him. 'My friend Asia said her mum did one for her grandma when she needed a new wheelchair, and she got loads of money.'

'You little genius!' I kiss him on the forehead and he swats me away. 'That's perfect. How much debt are we in?'

Mum laughs. 'Trey, do you really think people will donate?' She looks around the table at all of us. 'To this family?'

I nod. 'I do! How much do we need?'

Mum and Dad glance at each other.

'We'd need fifty thousand pounds,' Mum says, her mouth a tight line.

I gulp. *Fifty K?!*

'We need to cover the missed mortgage payments, bills, wages ... the water damage, replacing the stock ... *and* factoring in the next six months of payments,' Mum explains. 'You really think you can raise the money we need before Christmas?'

I tense my jaw. 'I want to try, and the showcase is a good place to start. It'll remind the community that we're here – that we've always been here.'

Dad looks at me, bewildered. 'What's a GoFundMe?'

'I'll show you,' Reon says, walking over to Dad as he searches on his phone.

'Trey, this all sounds great, but I just don't want you being disappointed when it doesn't work out,' Mum says.

Dad is busy with Reon, but I still lower my voice. 'I can't let Wonderland go without knowing that I tried everything, especially after how bad I messed up with the party. Wonderland belongs to us.'

Mum shakes her head. 'I'm not sure how you're going to pull this off when Christmas is almost here – and you better not lose us any more money. But if you think you can do it, then I won't stand in your way.'

'Thank you.' I rub my hands together. Now I actually have to get it done.

'So strangers give people money?' I hear Dad ask Reon. 'Why ain't we used this before?'

I'm on my bed, getting ready to film a video for TikTok. I figure that's one of the best ways to connect with book lovers – the BookTok community is huge on there. The GoFundMe is set up and ready to go, and I know I seemed confident with my parents earlier but I'm nervous now. Fifty thousand pounds is a lot of money. So many people helped during the height of BLM, but maybe that was just a moment in time. Do people still care now that the hype has quietened down? Before I can talk myself out of it any more, I turn my camera towards me and put on my best smile.

'Hey, guys, it's your boy, Trey Anderson. My family own one of the longest-running Black-owned bookshops in London, called Wonderland on Stoke Newington High Street. My great-grandad started it and it's been in our family ever since. Wonderland means so much to me and my family, but we've been having some troubles recently. My dad's injured and on bed rest, and a book discount shop has opened nearby and is taking our customers – which means we're close to losing our family business. We're putting on a Christmas showcase on Christmas Eve and I'd love for everyone to come. If you can, please donate via the link in my bio. Let's support Black businesses and save Wonderland!'

I watch it back, noticing that I'm not blinking enough, so I record it a few more times until it's perfect. Then I add the Christmas showcase details and the GoFundMe link to the description, and I post it. I do the same on Instagram and Twitter and then I take a deep breath.

Okay, now I'm really nervous.

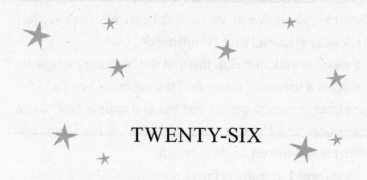

TWENTY-SIX

Ariel's playlist: 'Rain & Snow' by B2K

I was so hyped about our plans for Wonderland and my mural that as soon as I got home after the cinema I filled in my application form for the Artists' Studio. Now I just need to do the actual mural and hopefully get a place on the course.

To reward myself, I'm spending the night with Michael B. Jordan. Yes, I've watched *Creed* way too many times. Mum is still at work and Noah is getting ready for bed, so I'm lying on the sofa alone when my phone rings. My stomach flips when I see Trey's name on the screen, and I pause the film.

'Hey,' I say, the corners of my mouth lifting up in a smile.

'So, we have similar taste in music, but what about books?' Trey says, jumping straight in.

I sit up straight. 'You okay?'

'Yeah. I just posted about the Wonderland Christmas showcase.'

I have to see this. 'Wait, let me check,' I say.

'No, no, distract me – I'm nervous,' Trey replies quickly. 'So, guess what my favourite book series is.'

He's nervous and he's calling me and not his girlfriend? What does that mean?

'Ariel? You there?'

'Sorry, yeah . . . erm . . . I need some clues. Genre?' I ask.

'YA and it has a kick-ass protagonist.'

I stand up and walk to the bookcase in the living room, scanning my YA. I have a lot of options. 'One more clue.'

Trey's quiet for a moment, then he says: 'She's a symbol.'

I run my hands along a few of the spines and then select one of the books. This could be what he's talking about and it's definitely one of my favourites.

'*The Hunger Games*?'

Trey laughs. 'Yo, I didn't expect you to guess that so quickly! Do you have it?'

'Of course! And I'd like to think I'd survive the games, but I doubt I would . . . unless I camouflaged myself like Peeta did.' I laugh. 'I did not take you for a Katniss fan.'

'I like how complex she is,' Trey says. 'Plus, entering the games to protect her sister is some real shit. I'd do the same for Reon.'

'Yeah, same for Noah, even though I'd almost certainly be the first out. Okay. Guess one of mine. The clues are YA, sisters, love letters—'

'*To All The Boys I've Loved Before*,' Trey says before I can finish.

'What? How did you get that so fast?' I ask, shocked.

'The letters gave it away, and, no, it's not one of my favourites ... but if anyone's asking, I'm Team Peter.'

I burst out laughing. Trey Anderson reading about Lara Jean's relationship woes is just too funny.

He continues over the top of my giggles. 'I'm not a YA romance fan, but I like Nicola Yoon. I can tell you love all that swoony shit.'

I gasp. 'You did not just say "swoony shit"!'

'All that enemies to lovers and secret kisses in the library stuff.'

'Like you've never kissed in the library at college,' I respond.

'You think Blair steps foot in the library?'

I laugh even louder. YA romance is an underrated but amazing genre, and the fact that Trey's clearly a secret fan is everything.

'Did you re-read *Twilight* yet?' I ask.

'Nah, cause I have to mentally prepare myself for the nonsense I'm about to read.'

'Trey Anderson, I'll block you if you diss *Twilight* again.'

Trey laughs. 'Sorry. I'm just hating on Edward for having a girl that goes the extra mile for him.'

I'm surprised. Are Trey and Blair still fighting? 'Are you all right?'

Trey's quiet for a moment. 'Ignore me – I'm in a weird

mood. *Never Been Kissed* is on TV tonight. I'll watch that to lift my spirits.'

Now it's my turn to laugh. 'You're really not what I expected, Trey.'

He pauses. 'What did you expect?'

That you were an asshole. But I don't say that. 'I dunno, but I didn't think we'd be so similar.'

'I feel you. Hey, my mum said we can try out all the hashtag SaveWonderland ideas.'

'Oh, sick! Okay, so you posted about the Christmas showcase. Shall I get on with the book club? I know Jolie would love to help. We can run it on Wednesday?' I suggest.

'Yeah, cool, but I did say it would be an Estee Mase night. Let's play with the layout of the shop and add some discounts before college tomorrow. I hope we sell loads,' Trey says, and I smile at the enthusiasm in his voice.

'We defo will,' I say. Wonderland deserves some good luck. I can't wait to get started. 'May the odds be ever in your favour.' I try to do Rue's whistle, but all that comes out is air. So pathetic!

'What's that noise?' Trey asks.

'Nothing,' I respond and hang up quickly.

TWENTY-SEVEN

Trey's playlist: '12 Days of Christmas' by Gucci Mane

Twelve days till Christmas

My phone is buzzing on my bedside table. I reach over, still half asleep, to switch off my alarm, but it's Boogs. We haven't spoken properly since the day after the party.

'Hey, bro,' I say.

'Yo! Have you seen what's happening with your posts?' Boogs yells.

I sit up, my heart pounding, and quickly open up TikTok. I have one hundred thousand likes, over ten thousand comments and around forty thousand shares. I gasp. On Twitter I have fifty thousand likes, over thirteen thousand retweets and one hundred and sixty-two comments.

'What the ... ?'

I click on Instagram and this time see eleven thousand views and three hundred comments. I scroll through them.

Donated

Sounds amazing!

#BlackOwnedForLife

'How did this happen so fast?' I ask.

'Go on GoFundMe,' Boogs says, ignoring my question, and I immediately click on the link. I almost drop my phone. Five thousand pounds has been raised already.

'Bro, this is insane!' And then I do something so unlike me. I get up and jump on my bed, screaming 'Yes!' at the top of my lungs.

My door opens and Reon looks at me wide-eyed.

'Get Mum,' I say, and he runs to her room. 'Boogs, imma call you back.'

'No problem, man. And, Trey – this is sick!'

I hang up the phone just as Mum comes into my room.

'Trey, what on earth is happening?'

'Five thousand pounds, Mum! Look!' I jump off the bed and show her my phone.

She peers at it and covers her mouth with her hand. 'This is for . . . us?'

I nod.

'Oh my! Clive! Clive, you have to see this!' Mum takes my phone and runs down the stairs.

I grab Reon's hands and dance with him around my room.

'Can I jump on your bed?' he asks excitedly.

'Well, duh!' I say, a huge grin on my face.

We jump together and I feel like I can touch the sky. In fact, just let me go to Heaven and shake God's hand.

Dad is practically jumping in his seat when he sees me. 'This is incredible, son! Do you know the people who donated?'

I shake my head. There are a few names I recognize, but most are strangers. If people I don't even know believe in Wonderland then we're definitely going to reach fifty thousand.

Mum walks over to me with her arms open and she strokes my back as she hugs me. 'Well done, Trey. This is an incredible start.'

'Thank you, Mum.' We pull apart. 'Ariel's going to meet me at the bookshop before college to move some stuff around. Is that cool?'

Mum eyeballs me, but then grins to show it's okay. 'I'll be there in a bit.'

Ariel's already outside Wonderland in a black puffer jacket when I get there. She claps her hands when she sees me.

'Congratulations! I stayed up watching your posts gain traction.'

'You did?' I say, surprised.

She smiles. 'Yes and I donated too, although it wasn't much.'

'Ariel! You're already doing enough.'

She puts her gloved hand on my arm. 'I wanted to.'

I grin. 'Thank you. I know my family will appreciate it. Now, let's get inside – it's blitz out here.'

Once we're in, I go over to the heating, but when I press the switch the red light that signals that it's on stays black. I frown as I press it off and on again, but nothing happens. This cannot be happening – it's freezing in here.

I shoot a text to Mum before heading back to the shop floor, where Ariel is shuffling from side to side, trying to stay warm. 'Okay, so jackets on for now. The heating's not working.'

'Shit. Well, let's start moving stuff around to keep warm.' She gives me a sly smile and takes out her phone. 'A bit of music while we work? This is my fav playlist.'

We work diligently for just over an hour to Ariel's 90s playlist as we rearrange the shop window and the display tables. Mum wasn't down for the one-pound books, so instead we've gift-wrapped some slow sellers in Christmas paper and attached a teaser of the book on the gift tag. These we'll sell for a fiver. We're calling it 'Don't judge a book by its cover'.

Once we're done, I survey our work and there are discounts popping out from every corner. This is the first time I've seen Wonderland look different and it instantly makes the bookshop feel modern. Right now, we resemble Books! Books! Books!, but what we need is our own signature style. We'll soon have a sick mural from Ariel, but if we created a graphic novel section Reon could paint one of his superhero drawings too. That would look amazing *and* it would help us bring in a different crowd as well. Books! Books! Books! doesn't even stock graphic novels, so we can totally own that. Saving Wonderland is about more than keeping the bookshop in the family; it's about breathing a second life into it, one that will take the shop to a different level.

'What do you think of this?' Ariel asks, holding up a discount sign that she's drawn snowflakes on.

'Nice! That makes it really stand out.'

Ariel smiles. 'That's what I thought. I'll do the others – it won't take me long.'

I go around picking up the pieces of wrapping paper we left on the floor while Ariel is sitting back on her knees, doodling on the discount signs. Her hand moves quickly, creating effortless images of snowmen and angels. I stop for a moment to watch her. There's a small smile playing on her lips. She's totally in her zone and she looks so beautiful.

'You make that look so easy,' I say.

Ariel glances at me, but her hand keeps moving. 'My mum said I could draw before I could write.'

'Did you always want to be an artist?' I ask curiously.

'Yeah. It's almost like I don't have to try cause my hands just know what to do, if that makes sense?'

That's how I feel about singing. Without sounding big-headed, my voice is flawless; it's just my brain that makes me freeze up. But what if I trusted my art the way Ariel does hers? If I put myself out there and stopped second-guessing myself, maybe I could follow my dreams of being a professional singer.

Mum comes in and gasps when she sees us in just our T-shirts in the freezing cold shop – we took off our jackets ages ago from working up a sweat. She'd texted earlier to let me know an engineer can't come out until tomorrow, so I'm hoping the customers won't be too bothered by the cold.

'Looks good!' Mum says. 'You two make a great team.'

'Yeah, we do,' I say looking at Ariel, who blushes.

Hmm ... maybe she does like me? The thought makes my stomach somersault.

Mum claps her hands. 'You lot better hurry or you'll be late for class. Ariel, when did you want to start the mural?'

'After college this evening?' she asks, glancing at me, and I nod. 'I've made some posters for the Christmas showcase and the book club. I'll print copies and spread them around today.'

'Any update from publishers?' I ask Mum.

'A few indies offered some competitive discounts, so that's something,' she says.

'Nice! We're going to sell so much today,' I reply confidently.

We've got this in the bag. I'm already looking forward to coming back after college to see how much Wonderland has made.

TWENTY-EIGHT

Ariel's playlist: 'Just Ain't Christmas' by Ne-Yo

I hurry from sociology class to the library during my free period. I want to print out copies of my posters so I can put them up before lunch starts. As soon as I press print, Jolie runs in, breathless.

'Have you seen Trey's posts?' she asks.

I grin. 'Amazing, right? It's all thanks to you!'

Jolie blushes. 'If it keeps going this way, Wonderland might even break their target.'

I hadn't thought of that. Wonderland could make double what they need!

'How was the rest of your weekend?' Jolie asks.

'Trey and I took our brothers to the cinema.' I see Jolie's mouth drop open and I hurriedly press on: 'Keyword there is "brothers".'

'It still seems a bit date-like,' she says, slowly.

'No, it doesn't.' I know I sound defensive, but it wasn't a date!

Jolie picks up one of my posters. 'Do you need help putting these up?'

'Yes, please!' I reply, thankful she's changed the subject. 'Let's stick some around college and then the rest can go up near the bookshop. The book club is in two days and we have to get as many people there as we can. I'll text you the link to buy tickets.' I look around. 'Where's Annika?'

'She's working on her film project as it has to be handed in before we break for Christmas. Oh, also, Bebe asked us to sit with her at lunch today.' Jolie's smile is so big I swear I can count all her teeth.

I take my time gathering up all of the posters. My hands are sweating. What is Bebe up to? Our encounter at the cinema when she saw me and Trey is still replaying in my head, and I hope she's not going to do anything messy.

'Yeah? What did you tell her?' I ask, even though I know the answer.

'Yes, of course! Who doesn't want to sit with the popular kids?'

'Me,' I say, and Jolie laughs, but I'm not joking. 'I guess Trey and Boogs will be there.'

'It's girls only, she said. It'll be fun!' Jolie grins.

Great.

We put up posters around college before lunch, but the closer we get to the canteen, the more nervous I feel. I wish Annika was with us. She'd check Bebe if she said anything out of line. Bebe waves us over to her table once we have our food. Next to her are Blair, Santi and Yarah. Santi smiles warmly at us, Yarah waves and Blair ignores us. We sit down and Bebe grins.

'We were just talking about Wonderland,' she explains.

'I didn't even know Wonderland was in trouble,' Santi says to Blair. 'Did you?'

'Of course I did,' Blair replies, but I notice that she's avoiding eye contact.

'Well, I donated,' Yarah says. 'I really hope they make their target.'

'Me too,' Jolie pipes in.

Bebe has that weird smirk on her face like she did at the cinema. It's ironic that last night I was talking about *The Hunger Games* with Trey and now I feel like I'm being hunted.

'How was everyone's weekend? I went to the cinema – and I saw you there, didn't I, Ariel?' Bebe's eyes light up. 'With Trey.'

My stomach drops. Blair looks at me sharply and frowns. 'Trey?'

'Our little brothers are best friends,' I explain, my heart racing.

Bebe starts tapping her long nails on the table. 'I didn't see any kids with you.'

'They were in the toilet.' I look over at Blair and see she's still frowning at me, so I add, 'It wasn't a date.'

'Ooh, no one said anything about it being "a date",' Bebe sings, and I want to slap her.

Blair flicks her braids and shrugs. 'Well, of course it wasn't a date. Trey's taken and you're not his type.'

I feel like Blair just punched me in the gut. The only physical difference between me and Blair is that I wear glasses and I'm bigger than her . . . And we both know she's not talking about my glasses.

'Blair!' Santi snaps. 'Don't be rude.'

I'm grateful for Santi sticking up for me, but I'm already suffering from the impact of Blair's words. My head is filled with the sound of people calling me fat over the years, and I clench my fists under the table as I try to focus on my breathing. But the noise only seems to be getting louder.

'I didn't mean you're not his type cause you're big,' Blair says pointedly. I wish the ground would swallow me up. 'I just know Trey.'

She's right. Why would Trey like me when he has Black Barbie on his arm? Out of the corner of my eye, I see Jolie shaking her head, and I know she wants to say something, but she doesn't stand a chance against these girls and neither do I.

'But you didn't know Trey was at the cinema yesterday, did you?' Bebe says, and Blair's pretty face screws up into something ugly. 'Just like how he left you at my party and didn't tell you.'

That's when I realize that this isn't even about me. This is Bebe's weird power struggle with Blair. I'm just collateral damage.

'Bebe, can you stop?' Santi says, sounding tired. 'Of course she knew where Trey was.'

'Exactly,' Blair says, but for a split second I see her look uncertain. She didn't know. Blair stands up and hoists her pink bag onto her shoulder. 'If you'll excuse me, I'm going to find my boyfriend.'

'And I'm going to hang out with Boogs,' Santi says. 'Thanks for ruining lunch, Bebe.'

Blair gives Bebe a look before they leave the table. Bebe's jaw is tight, and I'm confused about what reaction she thought she was going to get from that situation. She stands up too and leaves without saying a word, her half-eaten lunch left behind.

Yarah sighs. 'Sorry about that, girls. I'm going to check on Bebe.'

Yarah walks away, and now it's just me and Jolie.

'What the hell was that?' Jolie says slowly.

I go to scoop up some rice, but end up dropping the fork on my plate. 'That was lunch with the cool kids. Next time just say no, okay?'

Jolie nods, her face etched with concern. 'Are you okay? That was so bitchy of Blair.'

I shrug as if it didn't bother me, but Jolie reaches over and squeezes my hand. She knows me well enough to know that it hurt a lot. I look down at my lunch of rice and fish and push it away from me, not because I'm not hungry, but because I need something more than this – something fried and greasy. What's the point of eating healthily? It doesn't matter how hard I work to lose weight, I'll still always be seen as the fat girl.

TWENTY-NINE

Trey's playlist: 'Ghetto Christmas' by Love Renaissance (LVRN), 6LACK and Summer Walker

I close my maths textbook and glance at the clock. I've got just enough time to grab some chips from the canteen before the end of lunch. I swing my bag over my shoulder and walk into the hallway, straight into Blair, who's glaring at me with her arms crossed.

'You went to the cinema with Ariel,' she says matter-of-factly before I even have a chance to say hello.

'No,' I say slowly. 'I was taking my brother and Ariel's brother to the cinema, and then Reon invited her. We went to see that stupid animal Christmas film.' I feel guilty that I'm hiding the whole truth – that I wanted Ariel to come and that I couldn't stop staring at her. 'It was just the cinema, babe.'

Blair breathes a sigh of relief. 'Bebe made it sound way worse. Why didn't you tell me earlier?'

'We haven't spoken since our argument. Plus, Ariel and I had literally just finished work yesterday and then Reon jumped in and asked her. It wasn't planned.' Over Blair's shoulder, I spot a colourful poster with *Wonderland* written on it. I walk towards it, reading the details about the Christmas showcase and the GoFundMe, and smile. Ariel did a great job. Blair stands next to me and I suddenly feel guilty for thinking about Ariel ... again.

'I wish you'd told me about Wonderland. I had to find out like everyone else,' she says with a pout.

Is she for real? She's forgetting that she was the one that didn't want to hear about it. But the last thing I want is another argument with Blair, so I swallow my anger and say, 'Sorry, I should have mentioned it. It was actually Annika and Jolie that came up with the hashtag—'

'Since when were you friends with Jolie?' she cuts in.

'We're not really. Ariel asked her and Annika to come to Wonderland to help plan the showcase.' A crease appears in Blair's forehead. 'But, hey, forget about all that,' I add hurriedly. 'The weekend's too far away, so how about we go out on Thursday? There's this cool place I want to take you to.'

Just like that, the frown disappears and Blair claps her hands. 'Where is it?'

'It's a surprise.' I tilt my head down and kiss her. It's warm and familiar and Blair. When I pull away, her eyes are still shut, like she's savouring the moment, but a movement down the hall catches my eye and I see a glimmer of red turn the corner. Ariel? A sea of guilt rushes over me even though I know I haven't done anything wrong. Why do I feel bad that Ariel may have seen me kiss my girlfriend?

'It's still going to voicemail,' I tell Mum.

I've called Ariel ten times. She's not working this afternoon, but she was meant to start on the mural. I send a quick text instead to check she's okay. Wonderland is packed right now. It feels like everyone in London has come to see the trending bookshop – yes, we're trending on Twitter! Isn't that insane? Authors and other indie bookshops have been retweeting like crazy, so Mum's been on the phone securing more discounts. Some authors have even offered to sign copies of their books that we have in stock. I just wish the donations were going up as fast as our social media followers.

Our discount signs are working well and bringing in some sales but a lot of people seem more interested in taking pictures in or outside of the bookshop, or strangely of me.

'Excuse me, I'd like to donate,' an elderly woman who I recognize from around the area says. No matter if it's rain or shine, she lives in her black fur coat.

'Oh, thank you. If you follow the link, it will let you donate online.'

She shakes her head. 'I don't use technology. Do you have a bucket that I can put some money into?'

'Erm ... one sec.'

Mum's too busy helping customers for me to get her

attention, and I have no idea if this is even legal, but I grab an empty hot-chocolate tin that was going to go into the recycling and write *DONATIONS* on it, before going back to the woman. She puts in a few pound coins and taps me lightly on the arm.

'I really hope this place sticks around.'

'Thank you. Me too,' I say with a smile.

I leave the donation tin out and hop on the till to ring up some purchases. A few hours later, once the footfall has quietened down and Mum is tidying up the till area, she notices the tin.

'Trey.' She gestures me over. 'What is this?'

I shrug. 'Some people don't like using technology but still want to donate.'

'Well, encourage them to buy a book at full price instead.' She picks up the tin and shakes it, before peering inside. It's full of pound coins and even some notes. 'Ignore me – we'll just leave this here,' she says with a laugh.

I'm finishing up serving the last customer, who is buying a handful of discounted books, when Blair and Santi walk in.

'One sec,' I mouth to them as I hand the customer their bag. 'Thank you for shopping at Wonderland. Merry Christmas!'

'Merry Christmas! I'll definitely be bringing the family to the showcase,' they say, and I grin.

I head over to the twins.

'Hey.' I kiss Blair and hug Santi. 'What are you guys doing here?'

Santi is practically jumping up and down. 'Guess who retweeted you?'

'Beyoncé?' I ask, smirking.

Blair laughs and Santi tuts.

'John Boyega?'

'An author, Trey!' Santi says. 'My favourite author of all time.'

There's no way ... Santi passes me her phone and Estee fucking Mase has retweeted my post!

'WHAT?' I hold the back of my head. 'This is mad!' Estee Mase is a Number One Sunday Times, New York Times bestseller, and she knows about Wonderland!

'You should get someone big like her to endorse the bookshop,' Blair says.

'What should I do?'

'Tell her to sign books at the showcase!' Blair and Santi say at the same time, before they look at each other and burst out laughing.

Now that *is* an idea! We still have boxes filled with her books. I'd hoped that we'd have sold more of them today. Even the book club ticket sales have been slow-going.

'Do you think she'll come?' I ask.

Santi nods. 'She's Black, she grew up around here, and she knows who you are and what you're trying to do for Wonderland. Look, let's take a picture of you in front of her books and ask.'

'Okay, let's do it!' I say excitedly.

I pick up her latest book and grin at the camera. Santi takes the shot and sends it to me. I quickly tweet it at Estee Mase and press send. If she actually comes, it would be so epic.

179

Santi squeals. 'I think I'll faint if I see her. How's the shop been today?'

'Busy, but a lot of people have just been browsing and taking pictures. There haven't been as many sales as I thought there would be.'

Blair links arms with me. 'It will pick up, don't worry. Ariel not working today?'

'No, she didn't show up. Did you see her around college earlier?'

'No,' Blair says quickly, and Santi looks at her but doesn't say anything.

The bookshop door opens and Boogs enters holding posters under his arm.

'A meet-up without me?' he asks.

'We were passing by.' Santi skips over to him. 'Trey just tweeted Estee Mase to ask her to come to the showcase!'

'Nice!' He gestures to his arm. 'I know Ariel made some posters, but I did a few and added a QR code. This way people can scan it and be taken straight to the GoFundMe page.' Boogs looks around. 'No Ariel today?'

I shake my head and look at one of the posters. It's amazing. Why Boogs dropped out of art is a mystery. 'Thanks, man. They're sick.'

'Hey, why don't you two come back to ours?' Blair suggests.

'Yeah, we haven't hung out together in ages,' Santi adds.

Me and Boogs look at each other and nod.

'Hang about and we can go once I finish. I won't be much longer,' I say.

THIRTY

Ariel's playlist: 'The Christmas Song' by Gregory Porter

I'm meant to go to Wonderland after college to start on the mural, but I don't feel like being around people. Blair's words are on a continuous loop in my head and, no matter how hard I try to forget about what happened at lunch, I can't. Seeing her and Trey kiss in the corridor reminded me that me and him is a stupid fantasy. They look right together, and I'm sure Trey would laugh if I told him that I was into him. Blair's right – I'm not his type.

So instead of going to the bookshop, I head to McDonald's, ignoring the voice inside my head telling me that I worked so hard to lose weight and that it's not worth ruining it now. But I don't care. I order a large Big Mac with two fries, chicken nuggets, a vanilla milkshake, an apple pie and an Oreo McFlurry. People glance at me as I struggle to hold all the food, but I ignore them.

Luckily, no one's home when I get back. I place everything on the kitchen table and I eat it so fast that I can't even taste it. I'm full halfway through the meal, but I force myself to eat until everything is gone and my stomach is painful and bloated. I pack all of the McDonald's wrappers inside a bin bag and chuck it outside so Mum doesn't see. Once I'm in my bedroom, I close the curtains, shutting out the world. I lay on my bed, allowing the tears to flow down my chin and stain my pillow.

THIRTY-ONE

Trey's playlist: 'You're Mine' by Jeremih

The twins live in a four-bedroom house in Angel, Islington, with their surgeon parents, who often work late. Their living room is triple the size of mine, and they have one of those cool TVs that sit on the wall and look like artwork until you switch it on.

'I vote for *The Best Man Holiday*,' Santi says. 'I mean, Morris Chestnut—'

'Hey!' Boogs says, and Santi laughs. 'Keep your knickers on, girl.'

'I thought you wanted them off?' Santi replies with a smirk, and Blair and I go 'Ooh!'

'Race you upstairs?' Boogs suggests, but Santi scoffs and presses play on the film.

Blair turns the lights off and cuddles up next to me. We're not even ten minutes in when I feel her hand slowly move up my leg. My body reacts instantly, but my eyes stay focused on the TV. I know where this is going – she's going to ask me to go upstairs with her. It's clear my body wants to, but for some reason I just don't feel like it today. I don't think I've ever not felt up for it with Blair. I grab her hand and hold it tight. She looks at me, surprised, and I don't blame her. By now I'd usually have run up the stairs, but I'm hoping she'll think I'm too engrossed in the film even though I've watched it a million times.

Santi and Boogs are quiet on the other side of the living room. I look over and realize they're not there. They must have snuck out at some point. Blair glances in their direction and notices too.

'One sec,' Blair says to me.

She stands up and closes the living-room door before walking back towards me, removing her top at the same time and revealing a lacy red bra that looks so good on her. She straddles me and starts to kiss my neck. Usually I'd respond by taking off the rest of her clothes, and although half of me is raring to go, the other half can't get into the right headspace. My arms stay by my side and I continue watching the film over her shoulder. Blair looks at me and follows my gaze before she jumps up like I'm on fire and runs over to the light switch. The bright bulb makes me squint my eyes.

'Are you kidding me right now, Trey?' she shouts. 'You're watching the stupid film!'

'No, no, I wasn't ... I mean, I didn't mean to!' I swallow nervously.

'What is wrong with you?' Blair picks up her top from

where she discarded it moments before. 'I'm practically throwing myself at you and you're not doing anything.'

'I'm sorry. I ...' I trail off pathetically and look down at my hands.

What's happened to us? I used to be able to tell Blair everything, and we always had this crazy sexual chemistry, but now everything just feels off. It has done since ... well, since Ariel came into the picture ... And now all I can think about is why Ariel didn't come to work and if she's okay. I shake my head. Thinking about Ariel, especially when Blair is standing in front of me half-naked, is a real dick move.

'I'm sorry,' I repeat. 'Maybe we should just—'

'What, Trey?' Blair whispers.

I look at her and see that her eyes are welling up. What exactly was I going to say? That I was dumping her? Do I *want* to dump her? I don't know what I want! Why is everything so complicated all of a sudden? Blair's holding her top over her chest and she looks so ... vulnerable.

'Nothing.' I stand up and hold her tight. 'I'm just really stressed about Wonderland.'

'Are we okay?' she mumbles into my chest.

Are we? I don't even know myself. So instead of giving her an answer, I put my finger under her chin, lift her head up and kiss her. I wait for that passion to come, the passion that's always been there, but it's not.

I'm walking down a quiet cobbled street under an arch of fairy lights. After what just happened with Blair, I felt awkward, so I made an excuse and left. She didn't stop me, so I know she was feeling uncomfortable too. I don't know how to fix us, and if I'm being honest with myself I don't know if I want to. I've texted Ariel a bunch of times, but she's still not responding. What is going on with her? I call her for what feels like the hundredth time and it rings out. I sigh and hang up, but my phone buzzes straight away, her name flashing on the screen.

'Ariel? Are you okay?' I quickly blurt out.

'Hey … Yeah, sorry, I'm fine. I wasn't feeling too great earlier. How was Wonderland today?'

'Don't worry about that. I was so worried about you. Do you feel better?' I ask softly.

'Better now.'

A car horn blares from the main road and it makes me wince.

'Where are you?' Ariel asks.

'Just walking down Upper Street. The lights are so nice here. Wait – let me send you a picture to cheer you up.'

The picture doesn't do it justice, but I send it anyway and I hear her gasp.

'Wow, it looks gorgeous. Are you on your way home?'

'No, I'm just walking around. I had a pretty weird evening,' I say.

'Can I join you on your walk?' she asks.

I smile. 'Yeah, I'd like that.'

It's freezing, like minus something, and I wish I had a balaclava because the cold wind on my face is not it. Ariel steps off the bus in a fitted winter coat with red gloves that match her hair. She looks tired, but her face comes alive when she smiles at me, and I can't help but feel crazy butterflies in my stomach. I haven't had that since I first started talking to Blair two years ago, but there's something about Ariel that feels different.

We walk up and down Upper Street a few times to keep warm. If it wasn't so cold, I'd stop and stare at the lights for ever.

'I want to show you something.' Ariel gives me a quizzical look as I take her back to the side street I was on. Her eyes widen when she sees the lights strung across in an arch.

'Wow.' She spins as she watches the lights.

'Cool, right? I like coming down here in the evenings sometimes.'

There's a bench nearby and we sit down on it. The cold seeps through my jeans. I put my hands in my pockets and Ariel gently nudges me.

'What's up?' she asks.

'Just relationship stuff.' I shake my head. I want to talk about anything but Blair. 'I tweeted Estee Mase ... asked her to come to the showcase and sign some books.'

'You did?' Ariel says, surprised.

I laugh. 'Hopefully she'll holla back.'

She takes out her phone and starts scrolling. 'Look at this.'

I lean over and everyone is tweeting Estee Mase, begging her to come to Wonderland.

'Whoa!' I scroll down further. 'I can't believe people care this much.'

'You guys deserve it. Have you checked GoFundMe recently?'

'I did earlier but we were still near the five thousand mark. The discounts haven't done as well as we thought.' I sigh. 'I dunno, maybe we need to try something else.'

'We still have the book club – how are we doing there?' Ariel asks.

'Only ten places have been booked so far, but it might change the closer we get.'

To be honest, I'd hoped we'd have sold out by now. Maybe we didn't give people enough notice? Ariel stiffens beside me and I glance at her. One of her gloved hands is covering her mouth, and her round eyes are bulging.

'What? What?' Then I see it on her phone screen.

Ten thousand pounds in twenty-four hours! 'OH MY DAYS!'

I jump to my feet, pulling Ariel with me, and I hug her tight, cheering at the top of my lungs. We're jumping up and down wildly, and the few people who are walking by stare at us, amused. But I don't care. This moment right here is perfect.

THIRTY-TWO

Ariel's playlist: 'Comin' for X-Mas?' by Usher

Trey's arms are round me. It's like Blair's comment at lunch and my later bingeing never happened. All that shame and hurt have disappeared into the starry night sky, and I'm so happy that I feel like I could float up into the air.

THIRTY-THREE

Trey's playlist: 'Come December' by Jordan Fisher

Everything about Ariel in my arms just feels right. Her eyes are alive and bright, her lips are full and inviting. I want to kiss her so damn much.

THIRTY-FOUR

Ariel's playlist: 'Merry Christmas, Darling' by Timi Dakolo and Emeli Sandé

I stop jumping when I see that Trey is staring at me. We're still holding each other tightly, and I want to reach up on my tiptoes and finally *finally* kiss Trey Anderson. Slowly, his face moves closer to mine. *Screw it!* I close my eyes and push up from my feet . . .

THIRTY-FIVE

Trey's playlist: 'Christmas With You' by Ceraadi

Her lips are so close to mine. If I lean down a tiny bit more, I can do what I've wanted to do since we were at the cinema. But suddenly my mind flashes back to Blair. Blair almost in tears and scared for our relationship. Kissing Ariel wouldn't be fair to anyone. I sigh and rest my forehead against hers.

'I can't,' I whisper, and I step back, creating a barrier between us.

'No, of course we can't,' Ariel says, looking away from me. 'You have a girlfriend.'

'Yeah.' I run my hand over my head. Neither of us says anything, and I wish Ariel would look at me instead of staring at the floor. Couples walk past us holding hands or taking selfies under the lights, and I realize I shouldn't have brought Ariel here. At this time of year, this part of London looks like a set straight out of a romcom.

Ariel looks my way with a smile that doesn't quite reach her eyes. 'I'm freezing. We should get a move on.'

I search her face, trying to see if I've hurt her feelings, but she's still smiling, and I have no idea what she's thinking.

'Yeah, let's go.'

We walk towards the main street, but the easiness we had earlier is gone. I keep glancing at her, but either she doesn't notice or she's purposely avoiding my gaze, because she doesn't look at me again until she waves goodbye to catch her bus.

THIRTY-SIX

Ariel's playlist: 'Santa Baby' by Rev Run ft Puff Daddy, Mase, Salt-N-Pepa, Snoop Dogg, Keith Murray and Onyx

I can't help but look back to see if Trey is still watching the bus, but he's already walking in the opposite direction, his hands in his pockets. It's loud downstairs and I just want to be alone with my thoughts, so I head to the upper deck, where, thankfully, it's pretty empty.

I rest my head against the cold glass and sigh, misting up the window. Why did I have to ruin things? I was so happy – *we* were happy – and then I decided to make a move. Obviously the wrong one. I thought that's what Trey had wanted too. Now that I think about it though – did I really want him to cheat on Blair with me? Blair is a lot of things, but getting with her boyfriend isn't okay. I know that, but in the moment I just didn't care. I wanted him all to myself.

There's a dull pounding near my temples and I gently knead them with my fingers. I'm giving myself a headache just thinking about everything. I close my eyes, lean my head back against the seat and try to tell myself to stop stressing.

It doesn't work.

THIRTY-SEVEN

Trey's playlist: 'Holiday Celebrate' by Toni Braxton

Eleven days till Christmas

'Morning, Trey,' Ariel says brightly when she walks into the office. Neither of us has college today, so I opened up early so she can start work on the mural.

'Morning,' I reply.

She turns her back on me as she takes off her coat and scarf. I've kept my jacket on because the heating still isn't fixed, but the engineer's promised to come later today. I watch her as she ties her red hair up into a messy bun. Her ripped jeans have paint on them and she's wearing a fitted top that hugs her in all the right places. I could stare at her all day. She takes out a bag filled with paints in all different shades and places it on the table. I've already filled up a container with water for her, and she grabs it along with her bag and heads for the door.

'Ariel,' I call out.

She stops and looks back at me, expectation written all over her face. I know she wants me to say something about last night, like I've changed my mind and I should have kissed her, but I can't. I wish I could tell her that I have feelings for her – that I think about kissing her a lot and that I'm at my happiest when she's around. But I need to work out what's going on with me and Blair. And I don't want Ariel to feel like she's second best, because she could never be. Neither girl deserves to be strung along.

'Erm . . . let me know if you need anything?'

Ariel doesn't need to say a word for me to know she's disappointed. She nods and leaves the office.

I follow her out onto the shop floor. Even though there are still a couple of hours until we open, there's already people outside the bookshop taking pictures. A girl around my age knocks on the window and gestures at her phone.

I shake my head and mouth, 'Later.'

The girl gives me a thumbs up and disappears. Ariel sees the girl and catches my eye, but she quickly goes back to her painting.

Mum thinks it's hilarious that people want to take a picture with me, but then I made a joke this morning that people will start asking to take pictures with the owner, and now she's at the hairdresser's just in case.

I grab my phone from my pocket and take some pictures for Wonderland's Instagram account. I've had it on silent the last couple of days because the number of notifications I'm getting is crazy. We went up from four hundred followers to fourteen thousand pretty much overnight. Now if only all those followers could give us a couple of grand each ...

I stand behind Ariel and take a photo of her mid-brushstroke, then send it to Mum to post before I tweet the same picture on my account.

Something special is happening @WonderlandBooks with local artist @ArielArt! #SaveWonderland #WonderlandBlackOwned #BlackBusinesses #BlackTalent

A notification pops up immediately.

Hi Trey, I'd love to do a feature on you, Ariel and Wonderland. It's amazing to see two teens from Hackney doing great things. When would be a good time to chat? Sarah Mills

I click on Sarah's profile picture and see she's from a major TV network. She wants to interview us?!

'Ariel! Come and see this!' I shout excitedly.

Ariel carefully places her brush down and runs her hands against her jeans. 'What's up?' She walks over to me, reads the tweet and gasps. 'We're going to be on TV?'

I want to hug her again, like I did yesterday, but I restrain myself. 'Are you cool with it? I hope it's not live. I literally won't be able to speak.'

Ariel touches my arm and a jolt goes through me. 'I'll be with you.'

We stare at each other and I don't want to look away. Ariel's the first to break the spell.

'Tell her to come by today for a chat,' she says.

Mum arrives a few hours later with her hair in perfect curls. She usually lives in jeans and a shirt, but today she's wearing a black knitted dress and heeled boots.

'Oh, so that's what we're doing?' I say with a grin, and Mum twirls.

'You look great, Mrs Anderson,' Ariel calls over.

'Thank you, baby. How are the sales going?'

'Better today. More of the discounted books are selling, but the full-priced ones are still on the slow side.'

Mum frowns. 'Let's give it a few more days. We need people to spend more.'

Just then, the door opens and a man in an expensive suit walks in. I recognize David Raymond straight away, and Mum tenses beside me. Mr Raymond does an exaggerated shiver and puts his hand up to the door heater, which clearly isn't working. He eyes up Ariel's painting and raises an eyebrow. There are only a few customers in the far corner, and I wish it was packed so he could see how much people love it here. He holds up one of the discounted books and twirls it in his hand.

'Mrs Anderson, how are you?'

'Fine, thank you,' Mum says stiffly, and Ariel looks up from her painting to watch.

'Good, good, and nice to see you again, Dre.' He dumps the book down carelessly and holds out his hand to me, but I don't shake it.

'It's Trey,' I say, but I can tell he's not listening as his eyes roam around the shop, lingering a second longer on the Christmas-wrapped books by the till.

Mr Raymond flashes a smile at us. 'I saw that you're fundraising for Wonderland. Fifty thousand pounds is a lot of money to raise in eleven days and, as you know, I'm very interested in this property. I thought you wanted to sell?'

Mum clears her throat. 'As much as I appreciate your offer, this is a family business and we want to do our best to keep it.'

Mr Raymond nods along as she talks. 'Oh, I understand wanting to keep something for the next generation, but I already offered you a generous price. However, allow me to sweeten the deal a little more.'

He pops open his briefcase on the counter and holds up a chequebook before taking out a pen and writing something down. He hands Mum the cheque and she has a sharp intake of breath. I look at it and my eyes widen at all the zeros. Is this guy for real?

'Now, Mrs Anderson, this offer expires at six p.m. on Christmas Eve. I can see you're trying very hard.' He looks again at the bargain box. 'But raising all that money will be very difficult so have a think, talk to your husband and let me know what you decide.' He smiles at us and closes his briefcase. 'I hope you get that heating fixed. It's not good for business. Have a good day.'

I take a step forward and Mum grips my arm, holding me back. What wouldn't I give to punch this guy! Mr Raymond walks out, a trail of expensive aftershave lingering behind him.

Once he's gone, Mum exhales deeply. The way he looked at the shop, like he knew we wouldn't make our target, makes my blood boil. But I know we can save Wonderland. We have to.

'It's a lot of money,' Mum says slowly, glancing back down at the cheque.

'Mum! You said we'd try everything we can!'

'I know I did, but, baby, this money is life-changing—'

'He's given us until Christmas Eve, right? So let's keep going until then. We're building momentum,' I cut in.

Mum looks around the now-empty shop.

'Tell her about that woman from the news,' Ariel chips in, and I could kiss her right there and then.

'News?' Mum frowns.

I quickly tell her all about Estee Mase and Sarah Mills, hoping it will change her mind about the offer.

'That's amazing! And what a great platform for Wonderland. Honey, I don't want to sell either, but I have to think about what's best for our family. Like you said, let's keep pushing until Christmas Eve, and when you talk to that reporter, keep the dialogue about this bookshop only. Don't name Books! Books! Books! We don't need hassle from them. You know how these reporters like to snoop and add fuel to the fire.'

I breathe a sigh of relief, thankful that Mum is still up for trying to save Wonderland. I hug her with one arm. 'Don't worry, Mum. I got this.'

THIRTY-EIGHT

Ariel's playlist: 'Cold December Nights' by Boyz II Men

'Do you have copies of *Love Struck*?'

I turn away from my painting and see a young, tall, handsome Black man in a tailored coat, skinny jeans and glasses looking at me. I catch my breath.

'You're Darren Acre,' I blurt out. As in bestselling YA author Darren Acre. No one writes Black love stories like him.

He smiles, a crinkle appearing by his mouth. 'I am. I was hoping I could sign some copies of my book, if you have it in stock. I saw Wonderland on Twitter and wanted to help.'

'Of course! That would be amazing! Let me introduce you to the Andersons. They own the bookshop.'

Darren looks over my shoulder at my mural. I'm only at the

beginning stages, but I've been documenting each step with a photo so I can use it for my Artists' Studio application. Right now, there are random blocks of colour and lines that wouldn't make sense to anyone but me. Nevertheless, he nods his head approvingly and says, 'I can't wait to see this. I've looked at your stuff online and I'm a big fan.'

I gulp. Darren Acre is a fan of *me*? I try to form words, but it's like my brain has left my body. My face is burning red and my hands feel clammy. Why can't I act cooler?

'Ariel? You okay?' Trey walks over, looking Darren up and down.

'Hey, man. I'm Darren Acre.' Darren holds out his hand and Trey's eyes widen as he shakes it.

'The author of *Love Struck*? Wow, I love your books. Thank you for coming through.'

'No problem. I was just telling Ariel that I wanted to sign some books,' Darren replies.

Trey grins. 'Ah, nice one. Follow me.'

They wander over to the till, and I know I should get back to my painting so I can finish it before the Christmas Eve showcase, but it's not every day a popular and fine author walks into my life.

'Are you working on anything new?' Mrs Anderson asks as she piles his books in front of him.

'Yeah, I'm thinking about setting my next one in Paris, just to break up the London setting. I've been living there for a few months now.'

'Oh, I love that,' I say, and everyone looks over at me. 'I

went to Paris once with my dad to see the Louvre, and it's one of the most beautiful places I've been.'

Darren grins. 'Paris is stunning. Maybe I'll make my protagonist a beautiful red-haired artist.'

'I'd read that!' Mrs Anderson winks at me. 'I'll be right back. There are a few more books in the storeroom.'

Darren hasn't turned away from me and my entire body goes warm. Trey is giving Darren a deathly glare, and I can't help the smile that plays on my lips. Darren notices.

'Oh, my bad.' Darren points at me and Trey. 'You two together?'

There's an awkward pause, and I look at Trey, who opens his mouth then closes it before shaking his head.

Darren reaches into his pocket and walks over to hand me a black card that has his name, number and email on it. 'In which case, if you're ever in Paris, hit me up.'

'Thanks.' I smile at him, holding the card in my hand. Trey glances at it and I notice his jaw tenses, but he doesn't say another word.

Once Darren has signed his books and left after we've taken a picture, Wonderland thankfully starts to get busy. We put the signed copies of *Love Struck* in the window and they sell out fast. The day goes by quickly, even though things are still a little bit awkward with Trey because of last night, but Darren Acre flirting with me in front of him has made me feel a whole lot better. Trey was clearly irritated by it. Darren is hot and talented, but my mind and my heart are stuck on Trey, and I don't know how to change that.

I'm distracted when Sarah Mills comes into the shop. She's a tall, thin white woman with blonde hair framing a plain face, and she's wearing a navy-blue tweed jacket and black trousers. I wave at her before putting down my paintbrush and rub my hands on my already colourful jeans. Trey and I walk over to greet her.

'Good to meet you both.' She goes to shake my hand but notices the fresh paint on them.

'Sorry, I didn't get a chance to wash it off,' I say, and Sarah shakes her head.

'Don't worry at all. I can't wait to see the mural once it's finished.' She looks around Wonderland. 'Wow – you're so busy.'

'Yeah! The response has been amazing. We're seeing more and more customers by the day,' Trey says. 'I'm really glad I shared those posts cause things would look a lot different for Wonderland without everyone's support.'

'I'd love to hear more about it,' Sarah says. 'Is there somewhere we can talk?'

'Yeah, I'll lead the way. Mum!' Mrs Anderson looks up as we walk towards her. 'We're going to the office.'

'Okay, baby. And nice to meet you, Ms Mills.' Mrs Anderson shakes hands with Sarah.

'The pleasure is all mine.' Sarah grins. 'It would be great to speak to you later too, if that's okay?'

Mrs Anderson strokes her new hair, and I make the mistake of catching Trey's eye at the same time. It takes so much effort not to laugh. 'No, that shouldn't be a problem.'

We sit in the office and Trey puts on the kettle. I'm

trying hard to scrape the paint off my hands and Sarah notices.

'I'd love to hear more about the mural,' she says.

So I explain my vision of having a wall of Black writers, and Sarah does a lot of nodding and agreeing.

'That sounds brilliant— Ah, thank you,' she says when Trey hands us all mugs. 'So, Trey, tell me about Wonderland and what makes it so special.'

Trey sits beside me with his leg brushing against mine and I try to ignore the tingle that travels up my body.

'Wonderland has been here since my great-grandfather opened it, and it's always stayed in my family as an independent Black business. The opening of another bookshop has affected us a lot, to the point where we were considering selling, but thanks to the public's support we'll hopefully raise enough money to keep the doors open.'

'That's brilliant! How did you feel about Wonderland being featured in *Rebel Pop* magazine's "Fifty Black-Owned Businesses to Support"?'

My mouth drops open. *Rebel Pop*? I glance at Trey, who looks as surprised as I do. How did we not know this? I've been so busy, what with Wonderland, the mural, the Artists' Studio application and college, that I can't remember the last time I even glanced at a magazine.

Sarah laughs. 'I guess you haven't seen it yet. Wonderland has been getting a lot of great support. It's been fascinating to see the momentum building.' She reads off a list of names, from authors to soap opera stars to television presenters, and

I'm buzzing that all these people are supporting us. And then she says, 'Rihanna.'

'Wait, wait, wait!' I hold my hands up and she falls silent. 'Are you saying Rihanna is supporting Wonderland?'

Sarah nods, like it's a totally normal and everyday occurrence. Trey is holding his head as if it's going to explode any minute. I don't believe it until I grab my phone and see it for myself. And there she is – @BadGirlRiri has just casually posted about Wonderland. This has made my ENTIRE LIFE! I show Trey and we scroll through the comments. He points at one from Wonderland thanking her.

'How did Mum see this and not tell us? Oh, we're going to have a big problem.'

Sarah laughs. 'This is what I wanted to talk about. You two are young, ambitious, community-focused teenagers. You're an inspiration. Wonderland is trending globally, and it shows no signs of stopping! I'd love for you both to be live on the six p.m. news on Friday to tell everyone why we should all get behind Wonderland. I really believe in what you're doing, and I think if Wonderland is on a prime-time spot it will help drive up the donations. Would that work for you both?'

'Yes!' I say. This is exactly what we need. I look at Trey, expecting him to be as excited as me, but he's completely frozen.

'It'll only be a few minutes,' Sarah adds. 'And we'll film it here, so you'll be in your element.'

'But it has to be live?' Trey asks, and I can hear the wobble in his voice.

I wasn't expecting Trey to look so nervous. He's Mr Popular, so I don't get why talking to a lens is so scary for him.

Sarah nods. 'You'll be great! Just bring that charm you showed off in your hashtag SaveWonderland posts.'

'And I'll be right beside you,' I say. Our hands are gently touching under the table and, without thinking, I grab onto his and squeeze it.

Trey looks down at our hands and then at me. He slowly smiles and I mirror it.

'Okay,' he says finally. 'We'll do it.'

I can barely focus on my mural. I'm going to be on the news, and Rihanna posted about Wonderland on her Instagram. The same Rihanna whose hair colour I copied and whose songs are on pretty much all of my playlists.

Is this even real life?

Someone coughs behind me, and I look over my shoulder. A group of people wave at me. I'm not used to painting with a big audience, but that's exactly what's happened. For some reason, we never thought that people would stop and want to watch me create, ask questions and take pictures. I mentioned it to Mrs Anderson and she suggested I wear headphones and listen to music – a pretty clear way of letting people know that I don't want to be bothered. So that's what I've been doing for most of my shift, unless Trey or Mrs Anderson waves to get my attention so I can help with a customer. Mrs Anderson has said if the bookshop stays open, I'll be made permanent and she'll till-train me. I really hope it happens. Wonderland has already become my second home.

I stand back, studying my work for the day, and smile, liking what I see. My hands are a hot mess and we're going to close up soon, so I better wash the paint off before it completely dries.

'Mrs Anderson, I'm just going to the toilet,' I say.

'Okay. Trey's sorting some stock for me. Can you tell him to come up? I've got to go relieve my sister from babysitting duties.'

'Will do!' I head down the stairs to the basement and pause when I hear a pitch-perfect voice singing one of my favourite songs – 'Cold December Nights' by Boyz II Men. It's such an underrated Christmas tune. Trey's got his headphones on and he's shifting boxes in a fitted T-shirt that shows off his muscled arms, his jumper discarded on the floor. Wow ... every time I hear Trey sing I get goosebumps. I could listen to him all day. He's so engrossed in the song that he doesn't notice me take out my phone and press record.

Half an hour later, Trey turns the OPEN sign to CLOSED, and I reach for my phone in my back pocket. It's been on silent all day because of the notifications, which is why I've only just noticed I've missed a call from Annika. I dial her back.

'Why didn't you tell me what Blair said to you at college?' she asks. That's Annika: straight to the point.

I hesitate. 'Oh, erm ... did Jolie tell you?'

'Yes, and why didn't you?'

'I don't know,' I mumble. The truth is that it hurt me too much to repeat.

'I'll be walking by Wonderland soon, so let's talk properly then. You got plans tonight?' she replies.

'No, but I look like a mess. My jeans are literally covered in paint.'

'I'm wearing two pairs of leggings cause it's so cold out here. You can wear one of them. See you in a bit.' And she hangs up.

I hope the leggings are stretchy.

I've cleaned up all my paints by the time Annika arrives twenty minutes later. Mrs Anderson's already left and Trey is tidying up the till area.

'You okay?' Annika asks, looking at me carefully, and I nod. 'I already called her and cussed her out.'

I gasp. 'You didn't?'

'Cussed who out?' Trey calls from the other side of the bookshop.

'You're g—'

I shake my head quickly and plead with my eyes for Annika not to say anything. For a moment, I think she's going to ignore me, but instead she smiles.

'Ignore me. Just girl talk. Do you mind if I steal Ariel? I'm taking her out to dinner.'

'Sure,' Trey says. He walks towards us. 'Are you coming to the book club tomorrow?'

'Of course! I'm always down to support – I just haven't read the book.' She flashes a grin.

'Annika!' Honestly, she could have at least read the first chapter.

'I've been busy! But don't worry – some blogger will have broken down the plot on Goodreads.'

I roll my eyes just as Trey says, 'Did Ariel tell you that Darren Acre came into the shop? You know, the author?'

I frown at him, because he says it so casually, like he wasn't bothered earlier, and now I'm confused.

'No way!' Annika says.

'Yep, and all of his books sold out. Also, we're going to be on the news on Friday!'

'You are?' Annika's mouth drops open. 'That's amazing!'

'Oh, and Rihanna posted about us,' Trey adds.

At this, Annika screams, and we both cover our ears. 'Shut up! Rihanna? "Work, work, work" Rihanna?' *Like there's more than one!* 'That is insane. Wonderland is going to completely smash the fifty-thousand target.'

I untie my hair from its messy bun and let it fall down over my shoulders.

'You've got some paint.' Trey leans over and gently rubs my jawline. He stops for just a second and keeps his hand there, before quickly withdrawing it. I glance at Annika and she has her eyebrows raised.

Trey clears his throat. 'I'll see you tomorrow. Bye, Annika.' And he walks off without another word.

'*Girrrrl.*' Annika looks at me up and down. 'We clearly have a lot to talk about.'

We end up at an Italian restaurant just round the corner. It's packed and loud, with gold tinsel everywhere and some weird accordion music playing in the background. Annika orders a huge bowl of carbonara that makes my mouth water, but I promised myself I'd eat healthier after my McDonald's binge, so I get a tuna Niçoise salad.

'Oh, come on –' Annika puts some carbonara on my plate – 'we're in an Italian restaurant, for fuck's sake.'

'I had a bad day yesterday ... after Blair.' I look down.

Annika's jaw hardens. She's known me for so long that she understands what my 'bad days' mean without me having to explain it.

'Honestly. Blair can be such a bitch,' Annika says. 'Where does she get off talking to you like that? And you know she tried to deny commenting on your weight, but Jolie isn't a liar. Also, you're a total hottie, so you're obviously every boy's type.'

I scoff. 'I don't know about that.' I twirl some carbonara on my fork and pop it into my mouth. It's so good.

'Hey!' Annika snaps, and I look up. 'Don't do that. Don't put yourself down. You are gorgeous and talented and lovely, and Blair should be worried. I saw the way Trey was stroking your face.'

'He was not!' I protest.

'I mean, who knows what would have happened if I hadn't turned up. You'd probably be getting it on the floor—'

'Annika!' I blush.

'Or going on another date,' Annika adds, and she gives me a knowing look.

'It wasn't a date,' I say.

She leans back on her chair. 'Is that what you're telling yourself?'

I grin. 'Maybe.'

We both start laughing. I'm smiling to myself as Annika bends her head to scoop up more pasta. It feels so good to be sitting here eating delicious food with my best friend and not feeling on edge like I did yesterday with Blair and Bebe. Annika really is the best.

THIRTY-NINE

Trey's playlist: 'Christmas Love' by Victory

It's busy on the high street as I walk home. It feels like everyone is in frenzied Christmas-shopping mode, even though we still have over a week to go. Luckily, my gifts are already bought, wrapped and hidden at the top of my wardrobe, behind my gym bag and out of Reon's reach. I swear if he goes snooping like he did last year, I'm refunding everything.

The zipper of my coat is open even though it's freezing, but I'm still hot because I have Boogs' jacket on under my own. I keep forgetting to give it back to him at college, but I'm going to drop it off now on my way home.

I think back to just before I left the bookshop and feel embarrassed all over again. Why did I need to wipe the paint off Ariel's face? And then I made it even worse by keeping my hand there like some weirdo. I saw Annika's reaction . . . I hope she doesn't tell anyone, especially Bebe or Blair.

I reach Boogs' house and ring the doorbell. He answers a few seconds later.

'What's good?' Boogs says, gesturing for to me to come in.

'Nothing much, man. I just wanted to drop off your coat.' I take off my own and his and hand it to him. I can hear voices coming from the living room. 'You got company?'

'Yeah. I texted you – James and Marcus are here,' Boogs replies.

I check my phone, but then remember it's dead. We head into the living room and there are beer bottles and snacks on the tables – the benefits of being an only child whose mum works late.

'Nah, I would do her for real,' James is saying, opening up a bottle before greeting me. His blue eyes look red. I sit next to Marcus, who puts his arm round me.

'Trey, you're famous!' he slurs. 'Can you get me Riri's number?'

'How many have you had?' I ask, and Marcus shrugs and starts laughing. I gently remove his arm from round me. 'Who would you do, James?'

'Bev Smith,' James says, and Boogs cracks up.

'How drunk are you? You already dated Bev, remember? During your break from Yarah,' Boogs says, still chuckling to himself.

'Me?' James says innocently, pointing at himself, and we all laugh.

'That party.' Marcus wags his finger at me. 'That party.'

We wait for him to say something else, but his eyes start to close.

James thumps his fist on the table. 'Ariel Spencer.'

'Huh?' I say, suddenly alert. *Does James know that I like her?*

'She is *fi-i-i-ne*. What's she saying, Trey? Is she single?'

Boogs throws a pillow at James. 'You're not single, dickhead.'

James flashes us a cocky smile. 'I'll dump Yarah tonight and get me that red-haired girl instead. You seen how thick she is?' James bites his fist. 'Now that's a woman. You know, I've never slept with a big girl before.'

'Yo, watch your mouth,' I snap, and Boogs looks at me and frowns.

James laughs and I want to punch him in the face.

'Don't they say big girls are always gagging for it?' he continues, and I get abruptly to my feet.

'Say something else,' I growl. James puts his hands up as if surrendering.

'What's your problem, Trey?' he asks with a smirk.

'Whoa, whoa, whoa.' Boogs puts a firm hand on my shoulder. 'Let's go outside, yeah?'

I'm breathing hard like I just went for a run, and my fists keep opening and closing. We step outside and the cold air hits me in the face. Boogs watches me carefully, but I deliberately look anywhere than at him.

'What was that about back there?' he asks, and I shrug. 'Trey?'

'He was being disrespectful,' I say bluntly.

Boogs cocks his head to the side and slowly his eyes widen. 'Oh shit! You like her.'

'What?' I say too quickly, too defensively. Boogs knows me.

He grins, his white teeth shining in the dark. 'You like Lil' Mermaid! Well, damn!'

'Keep your voice down,' I hiss, even though no one is paying any attention to us.

'I like Ariel. I actually like her for you ... more than I do Blair,' Boogs replies, serious all of a sudden.

'Really?' We've been a foursome for as long as I can remember, and Boogs has never said a bad word about Blair. I mean, I know she's his girlfriend's twin, but he's never suggested, not even once, that we aren't a good fit. 'Why?'

'I like Blair, but I dunno, man – this whole thing with Wonderland has put everything into perspective. I've seen how Ariel's been supporting you. You need a girl like that – one who cares enough to make an effort about what you're passionate about. Check me and Santi, right? I don't care about Whole Foods, I love meat and I'm not a big reader, but every time we hang out, I do things like buy her her favourite lentil crisps, or take her for dates to the most talked about vegan restaurant, or surprise her with the latest Estee Mase book and let her talk my ear off, cause that shit is important to her. When was the last time Blair even asked you what book you're reading?'

Boogs is right. I don't think Blair has ever asked me what book I'm reading. And isn't the whole point of being in a relationship so you have someone who's actually interested in you and who has your back? I haven't felt that from Blair in a long time. But Ariel? She's been there, riding with me from the day she started at Wonderland.

Boogs continues. 'She's been bitching to me and Santi about how much time you've being spending at the bookshop, and I'm like, Blair read the room – Wonderland could close down! Be honest with me, man – do you still want to be with her? Or are you with her cause people expect you to be? You're comfortable, I get it, but I think you'd be happier without her.'

Comfortable. Blair is that. Yeah, she can act spoilt, and sometimes I do wonder what we have in common, but I've always been able to tell her everything, and she's usually a great listener. We've had a lot of fun together ... but now I think about it, I can't remember the last time we had fun. We don't seem to be on the same vibe any more.

'I do like Ariel—'

'I knew it!' Boogs shouts.

I laugh. 'Can you relax?' Boogs mimes zipping his mouth. 'Ariel is great, like really great, but I've been with Blair for almost two years, and not being with her would just feel weird, you know?'

Boogs nods. 'Change is weird – I hear that. I left my old ends cause I wanted to change my life. I did a full turnaround for Santi, cause that girl makes me a better person. She's worth the change.' Boogs shrugs. 'Change can be good, bro.'

Is it time for a change? Am I ready for that? But I'm meant

to be taking Blair to The Grotto on Thursday and cancelling will only make our relationship even more strained.

'What you doing Thursday?' I say. 'I have a date with Blair, but we left things a bit shit the last time I saw her. Do you and Santi want to join us?'

'Yeah, just send me the deets,' Boogs replies. 'How's the fundraiser going?'

'I haven't had a chance to check since yesterday and my phone's dead now. Can you have a look?'

Boogs types on his phone and his eyes suddenly widen. 'Oh shit!' He holds the phone out to me. 'Twenty thousand pounds donated to Wonderland!'

'What?' I grab the phone in shock and scroll through all the donors and their comments. There are a lot of familiar author names, which is cool, and I see Darren Acre is one of them. Obviously, I'm grateful, but seeing him flirting with Ariel earlier really annoyed me. All that talk about Paris and how romantic the city is. Would he really base a character on her? I wonder if Ariel kept his card. I shake my head. I'm tripping. Ariel is single and can do what she wants, and I need to focus on my situation with Blair. But I really hope Ariel didn't keep his card . . .

'We should go live,' Boogs says, interrupting my thoughts. He takes back his phone and a minute later the red button appears on his screen. The viewer number starts to rise quickly. 'Wonderland just hit twenty thousand pounds! I'm here with the one and only Trey Anderson.' Boogs swings the phone around to me and I wave. 'We have thirty thousand left to raise by Christmas Eve, so come on, guys, do your thing and save Wonderland. The bookshop's located on Stoke Newington High Street in Hackney, so come through and buy a book or donate to the GoFundMe. Peace.' Boogs clicks off. 'Let's go grab a drink to celebrate, but please don't punch James when we walk back in there. I don't need an unconscious white boy in my living room when my mum gets home.'

I laugh, too buoyed up from the donations to be thinking about James. 'I'll try.'

We head back inside and Marcus is out for the count, snoring loudly on the sofa, while James has his back to us, a 2Pac song playing out loud. He's recording himself on TikTok lip-syncing to the words, and Boogs puts his finger to his lips. It takes everything in me not to burst out laughing. I grab my phone from my pocket to record James, but instantly see the black screen and remember it's dead. James steps backwards and trips over a bag on the floor, falling right into me. My phone slips in my hand, slams against the ground and what looks like hundreds of lines appear on my now-cracked phone screen.

FORTY

Ariel's playlist: 'Is It Morning Yet?'
by James Fauntleroy

'You like Trey,' Annika says matter-of-factly.

'No, I—'

Annika rests her hand on top of mine. 'You like Trey. Does he like you back?'

And suddenly I feel like I'm bursting and desperately need to tell someone about how I've been feeling, so I spill everything. Annika doesn't interrupt me once, but when I get to the part that happened yesterday by the light-covered arch and explain how we almost kissed, Annika gasps.

'We didn't though,' I clarify.

'But do you think he would have kissed you if Blair wasn't in the picture?' Annika takes a sip of her drink.

I copy her to give myself time to think rather than

because I'm thirsty. It's weird, but I can't imagine Trey without Blair. They've literally been *the* college couple since day one, yet when I think about me and Trey together it feels right.

'I think so.'

Annika puts down her drink next to her almost-empty pasta bowl. 'Damn.' She sighs. 'Look, you and Trey might end up together in the future, but I don't want you getting hurt. Blair is very territorial, and she doesn't play when it comes to him. I know it's tempting, cause – let's face it – Trey is hella fine, but he isn't single.'

'I know, I know.' Now it's my turn to sigh.

I wish we could start from the beginning and I could meet Trey before he even knew Blair existed. When will it be my turn to have the happy ending?

Annika claps her hands. 'Let's talk about something else. Are you excited for book club tomorrow?' But when I pull a face she says, 'Bloody hell, what now?'

'We've only sold ten tickets, and we were aiming for at least fifty. I had this vision of a room full of readers celebrating Estee Mase and buying more books, but even with Wonderland trending, the sales have hardly increased. Jolie's been a star and has been spreading the word, but it's not enough.'

Annika drums her long nails on the table. She clicks and points her finger at me. 'You need to go bigger – something to make people stop.'

I frown. 'Like what?'

'I dunno, something unexpected.' She shrugs.

Unexpected? What could we possibly do to make people pay to come to the bookshop tomorrow? It has to be something that screams *wow*. Then I remember the video I took of Trey singing. I look at Annika, who's twirling the last strands of spaghetti round her fork. Trey would kill me if I posted the video, but what if it was someone else . . . ?

'Have a look at this.' I pass Annika my phone and she presses play. Her eyes widen when she recognizes Trey.

She looks up at me. 'He has no idea?' I shake my head, and she grins. 'He looks hot in this video and he sounds amazing. Wait! What if we posted this—'

'That's exactly what I was thinking.' I love that we're on the same wavelength.

'And we can tell everyone Trey will be doing a private showcase after the book club!'

What did she say?

'No, no, no – Trey won't sing in front of people!'

Annika rolls her eyes. 'But they don't know that. All we need is for people to come and then we can say, I don't know, Trey lost his voice or something.'

I shake my head. 'I don't think—'

'Trust me, it will work. Girls will happily come out in the cold to hear this boy sing. Now, let me just . . .' Annika presses some buttons on my phone and her own phone beeps. Then her fingers fly over her screen. 'Okay . . . and done.'

'You posted it already?' I grab my phone to check her account.

'Duh! Book club's tomorrow, babe. I put it on a Finsta

account, so Trey probably won't even see it. I'll delete it after the event.'

But what if he does see it? He'll know it's me, I'm sure of it. And how am I going to explain that I filmed him secretly so I could save his singing on my phone? Creepy much? But I guess if book club sells out and makes money for Wonderland then it will be worth it. This is either the stupidest idea Annika has ever come up with, or it's genius . . . There's only one way to find out.

FORTY-ONE

Trey's playlist: 'O Come, All Ye Faithful' by Kirk Franklin and The Family

I don't know if he's high, drunk or both, but it seems to take James a moment to even realize how pissed I am.

'You've gotta fix it, bro,' Boogs says.

James nods in agreement, but then he says, 'I'm kind of short for money . . .'

'And I'm not?' I yell, making Marcus jump up awake.

'It's calm,' Boogs says, purposely putting himself between me and James, probably because he knows I'm ready to knock him out. 'Go see my boy Ahmed in Dalston. He runs a phone repair shop. Just say I sent you and he'll hook you up.'

'Thanks, man.' I shoot James a look and he drops his eyes to the floor. 'I'm gonna head out.'

I dap Boogs and walk out into the cold air, breathing hard.

James is such a dickhead. Between thinking about him, Blair and Ariel, I feel like my head is all over the place. I don't want to go home in this weird mood, especially because I know my parents are going to be happy about the GoFundMe and I don't feel like celebrating right now. I start walking with no real aim in mind.

There are loads of couples out tonight, holding hands, kissing under the fairy lights, giddy on Christmas spirit, and it's the last thing I want to see. I've been walking for a while now and I stop to take in my surroundings. I'm about twenty minutes away from home and by Newington Green roundabout. A 73 bus is coming, and I'm just about to put my hand out to stop it and head home when I hear singing. I can't see anyone, but then I spot a group of people crossing the road towards the small park and I have a feeling they're following the music. I trail behind them and see a crowd hidden behind the trees. In front of them are six singers, old and young, dressed in red and green and singing 'O Come, All Ye Faithful' in perfect harmony. It instantly calms me and I close my eyes, letting their voices wash over me.

'Would you like one, sir?' a woman asks me, holding out cups of mulled wine on a tray.

'Oh, I haven't got any change,' I say.

She smiles. 'Don't worry – it's Christmas, after all.' She gestures to me to take one.

'Thank you,' I say and she nods and walks off. I take a sip and it's hot and fruity, and warms up my entire body.

The carol singers are amazing, their voices effortless. Any

time I hear someone singing, I immediately think about the places where I could harmonize and ad-lib, putting my own stamp on the song. The carol singers sing a few more songs, and by the time they're done and I've finished my mulled wine, I'm feeling a million times better.

The crowd start to leave, some dropping coins into the collection bucket. I wish I had money to give them, but I have a better idea. I wait patiently as they talk to members of the crowd and eventually one of the singers sees me hovering.

'I just wanted to say you lot were great.' The man thanks me and shakes my hand. He looks about Dad's age with a full goatee. 'I was wondering if you'd be up for performing at Wonderland Bookshop's Christmas Showcase on Christmas Eve?'

The man's eyes widen. 'Are you the guy from the video? Of course! We love what the bookshop are doing. Anything we can do to help. I'm Michael by the way.'

'Nice to meet you, and thanks, man – that would be sick. Do you have a business card or something? My phone's broken.'

Michael digs around in his pocket and hands me a white card with HACKNEY COMMUNITY CHOIR written on it. 'Just let us know the time and we'll be there.'

I shake his hand again. 'Thanks, Michael. I'll send over the details once we've finalized everything. Have a good night.'

I pocket the business card and walk home with a smile on my face, humming Christmas carols for the whole journey.

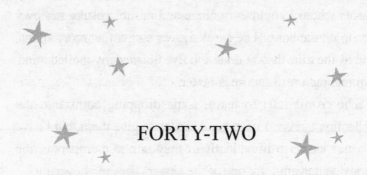

FORTY-TWO

Ariel's playlist: 'Eyes for You' by Justine Skye

Ten days till Christmas

Jolie and I hurry from college to Wonderland to set up the
book club. We only have half an hour after the shop shuts to
customers before people are due to arrive. There are already
a few eager girls waiting outside when we turn up, and I have
no idea why I questioned Annika's logic. She's always spot on.
That video of Trey singing has been viewed over five thousand
times, and we've completely sold out of tickets for tonight. The
comments took me by surprise though. Some girls are super
bold and have been shooting their shot. A few even declared
their love for Trey and have asked for a special song.

I've been anxious all day waiting for Trey to confront me
about the video because people have been tagging him in the
comments, but so far he hasn't mentioned it, which is weird.

I'm guessing he's just on a high about Wonderland hitting twenty thousand pounds . . . or maybe he somehow hasn't seen it yet. If he mentions it, I could always say it wasn't me that filmed the clip. It could have been a customer overstepping their boundaries, and he might go for it because there have been loads coming in recently to take pictures. But that sounds like a reach even to me.

Once we've finished setting up, Jolie pauses and puts her hands on her hips, surveying the shop. 'This looks great!'

We've lined up the seats in rows and each one has the latest Estee Mase book on it. We've placed pieces of white card on them too, each one with a different Christmas design hand-drawn on it. I managed to sketch them this afternoon, and Jolie's written *Merry Christmas from Wonderland* on the back in her pretty, loopy writing. The florist next door has also kindly donated flowers, so the room smells gorgeous, complementing the twinkly fairy lights and decorative tree in the corner. Estee Mase's backlist is on display by the till, and I really hope people take advantage of our half-price offer. The only problem is, it's still freezing, because, typically, the engineer didn't show up for the original appointment. They finally sent someone out late today, and Trey is in the basement with him now, but the heating should have been fixed hours ago.

'Should we let people in?' Jolie asks, looking at the time.

'Erm, let me ask Trey,' I respond, but then I hear him and the engineer coming up the stairs.

'Give it about ten minutes and the place should be warm again,' the engineer says.

'Thanks, mate,' Trey replies, walking him to the door.

I watch as the girls outside talk eagerly to Trey and I freeze, praying they don't mention the video. Trey closes the door and walks back over to us with a frown on his face.

'Everything okay?' I ask nervously.

Trey points over his shoulder. 'That was weird. One of the girls said she's excited for my show later. I have no idea what she's talking about.'

Jolie shoots me a look.

Thank God he hasn't seen it. 'Maybe she meant the Christmas showcase?' I suggest.

'Yeah, maybe.' Trey shrugs. 'Mum's asked me to sort some stuff out and tidy up the office, so I'll join as soon as I'm done. Give me a shout if you need me. It looks amazing in here, by the way. I really appreciate both of you.'

Once Trey's gone, I take out my phone and search for Annika's Finsta account. The video has been removed, but when I click on the #SaveWonderland, the video is up on multiple accounts.

'Ariel, I think you're going to have to tell him,' Jolie says.

I bite my lip. I know Trey is going to be pissed when he finds out, and I don't want to be on the receiving end of it. But everyone's bound to question him about his singing when he comes out of the office, so I don't think I can hide it much longer.

'I'll sort it,' I say unconvincingly. 'I will!' I add when Jolie raises her eyebrows at me.

She shakes her head. 'Let's start letting people in.'

*

Every seat is taken and I look around excitedly as people talk to each other animatedly. Even Boogs has come with Santi, although he's made it clear he hasn't read the book so we shouldn't ask his opinion – he's only here to support Wonderland. All the girls keep glancing at him approvingly, and I have no idea how Santi stays so unbothered by it all. I'm glad Blair didn't show up, but she definitely should have come to back Trey, even if books aren't her thing.

Jolie grins at me and I'm so glad that we pulled it off. The room is nice and toasty, and everyone's complimented us on how pretty the shop looks. I wish the crowd was more of a mix, but it's mainly people around our age to mid-twenties, and apart from Boogs, they're all females.

'Hi, everyone!' I wave from the front of the room. 'Thank you all for coming to Wonderland this evening. I'm Ariel Spencer, and this is my best friend Jolie Love-Jones. Welcome to our Estee Mase night!'

A cheer goes up around the room. One groomed-to-perfection girl with a fur coat, fitted red top and long curly hair puts her hand up. She came with two other girls in matching outfits, who were batting their eyelashes at Boogs, but when he didn't bite they sat in their seats and have looked bored ever since.

'Yes?' I say.

'When will Trey Anderson be singing?'

'Trey?' Santi hisses at Boogs, who's already on his phone showing her what I assume is the video. 'Has he seen this?' she asks.

'Erm . . .' I start.

'Right, we're already running late, so let's make a start,' Jolie says loudly, and I sigh in relief. The girl in the fur looks like she wants to say something else, but Jolie continues talking. 'Let's go around the room and everyone can share their first impressions of the book. Then we'll open up the session and discuss a set of questions. Okay, who wants to go first?'

I glance at the office, hoping Trey stays busy and loses track of time, then I return my gaze to the group.

Annika stands up confidently. 'I thought the book was brilliant.' She holds it and looks around the room with a smile. 'The protagonist isn't Estee Mase's typical choice cause of the tense relationship she has with her mother, but that's what really sets the story apart, and it's why we're rooting for Anthony to pursue her so she can have a happy ending.'

Jolie claps. 'Thank you, Annika. That's a brilliant way to kick us off.'

There's no way she read the story that quick, I think to myself. Annika sits down, looking very impressed with herself. She catches my eye and winks, and I can't help but smile. She totally copied someone's Goodreads review. Santi is practically bouncing in her chair and she puts her hand in the air to go next.

'Yes, Santi?' Jolie says.

Santi rises from her chair and the fur-coat girls look her up and down. She looks effortlessly chic with her floor-length brown-and-red-striped knitted dress, a huge belt tied round her tiny waist. She's grinning as she holds up the book. 'I'm the biggest Estee Mase fan and I think—'

But whatever Santi was going to say is drowned out by screams as the lights go off, leaving us in complete darkness.

'Okay, everyone – don't panic!' I shout, which only seems to make more people panic.

What the hell has happened? Has there been a power cut in the area? I faintly hear a noise coming from the office.

'Jolie, I'm going to find Trey,' I say in her direction.

'Put your phone torches on!' Jolie shouts over the screams.

'Lil' Mermaid, hold up.' The lights from everyone's torches are enough for me to be able to see the confusion on Boogs' face. 'Before you get Trey, does he even know about this video?'

'Erm ... well, no, but I guess the power cut has solved everything.' I giggle nervously, but Boogs crosses his arms.

'Trey will be able to reset the fuse, so, tell me: how are you going to fix the early showcase you've planned?'

'I-I don't know.' I fiddle with my hair.

This was such a stupid idea! I look over Boogs' shoulder and see people have already started to leave. What about all the Estee Mase books we need to sell? No, this can't be happening!

'This is a disaster,' I say, and Boogs turns around, noticing some of the audience already by the door.

'Okay, okay, don't panic. I'll sort them out. Get Trey to check the fuse and then grab the box of candles that his mum keeps in the office.'

I run into the office, the torch on my phone guiding the way, and I gasp when I see Trey lying on the floor.

FORTY-THREE

***Trey's playlist: 'Merry Christmas, Baby'
by Otis Redding***

One minute I'm putting the kettle back down, having made myself a cup of tea while J Hus's voice plays in my ear, and the next the lights have gone out and I've knocked over the mug. It flies through the air causing me to jump away from the scalding liquid, topple over a chair and land painfully on the floor.

'Trey!'

Red hair and a bright light looms into my vision.

'Are you okay?' Ariel asks, concerned.

'Yeah, I just tripped. Can you help me up?'

She takes my hand and lifts me up. The back of my head really hurts from the fall and tea has splattered my jeans, making my thighs feel sore and uncomfortable.

'Boogs mentioned candles?' she says. 'I can put them out until the power is fixed.'

'Boogs is here?' I ask, surprised.

As if on cue, I hear Boogs say, 'Who's ready for a show? Everyone clap and make a beat.' A cheer follows.

I frown. 'What's going on out there?' *Isn't this meant to be a book club?*

'I don't know,' Ariel says, looking at the floor. 'Candles?'

'Right, yeah, sorry. They're over there by the corner. I'll go to the basement and check the fuse ... Ah, damn it, I forgot my phone's at the repair shop. Stupid James broke it last night.'

Ariel grabs the box of candles. 'I'll help you. Just give me a second.'

As Ariel goes back to the shop floor, I look out of the window. I can see lights in the nearby houses and buildings, so it must just be Wonderland that's experiencing a power cut – typical. Can I have *one day* when something doesn't go wrong?

'Come on,' Ariel says when she returns, her torch on her phone lighting the way.

We walk slowly down the basement steps. There's a lot of cheering and foot-stamping going on upstairs and I really need to see what's happening. It's not helping my pounding head though, and I know I'm going to have a crazy headache later.

The fuse box is in the corner. When I open it, I can see some of the breakers are down, but when I push them back into place nothing happens. I do it several times, yet it makes no difference. I yell and slam shut the fuse box, making Ariel jump, and the light from her torch jerks around the room.

'Sorry,' I say. 'First the heating, then my phone breaks and now this. Give me a break, man.'

'I really don't want to add to your stress, and I know now isn't the best time, but I've got to tell you something.'

I groan. 'What now?' I look at Ariel, and I'm surprised to see how nervous she looks. 'What? What's happened?'

Ariel keeps her eyes on the floor. 'So, I sort of recorded you singing when you were in the basement yesterday, and, cause book club wasn't selling, Annika and I posted it on Insta, but then it got shared loads. So now most of the girls that are here tonight are expecting to hear you sing ...' She takes a breath. 'I'm so sorry, Trey. I really messed up. I wanted book club to go well to help Wonderland, but now this power cut has happened and people are about to leave without having bought any books. And I'm sure they'll ask for a refund cause I lied about you singing. I think Boogs is dancing or something to stall, but there are some adamant girls upstairs who want to see you perform.'

A recording? People are here to hear me sing? Refunds? Boogs is dancing ... ?! Ariel passes me her phone and my voice fills up the basement. I sound good, more than good actually. I click the comments, feeling weird that over five thousand people have heard me sing. The comments are really nice, with a few people asking if I'm professional. For a moment, it makes me think that maybe I'd do well in a singing competition, but then I remember that this video only exists because Ariel filmed me without my consent and then posted it online.

'Trey, I'm sorry,' Ariel says again, and her eyes start to well up. 'I feel really shit about it all.'

'Why were you filming me in the first place?' I say in this super calm voice, even though I can feel a slow heat rising through my body.

'I just . . . I came down to the basement to call you, but then I heard you singing and I started recording without thinking. It was wrong, I know that,' Ariel mumbles nervously.

I can feel the heat creeping up my neck and onto my face. 'But not only did you post it online, you then told people that I'd sing for them. Even though you know I don't like to sing in front of crowds.'

Ariel bites her lip. 'I really wish I hadn't done it.'

But she did. The way my luck is going, of course there's a viral video of me singing; of course there are people here wanting to hear my voice. The familiar feeling of dread sinks its claws into me. There's no way I'm doing it.

'This is so fucked up,' I say, my voice rising with each word, and Ariel flinches. 'I confided in you about something and then you put it up on the internet for everyone to see. I'd never do something like that to you.'

The truth is, it hurts. And I want to tell her that, but I'm so pissed that I can't even think straight.

Ariel wraps her arms round her body as if she's protecting herself from me. 'Trey—'

'The lights aren't coming back on any time soon. Everyone needs to get out,' I say over her.

'But, Trey—' she tries.

'But nothing!' I snap. 'This is your mess, so fix it.'

I peek my head out of the office door to look at the shop floor. The bookshop is packed. There are candles everywhere, which makes the whole room look magical, but I can see the furious looks on the girls' faces as Ariel tells them I won't be singing. Boogs catches my eye and he whispers something to Santi, who flashes me a sympathetic smile. He grabs one of the candles and walks towards me. I head back into the office and Boogs closes the door behind him, blocking out the raised voices.

'Well, book club went south real quick,' Boogs says, placing the candle on the table so a warm glow fills the office.

I tut in response as I sit down. Boogs sits opposite me.

'I don't think Ariel meant anything bad by it,' he says. 'I'm not saying it was cool of her,' he adds when he sees me about to object.

'Who does that? I'd never take a picture of one of her artworks without her permission and then share it online.'

'Yeah, I hear that still, but she was trying to help,' Boogs responds.

That's what makes it worse! She thought she was being helpful, despite crossing some serious boundaries.

'I tried to keep the crowd entertained with my dance moves, but you know I had to hold back. I don't want to make the girls go too crazy.'

Despite my annoyance, I laugh. 'When Ariel said you were dancing, I was like, *what?!*'

'Any excuse, right?' Boogs laughs. He looks at the table, drumming his fingers on it. 'You know, it wouldn't have been the worst idea to sing tonight. Singers do sing in front of people.'

I avoid his eyes. I know he's right, and it's not like I sounded shit on the video, but I don't want to be forced to do something I'm not ready for. When I do sing in front of a crowd, it will be my decision, and only mine.

I shake my head. 'She shouldn't have put me on the spot. There's nothing cool about that. Look, can you make sure everyone leaves, including Ariel, and then help me clear up?'

Boogs nods and stands up. 'No problem, man.'

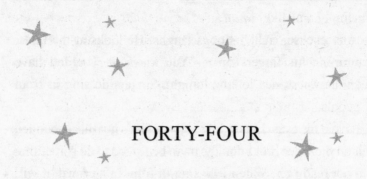

FORTY-FOUR

Ariel's playlist: 'Do You Hear What I Hear?'
by Destiny's Child

Nine days till Christmas

I'm an idiot. What did I think was going to happen? That Trey would be happy to sing on the spot? I groan at the memory, and Ezekiel looks over at me from his table, an eyebrow raised.

'I'm fine,' I say, and he goes back to his painting.

Book club was a complete disaster, and there were so many refunds! Trey didn't even come out of the office to say goodbye. All I wanted to do was apologize again and help clean up, but Boogs told me to leave it. Clearly that was Trey talking. He didn't respond to my many text apologies yesterday evening, but after the fifth one I remembered him saying his phone was broken.

Focus, Ariel!

I take out the Christmas cards for The Grotto tonight, having completed one of my art portfolio pieces during the lesson. Rubbing my hands together, I sprinkle some glitter on the cards. I've learned that the sparkly ones tend to sell more. Eden is at her desk, looking through my application form for the Artists' Studio to make sure I've filled it in right.

There are a few other students still here finishing off their work before we break for Christmas next week, and the radio is playing in the background. I love how the teachers are always more chilled in the lead-up to a holiday. I'm humming along to the song under my breath, trying to ignore the weird feeling I get every time I think about Trey and Blair coming tonight. Maybe the festive spirit at The Grotto will put him in a forgiving mood and we can make up, away from Blair's prying eyes. He definitely needs cheering up now that Wonderland is missing a day of trading because of the power cut.

'Ariel?' Eden waves me over.

'Is it okay?' I ask nervously as I sit opposite her.

'Your application form is brilliant, and the mural at Wonderland will really seal the deal. I feel like at this point you'd have to be living under a rock to not know about that bookshop.' Eden smiles. 'This is for you.'

She hands me back my form, but on top of it is a letter. I frown as I look at it, skimming over the words. *Brilliant*, *rising star* and *true gift* are jumping out of the page, and I can't believe Eden wrote this about *me*.

'Thank you so much, Eden.' I want to cry, but I hold it together.

'I mean every word,' she says before lowering her voice. 'You've always been my favourite.'

And in this moment, I really wish Dad was waiting for me at home, painting in front of the fireplace, so I could share the good news with him. I smile at Eden. 'You're mine too.'

I leave college with a wide grin on my face and head home to change into a Santa hat and candy-cane Christmas jumper before making my way to Shoreditch. When I get to The Grotto, the loud festive music hits me right in the face and I can't help but get excited. I know it won't be the same without Dad, but I'm determined to sell all my cards and do him proud.

We've been here for a few hours now and The Grotto is heaving with people. I'm on the stand with my dad's friend Matty, a short, stocky, middle-aged white man with a perma-tan. He hands me a cup of hot mulled wine. I take it eagerly. Even though I'm layered up, I'm still freezing.

Matty blows on his drink. 'Good turn-out so far.'

Christmas music is blaring from the speakers, fairy lights are hanging from every available space, and there are tons of food stands, art stands and sweet stands dotted around. The famous marshmallow fire pit is the busiest. They sell different-flavoured marshmallows for customers to cook over an open fire and it's always a hit. Down the other end of The Grotto are a group of carol singers by the ice rink, as well as an ice bar for over-eighteens. I can't wait for next year when I can go and check it out.

My Christmas cards and Noah's are laid out on the table,

and they look gorgeous. Some sellers like to group the same cards together, but I like mine to be mixed up. I find that people spend more time looking at a pile of cards when they realize that the one underneath the top one is different.

Matty isn't an artist, he's actually a butcher, but he was friends with Dad for years and his cousin runs The Grotto. He helps us to secure a stand every year. Dad used to give him a cut of his sales to pay for the stand, but this year Matty said he'd cover it. I thought it would be weird without Dad here, but it's actually really comforting because I have so many good memories of being at The Grotto with him. Plus, I've known some of the standholders for years, and I only ever see them once a year on nights like tonight. Even without Dad, everyone's been so lovely and welcoming.

'Thanks again, Matty,' I say, and Matty holds up his drink to me.

'It's what your old man would have wanted. He would have been proud of you. Applying for the Artists' Studio and getting on the news – that's good stuff!'

'Thank you.' I take a sip of the mulled wine. It's fruity with a hint of cinnamon – *delicious!* – and it instantly warms me all over.

Matty rubs his stomach. 'Cor, I'm hungry. I'm going to run and get a burger. You want one?'

'Yes, please, but no cheese.' I've been trying to stay healthy, but the only proper food you can get at The Grotto is chips, burgers and pies, so I don't have much choice.

Matty gives me the thumbs up and disappears into the

crowd. I take a few more sips of my mulled wine, checking my phone at the same time, and I almost choke. A message from Trey! My heart starts to race as I open the text. I'm praying he's decided we can be friends again.

> Hey, my phone's been fixed and I saw your messages. I'm at The Grotto with Blair, Boogs and Santi.

Okay, at least he messaged me back, but I wish he wasn't here with Blair. Maybe that's my punishment.

FORTY-FIVE

Trey's playlist: 'Give Love on Christmas Day' by SWV

How have I never been to this place? The Grotto is busy and festive and colourful. It's like it puked up Christmas in the middle of Shoreditch, and everything about it is brilliant. Thankfully, the headache I had all day from yesterday's fall has gone, so I can enjoy myself. I put my now-fixed phone back in my coat pocket and grab Blair, who's holding onto my arm because she was determined to wear her new heels. I told her it would be busy and we'd be walking for ages, but she didn't care. At least I have enough money so that we can treat ourselves to the fire pit marshmallows I spotted as soon as we arrived.

'It's gorgeous here,' Santi says, her eyes bright as she looks around in wonder. 'Who told you about this place, Trey?'

Everyone looks at me.

'Oh, someone mentioned it in passing – I can't remember who,' I lie, because I don't want to mention Ariel in front of Blair.

I'm still kind of pissed off with Ariel, but I don't want to create bad vibes tonight, especially when this is the first time she's here selling cards without her dad.

'I want to see everything,' Boogs says. 'Where should we start?'

'It's so cold,' Blair moans. 'I need to sit down. My feet hurt.'

'Blair, we literally just got here,' I argue back.

'No one told you to wear those shoes,' Santi says. 'Get in the Christmas spirit!'

Blair pouts and grips me tighter. 'Walk slower.'

I roll my eyes but hold my tongue. We haven't spoken about what happened the other day at hers, and things still seem a bit weird between us. I wasn't sure how she was going to react when I said Boogs and Santi were coming tonight, but she seemed relieved, which made me think she was feeling uncomfortable about hanging out with me too. Despite the inappropriate footwear, she looks beautiful dressed in all white. Her long braids frame her face, and the cold is bringing a natural flush to her cheeks. I'm definitely still physically attracted to her, but there's a barrier between us that I can't seem to tear down. In the past when we haven't seen eye to eye and ended up on one of our breaks, I'd go all out trying to fix things. But this time, I don't know if I should . . .

We stop to get Santi a vegan burger, which she makes everyone take a bite of to prove that vegan food is delicious.

I'm convinced it's going to be nasty, but it's actually so good that I order one myself.

'I heard there's an ice bar,' Blair says. 'Can we check it out?'

'You know ice is cold, right?' Santi replies, and we all laugh. Blair sticks out her tongue at her.

'It's for over-eighteens only so they won't let me and Boogs in,' I add before Blair gets carried away.

I glance around The Grotto, eyeing each stand, and then I spot Ariel at a table, holding a paper plate of food and looking cute in a Santa hat, and my heart leaps.

'Let's look at the Christmas cards,' I suggest, and we walk over.

Boogs gives me an 'Are you sure?' look once we get closer and I nod. I just want to say hey and buy a couple of cards like I promised.

Ariel's whole face lights up when she sees me. She quickly puts her burger down to the side. 'Trey! Hey, everyone.'

'Someone's happy,' Blair mutters under her breath, but I ignore her.

'Wow, these look incredible.' I pick one up and the detail is next-level crazy.

'Thank you. Look, these ones are Noah's.' She hands me one of Mary and Joseph in the manger. 'My brother,' she adds to the others.

He has the same style as Ariel and he's already so talented for someone his age.

'How long have you been selling cards here?' Boogs asks her. 'This place is great.'

247

'I've come here with my dad since I was about twelve, but this is my first time alone. This is Matty.' She points at a short, weathered-looking man, who looks up from the customer he's helping and waves. 'He helped me get the stall.'

'Hey, you're the guy from hashtag SaveWonderland!' Matty grins at me. 'I've donated to your GoFundMe.'

'Thanks, man,' I say smiling.

'This is your first time selling cards alone?' Santi asks, and Ariel nods. 'We absolutely have to support you!' She reaches into her purse and Ariel smiles. 'Come on, Blair, pick one.'

Blair hasn't said a word to Ariel, but if Ariel is offended by it she doesn't show it. Blair quietly skims through Ariel's designs.

I pick up one of a Christmas tree, and the star on the top is bursting with different-coloured rays. 'My mum and aunty will love these.'

'Trey,' Ariel says, loud enough just for me to hear. I look up. 'I'm really sorry for yesterday. I promise never to do anything like that again.' Her face is etched with worry, and she looks sincere.

'I accept your apology,' I reply, and she beams, making my stomach somersault. But then I see Blair from the corner of my eye and instantly feel guilty.

'Has the power been fixed at Wonderland yet?' Ariel asks, sipping her drink.

'Yeah, but the bill was crazy. Mum's pissed, but at least there won't be any new pictures of you from today, mid-talking and trying to paint.'

Ariel laughs. She looks down at my hands that are holding a stack of cards. 'Trey!'

'Who are all those for?' Boogs asks, eyeing me.

'Just family,' I mumble. I don't even know how much they are, but I want to support Ariel in any way I can.

She takes the cards out of my hand and puts them all back, apart from two that I said my mum and aunt would like. Then she puts them in a paper bag and says, 'On the house.'

'No, I want to—'

'You and your family have done so much for me, so this is a gift from me to you.'

She presses the bag into my hand and our skin brushes against each other's. A jolt of electricity races through my body. I catch her eye and search her face, not caring that we're not alone, and wonder whether she felt it too.

FORTY-SIX

Ariel's playlist: 'What Christmas Means To Me'
by Stevie Wonder

I quickly turn away from Trey and check on Santi, who has a few cards in her hands. My cheeks feel flushed, and it's not from the cold. When our hands touched, my whole body came alive. I wish we were here together, just me and him.

'I'm almost done,' Santi says. Her pretty face screws up in concentration, and I appreciate how seriously she's choosing the cards.

'Call me when you're ready,' I say to her.

'I will. Boogs, come help me! I need your artistic eye,' Santi says.

I hesitate before I go over to where Blair is standing. She's wearing a white coat and looks like a beautiful ice queen, but she couldn't look any less interested if she tried. She's flicking through the cards with no care, and I spot some of the glitter falling off. I wince, like she's physically hurt me, and it catches her attention.

'Sorry,' she says, not sounding sorry at all.

'Anything taking your interest?' I say brightly, because the customer is always right, even if the customer is Blair.

'No, nothing . . .' She trails off and holds up one of the cards, but I can't see which one. She's frowning at it and turning it round so that she's looking at it from different angles. I'm confused; none of the cards are complicated. Then she slowly looks up at me with wide eyes and my heart starts to race, even though I don't know why.

'Is this you?' she asks slowly.

She turns the card over and it's like someone has poured ice water all over me. It's the sketch I drew of the couple in the bookshop – the couple that look like me and Trey, *is* me and Trey. But how did it get here? I thought I'd thrown it away. No one was ever meant to see it.

'Of course not,' I say and laugh, but it's high-pitched and sounds nothing like my normal laugh. Blair stares at me coldly, like she knows I'm lying.

'Are you sure?' She glances at it. 'It really looks like you, and this boy looks like Tr—'

'It's not,' I say loudly, and now everyone is looking at us. But what's worse is that I know I sound guilty.

'What did you pick?' Trey asks, walking over to Blair, who goes to hand him the card.

Trey cannot see that card! I reach over the table, snatch it from Blair, scrunch it into a ball and throw it on the floor so it lands by my feet.

Trey, Boogs, Santi, Matty and even a few of the other customers look at me alarmed.

'Sorry, there was a random card out,' I say easily. I try to smile, but my mouth isn't working properly, so it doesn't come out as friendly as I'd intended.

Blair is still staring, her eyes narrowed and nostrils flared, like she's a moment away from jumping over the table and scratching my eyes out.

'You okay?' Trey asks, finally noticing Blair, who's refusing to look away from me.

'Yes,' she says eventually in a calm, very unlike-Blair voice. 'It all makes so much sense now.' And the look on her face tells me everything. She knows I like Trey and she's not going to let it go any time soon.

FORTY-SEVEN

Trey's playlist: 'Another Lonely Christmas' by Prince

What happened with Blair and Ariel back there? I go to ask her, but the crowd distracts me – it seems even more packed as we make our way over to the marshmallow pit. I'm trying to use my size to make a clear path through, but people keep bumping into me. Blair's holding my arm, and Santi's holding onto her, and then I feel myself being pulled back. I turn to see Santi looking around.

'Where's Boogs? Boogs!' she yells.

I cup my hand around my mouth. 'Boogs!'

'Sorry, I'm here.' Boogs joins us, sounding breathless. He looks at me. 'I dropped something back there.'

We finally reach the marshmallow pit and there's a huge shelf of jars containing different-flavoured marshmallows – vanilla, chocolate, salted caramel, candyfloss, cola. I've never seen anything like it. There are loads of fire pits, and people are standing around them with marshmallows on sticks, melting them over the flames.

'What flavour do you want?' I ask, but Blair is staring into space. 'Blair?'

She blinks. 'Huh?'

'You cool?'

Blair shakes her head and smiles at me. 'Yeah, sorry. Ooh, these flavours are fab. Now which one?'

Once we all have our marshmallows, and I'm out of money, we nab one of the empty fire pits. The heat on my face is the best feeling ever.

'Let's get a picture!' Blair says, pulling out her camera. 'Marshmallows up.'

We do as we're told until the camera flashes, and then go back to toasting. I'm the first to try my marshmallow and it's hot, sweet and, oh my days, delicious.

'Mmm,' Boogs moans. 'Where has this been all my life?'

'Trey, did you hear back from Estee Mase yet?' Santi asks as she continues toasting her marshmallow.

I grimace. 'No, she hasn't read my message.'

'Ah, man! I really hope she comes,' Santi replies at the same time as Boogs sneaks a bite from her marshmallow.

'Hey!' She holds her stick protectively. 'Try that again and I swear to God . . .'

I turn to Blair, who's looking at her phone, the glow from the fire lighting up her face. 'Have you read some of these thirsty comments?' Blair shows me her screen. Most people are showing their support for Wonderland, but a few girls and guys are flirting with me. 'I hope they know you're taken.' She gives me a look.

'You're the only girl on my feed,' I say.

'And Ariel.'

I freeze. Fuck. Did I post Ariel by accident?

'There's one of her painting,' Blair explains.

Now I remember the picture, and I internally sigh in relief. 'Yeah, but that was for Wonderland.'

Blair shrugs. 'Some girls get confused when you're too friendly.' She puts her phone back in her coat pocket. 'They can get the wrong idea.'

I wave at my marshmallow, trying to cool it down so I can eat it, but Blair is still staring at me.

I frown. 'What?'

'Do you agree?' she asks bluntly.

'Yeah, I guess,' I mumble, and she smiles, satisfied. *Where is this even coming from?*

'So, the news tomorrow,' Boogs says. 'Do you know what you're going to say?'

I shake my head. I've been trying to memorize key points about Wonderland so I don't forget anything. This is the only chance we'll get to give the fundraiser a massive push and hit our target. Every time I think about the fact that millions of people are going to be watching me, I feel my stomach twist. I really don't want to make a fool of myself, and I just hope if I freeze up or get tongue-tied Ariel will jump in.

Blair cuddles up to me and I put my arm round her.

'Is it just you being interviewed? Or you and your family and Ariel?' Santi asks.

'It's me and Ariel.'

I sense Blair stiffen, but the next moment I think I must have imagined it, because when I look at her she's smiling at me. 'You're going to be great,' she says. 'I'll be rooting for you.'

'Thanks, babe,' I say, before finishing my marshmallow. Damn, I wish I had money to get more.

I get home just after ten and Dad is up on the laptop. There isn't much to do on bed rest, so Dad has been monitoring the donations coming in, as well as answering emails from the media, well-wishers and people asking to perform at the Christmas showcase.

Mum and Aunt Latrice spent the day giving the shop a good clean and clearing a space for a seating area for customers. Mum figured we should do it before they film the item for the news so the shop looks good on TV. After filming tomorrow, the three of us, plus Jolie (I asked her because I was impressed with how she directed my social media) are going to audition the showcase acts. Aunt Latrice is pretty brutal, so I'm sure she'll be bringing Simon Cowell energy to the judging panel. I didn't ask Ariel because I assumed she'd want to stay working on the mural.

The number of people who want to help Wonderland is overwhelming, and it must be even more so for Dad. He seems a lot happier these days, and I think all the worrying about Wonderland not doing well was getting to him *way* more than he let on. I wish we were getting more donations, but we've still got time to reach our target.

'Hey, son,' Dad says when I walk into the living room. 'How was it?'

'Really cool. We should go next year when you can walk about again. How we doing?'

Dad turns the laptop towards me and we're at twenty-five thousand pounds. 'Tomorrow after you're on the news it will definitely go up. Oh, I've got something to show you.'

Dad clicks on the TV and presses play on a recording of one of the morning shows. Wonderland immediately appears on the screen, and they're talking to Dad! I look at him, bewildered, and he grins at me.

'They kept emailing to ask if they could talk to me, and eventually I told them you're going to have to come to the house.'

'When did you film this?' I ask, amazed.

'A few days ago when everyone was out.'

I watch the footage and Dad does a great job. His passion and love for the bookshop shines through. He talks about our family and Black businesses and the community. He doesn't even slag off Books! Books! Books!, which I'm surprised about. If I didn't know him, I'd feel so compelled to help out the Anderson family, and that's what I want to achieve tomorrow. That easy, passionate, yet humorous energy that Dad has.

'Just be yourself tomorrow,' Dad says, looking at me. 'Be that charming boy that I know.'

I sigh. 'I'll try.' I stand up and Dad grabs my arm.

'Trey, I just wanted to say thank you for all you've done. Regardless of what happens with Wonderland, I'm so proud of you, and I'm really glad that we've done everything to try to save it.'

I smile. It means a lot to hear those words coming from Dad's mouth, but while he seems lighter, I feel a massive weight on my shoulders. If I don't nail it tomorrow then we probably won't make enough to save Wonderland and it will be all my fault.

'Yeah. Me too,' I say eventually.

Please, God, let this not be in vain.

FORTY-EIGHT

Ariel's playlist: '8 Days of Christmas' by Destiny's Child

Eight days till Christmas

I didn't sleep at all last night. How did that card end up in the pile? And of all the people to find it, why did it have to be Blair? It was like a bad dream! God knows what everyone thought of me reaching over and scrunching it up like that. The worst part is, I couldn't even find it afterwards. But as long as Blair doesn't have it to show Trey then I think I've got away with it. And if she tries to bring it up, I'll just deny it and pray that Trey believes me. I'd die of embarrassment if he knew I was drawing pictures of us together.

I walk over to the mirror in my room and see my eyes looking tired and red. They definitely aren't interview-ready. I take my time putting on my make-up so my skin looks flawless and is highlighted in all the right places. Then I rummage around in my wardrobe for my best black jeans and a cream low-scooped jumper that gives just the right amount of cleavage. No painted jeans for me today! I add some gold hoops and rings to complete the look. With my red hair, I look smart-casual with an edge of funky. The butterflies in my stomach take flight when I think about little ol' me being on TV. Even Mum's boss, who can be a bit of a dick, said they'd tune in from work. This news footage will only strengthen my application form for the Artists' Studio so I've got to bring my A game.

The butterflies are still there when I get to college, and it doesn't help that people keep stopping me every few minutes. It seems like the whole school knows about me and Trey being on the news this evening. Everyone is wishing me good luck, even people that I don't know. *This is what it must feel like to be popular*, I think to myself. But I'm not sure I like the attention as much as I thought I would. I reach the art room and Annika and Jolie are already waiting for me outside with a gingerbread latte for me.

'You look gorgeous,' Annika says, hugging me.

'Thank you,' I reply, my cheeks flushing.

'I can't wait to watch you both today.' Jolie claps excitedly. 'How are you feeling?'

'I'm nervous, but I'm looking forward to it,' I say, taking the cup. 'I really hope we reach our target after this.'

'Of course you will! How was The Grotto?' Annika asks.

I hesitate. 'It was good. I sold out of my cards.'

'That's brilliant!' Annika gushes, but quickly frowns. 'Do you want to tell your face the good news?'

'Yeah, why don't you sound happy about that?' Jolie asks.

'Come inside.' I open the art-room door and walk in. The first art lesson doesn't start for another hour so it's empty. We sit down and I tell Annika and Jolie about last night, even though I promised myself I'd forget about it.

Jolie gasps. 'You and Trey?'

'Well, there's not really a me and Trey—'

'There totally is,' Annika interrupts. 'But now you think Blair knows?'

'Trust me, she knows. Has she said anything weird?' I question, trying to hide the worry from my voice.

Annika shakes her head. 'I saw her this morning and all she said was that she had a really good time last night. She seemed fine to me. Did you see the picture she posted on Insta? Oh, wait, you don't follow Blair.'

Annika takes out her phone and shows it to me, and my heart drops to my stomach. Trey, Blair, Boogs and Santi are sitting by a fire pit holding up their marshmallows and looking like the most stunning foursome ever, with their perfect smiles and the festive lights behind them. The caption reads:

Date night with my favourite people. Best boyfriend eva!
@TreyAnderson #SaveWonderland #HandsOffHeIsMine

I'm so stupid. Trey looks totally into Blair.

'Look at the time stamp,' Jolie says. 'Was this after they saw you?'

I check and realize it was posted not long after they came to my stand. 'Yeah, I think so.'

'Then she probably posted it on purpose. Look at the hashtag – subtle much?'

Jolie is being way too nice. It's laughable that Blair would ever be threatened by me.

We walk out together and Annika turns off to go to media, while me and Jolie head to sociology. I'm barely paying attention in the lesson as I'm thinking about the news interview to come. Once it ends, Jolie hugs me and leaves to go to drama while I go to English. Everyone including my teacher, Mrs Taylor, is asking me about the feature later and they promise to tune in.

I head to my last class of the day after lunch. The level of noise today in art is at an all-time high because everyone's asking me about the news tonight. Eden, who never raises her voice, shouts over everyone to settle down, and I'm grateful I can now get on with my work in peace. I start on a new piece for my portfolio, sketching out the image in pencil. I'm avoiding paints as I don't want the whole world to see my messy hands.

The time flies by and before I know it art is finished and I only have two hours until the interview.

'Remember to watch Ariel and Trey on the news at six p.m.!' Eden calls to the class as everyone prepares to leave.

'And donate! More than once, please,' I say, before turning to Eden. 'Do you mind if I stay here and work to kill some time?'

'Of course,' Eden says on her way out. 'But leave the door

open.' One time, Bebe and Jerome Michaels were caught pressed up against a wall in a closed classroom, him with his shirt off. So, yeah, doors are always left open unless you want to get in trouble.

I prop up my phone on the table ready to record myself. My followers on Instagram have massively gone up since Wonderland trended and customers started posting photos of me. It's crazy that I now have eight thousand followers who care about my art. I press record so I can share my artwork process later once I've edited the video. I grab a piece of paper and sketch out the finer details of Toni Morrison's face, which I plan to use as a guide for the mural. Plus, I can add it to my portfolio.

I'm working away for a few minutes when the door slams, making me jump.

'Bloody hell, you scared me!' I say, looking up.

Standing in front of the closed door is Blair, hands on her hips and her eyes narrowed. I know this isn't going to be good.

'You know, I've been thinking all night about that card,' Blair says, walking towards me. I stand up, my pencil falling from my hand. 'And I still don't understand why you drew that picture. Why you and Trey? Do you like him? Is that it?'

Shit! 'No, we're just friends,' I reply quickly.

Blair laughs, but not in a nice way. 'Do you draw all your friends cosied up holding hands? I think you're mistaking Trey's niceness for something else.' Blair leans on my desk and glares at me. Her face isn't far from mine and I start to shrink under her gaze. 'He will *never* like someone like *you*.'

You. Like I'm not even a person. Like I'm something disgusting and unattractive. I can feel the anger rising from the pit of my stomach. All the times Blair has ignored me, dismissed me and just been plain rude to me are bubbling to the surface. Her words have hurt me so badly that she's pushed me to the point of bingeing again. No more.

'Trey does like me,' I say before I can stop myself, and Blair jerks back like I've hit her. 'He likes me a lot. But he's a good guy, an amazing guy actually, who's doing everything he can for his family. And what have you done to help? It's beyond me why he's with someone like *you*.' I copy the way she said 'you', and to my surprise Blair flinches like I've touched a nerve. 'You look at me and see someone who's bigger than you, and in your head that makes me unattractive. But I know my worth. I'm beautiful and your words mean fuck all to me.'

Blair's mouth opens and closes like the comeback is stuck in her throat, and for once I feel confident and fearless. Who the hell is Blair Bailey anyway? Why did I ever let this girl make me feel so small? I reach for my phone on the table, ready to leave, but Blair beats me to it. She holds it up like a prize, her face twisted in an ugly snarl.

'Give me my phone,' I demand, putting my hand out.

Blair points at me. 'Stay away from my boyfriend! I know you don't care about Wonderland. You're only doing this to get close to him.'

'You're delusional, Blair! Now, give me back my phone,' I yell, but she ignores me.

'All everyone talks about these days is Ariel the talented

artist and I'm sick of it. I'm sick of you. I even saw some comments online saying you and Trey make a cute couple, which is a complete joke. Me and Trey are solid and I'm not going to let you and your desperate, pathetic self ruin my relationship.'

'Give it!' I lunge for my phone, but Blair is quicker than me and she runs to the door, slamming it in my face. Then I hear an unmistakable click. I pull at the door, but it doesn't budge. No, this can't be happening! Blair's locked me in! And she has my phone!

'Hey!' I bang on the door with my fist. 'Blair, open the door right now!' I look out of the small glass window but Blair's nowhere to be seen. The hallway is empty.

I push against the door with all my weight. Nothing. My heart starts to race as I try again, but the door doesn't budge.

'Help!' I yell, hitting the door. 'Someone help me!'

My eyes well up and I wipe them away aggressively. I need to get out of here. Trey needs me. I have to get to Wonderland.

'Help.' My voice is hoarse and my fists hurt from banging on the door. I slide to the floor, not even bothering to wipe my tears. My coat and scarf are in a heap by my feet.

I can't believe I'm still stuck here. I swear when I see Blair I'm going to kill her. The clock on the wall is ticking loudly, reminding me that I'm completely screwed and the interview is going to start in twenty minutes. I bet Trey is going out of his mind. He must know that something bad has happened because I wouldn't miss today for anything.

I'm still wondering how Blair got a key for the art room. Had she been waiting for me to be alone? And where the hell has she taken my phone? I push the questions out of my mind and resentfully look at the windows opposite me. What kind of college bolts the windows, for fuck's sake? We're practically adults.

A faint sound outside the door makes me scramble to my feet. I press my face against the glass to see who's there and notice someone walking down the corridor, whistling.

'Hello?' I bang hard against the door. 'Help, I'm stuck!'

The whistling stops, and for a second I think I've imagined it, but then a voice says, 'Hello? Is someone in there?'

'Yes! I'm locked in the classroom. I need help!'

I hear quick footsteps and see his Afro before I see him. Ezekiel's eyes widen when he spots me.

'Ariel?'

'Ezekiel! I'm locked in!'

He tries to push the door open, but it doesn't budge. 'How?'

I shake my head. 'It doesn't matter. I just need to get out. I'm meant to be on the news in less than twenty minutes.'

'Oh shit.' He tries the door again, and I want to scream at him that it's obviously locked. He bends down and disappears from view, reappearing a second later holding a phone. My phone!

'That's mine!' I shout, relieved.

Ezekiel frowns. 'But why is it out here?'

'It's a long story. Ezekiel, please can you find someone to open the door?'

He nods. 'I'll be back.'

I breathe a sigh of relief. My biggest fear was that no one was going to find me until the morning. I pace the room impatiently, willing Ezekiel to return quickly, but he doesn't come back for fifteen minutes. Finally he returns with an older white man, who I recognize as one of the cleaners.

The door clicks. Thank God! I pull on my coat, scarf and bag.

'You have to report this,' Ezekiel says, handing me my phone, which is dead. 'If someone locked you in here, the college need to know about it.'

'I will, but I need to go right now. Thank you both so much.'

I'm not a runner, but I run out of college so fast, heading straight for the bus stop to take me to Wonderland. I've got to fix this before it's too late.

FORTY-NINE

Trey's playlist: 'The First Noël' by Whitney Houston

I'm trying really hard not to panic, but I keep checking my phone every few minutes. The news team are here setting up and Ariel's totally MIA. There are a few customers inside the bookshop who have agreed to be filmed for the interview and a line of people outside, some here to audition and some just hoping to get on camera.

Wonderland looks like a Christmas picture. Mum has put some of the slow sellers in a book stack, wrapped them in gold ribbon and surrounded them with bright Christmas baubles, and the fairy lights strung up around the shop are twinkling. She and Aunt Latrice wanted to watch me be interviewed, but there's no way I could have done it with them staring at me, so they've stepped out to grab some food before the auditions. Although, now Ariel isn't here, I'm wishing they'd stayed.

Where is she?

I have a card of notes in my hand that I know I can't use on camera, but I've been reciting what's on them all day. Sarah Mills was kind enough to tell me in advance what she was going to ask us. *Us* ... What am I going to do if Ariel doesn't show up?

'Any luck?' Sarah comes over and asks. I shake my head. 'I'll try one more time.'

I've been calling Ariel back to back, and at first it rang, but now it's going straight to voicemail. Maybe her phone died? When I called Jolie to see if she knew where Ariel was, she said they'd chatted earlier at college. But there's no way she can still be there now. I run my hand over my head. Reon told me this morning that over fourteen million people watch the news and that fact has been stuck in my head all day. I cannot talk to a camera by myself, knowing that fourteen million people are watching.

'You okay, Trey?' Sarah puts a hand on my shoulder. 'You're looking a little pale.'

'I am?' I swallow hard. 'What do we do if Ariel doesn't turn up?'

Sarah frowns. 'Well, we have to fill in the time, so I can ask you a few more questions.'

More questions? I shake my head. 'Sorry, can you give me a minute?'

I don't even wait for her to respond before I head to the office, close the door and take in big deep breaths. I try Ariel again, praying she'll pick up this time, but no luck.

Someone knocks gently on the office door.

'Yeah?' I answer, trying to calm my breathing.

Blair pops her head round and I stare at her, surprised. Blair's the last person I expected to see. She's wearing tight-fitting jeans and a white T-shirt that says #SaveWonderland.

'Hey.' I hug her tight. 'What are you doing here?'

'I wanted to wish you good luck. Are you and Ariel ready?'

I shake my head. 'She's not here. I've been calling her, but no answer.'

Blair gasps and covers her mouth. 'Oh no, I hope she's okay.' She rubs my arm. 'How are you doing?'

'I'm stressing out. I can't do this by myself.'

'Oh, baby, I'm here. I can stand by your side and help if you need me?'

'Really?' Blair hasn't shown interest in Wonderland … ever. I'm not sure she's the best person to fill in the gaps if I get stuck. Maybe she's just saying this now so she can be on TV? 'That's really nice of you to suggest, but—'

'Estee Mase is your bestseller and we want her to come to Wonderland to sign some books,' she says quickly. 'We've made changes to the bookshop so customers can relax and take their time finding the right books. By Christmas Eve there will be a mural celebrating Black writers.'

I look at Blair, surprised, and she smiles smugly.

'Santi's been schooling me. I'm really sorry that I haven't been present or supportive enough, but I'm here now and I'm not going anywhere. All you need to do is talk about why Wonderland means so much to your family and this community. I'll jump in if you need me.' She looks down at her top. 'I even made this last night to show my support. It's not the neatest—'

'It's great – you're great,' I say earnestly. Yeah, Blair's pretty late to the party, but it means a lot that she's here now. I touch one of her long braids. 'You're sweet to do this for me.'

Blair tiptoes and kisses me. 'I'm your girl. No one has your back more than me.'

She holds my hand and I instantly feel calmer. I can do this. I can talk about the bookshop. I can get us to fifty thousand pounds and save Wonderland. Despite what we've been going through, Blair showed up for me when I really needed her, whereas Ariel is nowhere to be seen.

As instructed, I keep my eyes on Sarah, who's standing by me with an earpiece on. Blair has her hand on the bottom of my back and it's comforting. I can do this.

A guy holds up his hand and mouths, 'Five, four, three, two—'

'Those of you that have been keeping up with social media will have seen a little bookshop called Wonderland on Stoke Newington High Street in Hackney that is fighting to survive. A Black-owned family business had been left with no choice but to close its doors by Christmas Eve, until Trey Anderson, whose parents own the bookshop, decided to share a video online explaining Wonderland's troubles. That video has been viewed over a million times, with support from bestselling authors and celebrities like Rihanna. Now the GoFundMe page is halfway to its target of fifty thousand pounds with seven days to go. I'm here with Trey Anderson and his girlfriend, Blair Bailey. Now, Trey, can you tell us a little more about Wonderland?'

Fourteen million people.

I know I need to speak. Sarah's giving me an encouraging nod and Blair's gently tapping my back, but it's like my mouth can't move. My armpits feel hot and sweaty. Shit! Do I have sweat patches on live TV?

'Wonderland was opened by Trey's great-grandad, before his grandfather and now father took over,' Blair says and I look at her. 'Wonderland has made such a positive mark on this community. Right, Trey?'

'Yeah— Yes, that's correct. Wonderland is more than a bookshop. It's a Black-owned family-run business that has been suffering recently.' And suddenly I'm off, telling the world about why Wonderland is so important, and how concerned we are about it potentially closing down, and how I didn't expect my video to go viral. 'We're getting closer and closer to meeting our fifty-thousand-pound target each day, so please, if you haven't already done so, donate to our GoFundMe.'

'That's brilliant, Trey. And tell us more about the Christmas showcase,' Sarah says.

'It's on Christmas Eve. Originally, we set it up as a fundraiser, but now we're going to use it as a special day to celebrate Wonderland, Christmas and the community. I'm hoping author Estee Mase will come down. She grew up around here.'

'Now that would be great!' Sarah smiles at me. 'What are the chances, do you think?'

'Hopefully she'll watch this and respond to my DM!' I say, and Sarah and Blair laugh.

'And lastly, Trey, there's a video going around online of you singing so brilliantly. Can we expect you to perform on the day?'

Why did she have to bring up the singing video? My stomach flips and I place my hand on it to try to calm myself down. 'Oh ... erm ...'

'You'll have to show up to see!' Blair says quickly. 'The line-up for the showcase is incredible. Everyone should be there to show their support for the talent in Hackney.'

Thank God for Blair. The tightness that's been in my chest all day loosens as Sarah explains how to donate to Wonderland. I smile into the camera and then we're done.

'That was great.' Sarah shakes my hand and then Blair's. 'I'm so glad we did this, and I really hope Wonderland reaches its target. It's a beautiful bookshop.'

'Thank you, Sarah, for everything,' I say.

Blair squeals and I wrap my arms round her, lifting her off the ground. I did it!

FIFTY

Ariel's playlist: 'Soulful Christmas' by Faith Evans

The bus pulls up and I run off it, heading straight towards the bookshop. There's a long line outside that I assume is for the auditions after the interview. I'm sweating and I don't need to look in a mirror to know my make-up is smudged and my baby hairs are no longer laid. Plus, my chest is still hurting from running out of college. People in the queue call my name as I run by, but I ignore them and hurry to the front. As soon as I reach the doors, I'm stopped by a burly man.

'Filming is in progress, miss.'

'I'm meant to be in there,' I say, breathing heavily. 'Ariel Spencer.'

The man shrugs. 'No one can go in until they've finished up.'

'But I'm meant to be on the news!'

The burly man doesn't move and I groan. This is bullshit!

I peer through the window and see people moving around, packing up equipment. My heart sinks. I missed it! I can see Trey swinging a girl around, and I press my face closer to the window and gasp.

Blair!

FIFTY-ONE

Trey's playlist: 'K for Christmas' by Lil Mosey

'Why don't I help you guys set up for the auditions?' Blair says when I put her back on the floor.

'Thanks, that would be cool,' I say. 'We're going to do it in the basement.'

'The basement? Is the floor sorted now?' she asks.

'It's dry, but we're still going to have to replace it. We're doing the auditions down there to give Ariel space to work on the mural.' I shrug. I don't want to think about Ariel. 'Thank you again for being here.'

Blair strokes the side of my face, and I grab her hand and kiss it. Because of her, I managed to speak about Wonderland in front of fourteen million people and not choke up. I owe her everything.

She goes downstairs and I watch her walk away. Damn, she looks good in those jeans. She smiles at me over her shoulder and winks, almost as though she's read my mind. I turn back to look at the shop floor and freeze when I see red hair at the window. Is that Ariel? I walk to the door and pull it open and Ariel's there, her hair matted to her forehead and mascara running under her eyes. She's arguing with the security guy, who steps aside when he sees me.

'Trey!' Her eyes widen when she spots me. 'Let me explain.'

I cross my arms over my chest. 'So explain.'

She glances at the queue of people who are watching us and I see a person take out their phone. I really don't need a video going viral for the wrong reasons. I grab Ariel's arm and pull her into the bookshop.

'Where were you? I was calling you for ages.' I'm surprised to see her eyes welling up.

'Blair locked me in a classroom and took my phone.'

I don't know what I expected Ariel to say, but this was definitely not it. Why would Blair do that? It doesn't even make sense. I glance at Ariel's hand, which is holding her phone tightly. If Blair took it, then how does Ariel have it? She sees me looking and her mouth drops open.

'She left it outside the classroom and when I got it back it was dead.'

'Right,' I say slowly, nodding my head. 'You know what, I don't know what happened today, but you knew how important this was for Wonderland and how much support I needed to be able to speak live. And, even then, you still decided to go

AWOL, and now you're trying to blame Blair! She actually came through today and helped me.'

Ariel's eyes bulge. 'She did this on purpose!'

I scowl. 'Why would she?'

Ariel bites her lip and looks away from me. She wipes her tears and, for some reason, the gesture really pisses me off. What has she got to cry about? Today could have been a disaster if Blair hadn't come to my rescue.

'I've got auditions to prepare for, so if you want to do your painting or whatever, go for it, but I'll be with Blair getting everything ready.'

'But, Trey—' She grabs my hand as I go to turn away.

'WHAT?' I yell, shaking her off, and everyone looks at us.

I'm breathing hard and I can feel fire bubbling inside me. To be honest, I'm more annoyed with myself because I thought Ariel understood how important this was to my family, to me. I thought she got me, but she's let me down again. First the video and now this. How did I get her so wrong? I was stupid to even think about throwing away what I have with Blair.

I walk away from her without looking back.

FIFTY-TWO

Ariel's playlist: 'In Love at Christmas' by K-Ci and JoJo

All the TV people are looking at me, including Sarah Mills. She gives me a sympathetic smile and starts to walk towards me. I want to quit this job, leave and never talk to Trey again. How can he think I would miss this on purpose? I thought he knew me.

I head for the door, but then I see the mural that's half finished and I think about Mrs Anderson, who gave me a job when I needed one and has been nothing but nice to me since I started.

'Ariel,' Sarah says. 'I'm so sorry you missed the filming.'

'It's okay,' I say brightly, forcing myself to smile. 'There were some issues at college. Did it go well?'

Sarah nods. 'Hopefully when we do a follow-up piece we can speak to you.'

'That would be great, thank you.'

At least I haven't messed up that relationship. I go over to the painting and take off my scarf and coat, wishing I could drown everyone out, but I can't play my music on a dead phone. I sigh and plug it in to charge.

It doesn't take me long to get into the rhythm of painting and I glance at the drawing of Toni Morrison every few minutes to guide me. I'm busy sketching away when the bookshop door opens, letting in a rush of cold air.

'Ariel, what happened?' Jolie rushes in, her cheeks red from the cold. 'Why was Blair on the news? I've been calling you.'

'Shh.' I glance towards the stairs. 'She's downstairs. It's a long story, but I'll tell you about it later. Trey's angry with me again though, so that's fun.'

'I'm sorry.' Jolie hugs me. 'I know you were looking forward to it.'

In her arms, I want to burst out crying, but I need to hold it together. I just want to get this done and get out of here.

'Can you do me a favour?' I ask, and Jolie nods. 'If someone needs to run upstairs to fetch people for the auditions, can it be you?'

I don't want to see Trey, and God only knows what I'll do if I see Blair.

'I've got you,' Jolie says. She looks at my painting. 'This already looks amazing.'

Usually I light up when someone compliments my

work, but today nothing happens. I'm not angry or upset, just numb.

'Here.' Jolie reaches into her pocket and passes me a candy cane. 'They were giving them out by the bakery.'

'Thanks.' I twirl the red-and-white sweet in my hand.

'I've got to head downstairs. Are you going to be here for much longer? We could get some food later and you can tell me what happened.'

I hesitate. I was planning to go before the auditions finished so I didn't need to see anyone, but the need to offload is stronger. I remember how good it felt to tell Annika about Trey at that Italian place.

'Yeah, we'll get food.'

Jolie smiles. 'I'll see you in a bit.'

I wave at Mrs Anderson and Trey's aunt when they enter the bookshop and they head towards the basement. Once I have my AirPods in and K-Ci and JoJo's beautiful harmonies are playing through them, I'm lost in my own world. I have a zillion messages and missed calls that I ignore, instead focusing on the mural, which is looking great. You can now see Toni Morrison, Alice Walker, Maya Angelou and Estee Mase. I'm going to start on James Baldwin and some other Black male authors next time. Maybe I'll add some quotes from their books to the painting to really bring it together.

I go to the office to wash my hands in the sink and almost bump into Trey. He jumps to the side like I have cooties or something and walks out without saying a word. I ignore the way my heart is thudding and turn on the tap, watching the red, yellow and brown paint merge into a swirl before they disappear down the drain.

I'm lying on my bed. Mum is working late and Noah is staying at a friend's. The house was quiet when I got home, and I really wish it was filled with noise to drown out my thoughts. Mum's millions of text messages asking why I wasn't on the news remain unanswered on my phone. What do I even say? I eventually text back explaining I changed my mind. It's a stupid excuse and I know she'll drill me about it later.

I'm watching Trey's interview for the sixth time. I don't know why I'm torturing myself like this, but I can't stop. I'm still in shock that Blair made me miss it and that Trey doesn't believe me. Jolie is the second person to tell me to make an official complaint about Blair to college, but the more I think about it, I don't see the point. She'll just deny it. No one saw her in the art room to my knowledge and it will be her word against mine. She'll probably tell everyone that I'm in love with her boyfriend and that I'm making this all up so she looks bad.

Am I in love with Trey? I watch him carefully. My heart yearns to be there in that moment when Sarah asked him a question and he couldn't seem to catch his breath. But then he gets into the flow of talking and his eyes are shining and *that* smile. There's something about his smile that makes me feel warm all over. How do you know if you're in love? When I was fifteen, I dated a guy called Damson Raynes who was into anime. I really liked him, but that lasted about two weeks, so that definitely wasn't love. I wonder where Damson is now. I find him on Instagram and he's still fine but he has a girlfriend. Of course he does. Is every attractive guy boo'd up?

I sigh and toss my phone to the side.

FIFTY-THREE

Trey's playlist: 'Coming Home for Christmas' by Luke

Seven days till Christmas

I wake up in a pink bedroom with a brown arm draped over my torso. I look to the side and Blair is sleeping soundlessly. When she asked me to come over after the auditions, I jumped at the chance, and it felt good to be close to her again.

The interview's been shared on social media and has been viewed thousands of times. Mum and Dad were so happy with how it went and I am too, despite my nervousness at the beginning. Plus, it massively helped with the donations – we're at just under forty thousand now! Hopefully Estee Mase watches the news and gets back to me. Everyone would be so buzzed to meet her in person. It's less than a week now until the showcase and the GoFundMe closes, so we need a big final push.

Mum asked me why Ariel wasn't interviewed, and I lied

and said she hadn't been feeling well earlier. I didn't want to tell her what she actually said about Blair, because I'm sure Mum would have flipped out. She likes Blair, and she knows she'd never do anything like that. Despite me being annoyed with Ariel once again, I don't want to cause any conflict between them.

When we were done with the auditions and I went up to the shop floor, I was surprised to see Ariel still there painting with her headphones on. I watched her for a bit, and a part of me wanted to go up to her and ask her to tell me what really happened. I would have understood if she'd said she'd got nervous and changed her mind, but to make up a story about Blair locking her in a room and taking her phone is another thing.

I carefully get out of the bed and put my clothes on.

'Are you going?' Blair sits up, exposing her tits, and I'm distracted for a moment. She notices and gestures to me with her finger to come back.

I groan. I'd love nothing more than to spend the whole day with Blair, but I'm opening up. I don't risk leaning over to kiss her, because I know it won't take long for both of us to be naked again. Instead, I blow her a kiss.

'I'll call you later.'

She pouts as I wave her goodbye.

I head down the stairs, and – thankfully – Blair's parents are both already at work so they don't know I snuck in last night. Santi is in the living room in striped pyjamas, eating a bowl of cereal.

I peep my head in. 'See you, Santi.'

'Wait!' She jumps up. 'How's Ariel?'

I frown. 'I dunno. I'm not really speaking to her after yesterday.'

'Oh,' Santi says in a quiet voice. She sits back down, putting her full cereal bowl on the table.

I walk over to her. 'You cool?'

She opens her mouth, then closes it. I've known Santi for a long time, and I don't think I've ever seen her like this. It's almost like she's fighting with herself over something.

'Is it Boogs?'

Santi's eyes widen. 'What? No, it's nothing to do with him.'

'You're still here?' Blair bounces into the room in a dressing gown, and Santi grabs her cereal bowl and begins eating. 'You're going to be late.'

'Yeah.' I glance back at Santi, but she's gone back to watching TV and is ignoring me. I kiss Blair on the cheek and head out.

FIFTY-FOUR

Most people wouldn't find it fun being surrounded by thirty screaming kids covered in paint, but I love it. I've been volunteering at the community centre for a few years now. Today they're painting Christmas cards that we're going to hang around the room. Some of the kids aren't naturally artistic, and you can tell they've been forced to come by their parents because they want a few hours of peace, but there are others who are exceptional, like Noah and Reon.

When I arrived this morning, I had an irrational fear that Reon would act weird with me because of Trey, but he greeted me with his usual hug. I'm not due to work at Wonderland today, so I can't wait to go home and chill out for the rest of the day. Maybe I'll go to the shopping centre and buy some bits for Christmas. I already know the perfume Mum wants

287

and Noah's asked for more art equipment, but I just haven't got round to buying either of them yet.

'Can I show you something?' Reon asks and I nod. He reaches into his backpack and pulls out a drawing.

I gasp. 'Is this me?'

Reon nods. 'And Trey.'

He's drawn me looking like Storm from X-Men and Trey as Captain America. We're mid-battle, fighting against green monsters who are surrounding Wonderland. I trace my finger along the brilliant artwork, taking in all the detail.

'Do you like it?' Reon asks nervously.

I grin. 'I love it. Can I keep it?'

Reon smiles, and it reminds me so much of Trey. 'Yeah! I showed Trey earlier and he told me to show it to you.'

'He did?' *So he was thinking about me. That has to be a good sign, right?*

Mr Arnold, who runs the community centre, walks into the art room and all of the kids start calling out for him to come and look at their cards. I like Mr Arnold. He reminds me of Santa Claus with his big, round belly and white beard.

'One second, guys, I just need to speak to Ariel.'

I follow him to the corner so the kids can't interrupt.

'Mrs Anderson said she's been held up at the bookshop and asked if you could bring Reon over after class?'

'No problem,' I say, even though it *is* a problem, because now I have to see Trey.

Mr Arnold smiles. 'Thank you, Ariel. I'll let her know.'

*

The boys talk a mile a minute as we walk to Wonderland. I decided to take the scenic route to delay seeing Trey, which means we go past the square. A huge undecorated Christmas tree has been erected, and we stop and stare. For the past few years, the council haven't put one up because apparently there's been no money for it, despite all the residents' complaints. I wonder why they've managed to get one this year.

The boys race up the familiar high street, ignoring my shouts to slow down. By the time I walk into Wonderland, they're already in the children's corner, leafing through the books. Mrs Anderson, Trey and a young Asian woman with long black hair are talking in the middle of the shop floor.

'Ariel!' Mrs Anderson waves me over.

Trey greets me with a nod, and the Asian woman holds out her hand for me to shake.

'Great to meet you, Ariel. I'm Gita Agarwal, and I work for Hackney Council. I was just saying to Mrs Anderson and Trey how amazing it is that so many people are excited for the Christmas showcase. We actually wondered if you wanted to host it on the square to accommodate more people.'

'Really?' I gasp. In all my seventeen years living here, I've never seen a performance on the square.

Gita nods. 'I don't know if you've seen the Christmas tree we've just put up?'

'Yes, I literally saw it on the way here,' I say excitedly.

'Good! Well, next to it, we can put up a stage with lights for the showcase. We can get the whole community involved and I'll make sure the press are there to cover the event. It's going to be brilliant. We also want to start up an artist spotlight to celebrate the amazing talent in our community and display it like the Ridley Road Stories exhibition in Dalston. We wondered if we could take some pictures of the mural here and the stunning courtyard painting that you did for Corden College? Of course we'll credit you, and every month we'll pick a new artist to highlight.'

'You want to spotlight my work to the whole of Hackney?' I ask slowly, afraid I didn't hear her right.

'Is that okay?' Gita asks.

Is that *okay*? This is *epic*! It'll be my first art exhibition, and I know Dad is punching the air up there. This is so perfect for my Artists' Studio application!

Mrs Anderson rubs my arm. 'I'm so happy for you, Ariel. You deserve it.'

'Thank you.' I look at Trey, who gives me a brief smile, but it doesn't reach his eyes.

'Can I just say, Wonderland has brought so much positive attention to Hackney. We're all behind you,' Gita says. 'I don't know if you've seen, but the council donated a grand this morning.'

'They did?' Mrs Anderson puts her hand on her chest, and Trey puts an arm round her. 'That's amazing! Thank you!'

'You're so welcome. Mrs Anderson, would you mind walking me through the acts performing at the showcase? And is there any update on Estee Mase?'

'Let's go to the office,' Mrs Anderson says, leading the way.

Trey and I are left alone. He has his arms crossed over his body, looking anywhere than at me, and I hate it.

'This is really cool,' I say, trying to break the ice.

'Yeah,' he mumbles.

I sigh. 'Come on, Trey, we have to work together. Can we at least be civil?'

Trey nods slowly. 'You're right. Let's keep this strictly business. You're an employee at Wonderland and, unless it's about the shop, I don't think we have anything else to discuss.'

I hardly recognize this cold person in front of me. Trey knows what a big deal it is for my work to be featured by Hackney Council, and he doesn't seem to care one bit. I look him up and down. 'No problem.' I head towards the front door and shout over my shoulder. 'Come on, Noah. Let's go.'

Once I drop Noah off at home, I head to the shopping centre and buy him and Mum their gifts, as well as two plain jewellery boxes, for Annika and Jolie, that I'm planning to decorate myself. I'm also going to make a card for the Andersons.

I'm starving when I get back, but luckily Mum is dishing up lunch.

She smiles when she sees me. 'Hi, darling. What did you get?'

I check to make sure Noah's not within earshot. If he hears the word 'presents', he'll be begging to know what they are.

'Just your gifts for Christmas.' I put the bags down in the cupboard in the corridor. 'I've got to tell you what happened today.'

I fill Mum in on the council, and she claps her hands in delight.

'That's amazing! You're going to get that scholarship to the Artists' Studio, you know that, right?'

'I don't want to jinx it,' I say, taking my plate of food from her. 'But I definitely have a stronger chance now. I'm going to their open day on Tuesday – do you want to come with me?'

'I'd love that. Let me see if I can swap my shift.' She turns towards the stairs and yells, 'Noah! Lunch!'

'Coming!' he shouts back.

Mum and I sit down with our food, while we wait for Noah. 'We haven't spoken properly about the news interview. You said you changed your mind?' she says in a tone that screams *Bullshit!*

'I was actually late getting there.' A half-truth. 'The important thing is, Wonderland got its moment. I was annoyed that my art wasn't mentioned, but now that the showcase is even bigger than we first thought, I guess it's worked out okay.' *Except Trey hates me and is dating a crazy person.*

I bite into my salmon, avoiding Mum's gaze because I really don't want her to dig. I can't talk about Trey and Blair. My phone beeps, and when I check it I see a DM from a sender called Estee Mase. I drop my cutlery.

'What's wrong?' Mum asks.

There's no way it's her. There's no— Oh my shit, it's her! I read the message quickly.

'Mum, look!' I pass her my phone, and Mum gasps. 'The

Andersons are going to be so happy!' I'm almost jumping up and down in my seat.

Trey isn't going to believe this! I know we're not getting along right now, but this is going to change everything for Wonderland. I can't wait to see his face when he finds out.

I type back quickly.

That would be amazing. Thank you so much! I promise I'll keep it a secret.

FIFTY-FIVE

Trey's playlist: 'My Christmas' by Tony! Toni! Toné!

Six days till Christmas

We're at forty-one thousand pounds now and I don't understand how we're not at our target despite being on the news. What are we doing wrong? We can't let Raymond & Raymond buy us out after all this hard work, but Christmas Eve is coming up fast and we're running out of time.

The bookshop is as busy as it usually is now, and it's weird to think that this is the new norm. Aunt Latrice took Reon to the Christmas guest service at church so Mum could help me with the footfall. Mum's on the tills and I'm floating around, helping customers, encouraging them to buy more books and picking up stray ones that have been discarded carelessly.

We're trying to leave Ariel alone to finish the mural. There's a sheet blocking most of it from view because she said she wants to surprise us, but at an angle I can catch a glimpse of her and a part of the painting. She's on top of a ladder with her headphones in and she can't see me looking at her. I haven't told her yet, but what I've seen so far is stunning. I thought the artwork I'd seen her draw was beautiful, but this is by far the best thing she's created. The detail and colours are so incredible. It literally looks like these great writers are here, jumping off the wall.

At first I'm looking at the mural, but then I'm watching her, my eyes running over the way her apron ties in at her waist and how her long red hair falls down her back. I miss her. I hate that we're in this place, but how do we move on from this?

The door opens and Boogs and Santi come in. It's so warm in here that I'm in a light shirt, but they're in puffy coats and hats with gloves.

'What's up?' I nod at Boogs and hug Santi.

'We were just passing by and . . .' Santi trails off as she spots a glimpse of Ariel's mural. Boogs follows her gaze and they both stare wide-eyed.

'Damn,' Boogs says under his breath.

'Are you two speaking yet?' Santi asks hopefully.

'Nah, not really,' I reply glumly.

'Maybe you should hear her out,' Santi says.

I frown at her. 'She was saying shit about your sister. You know that, right?'

Santi averts her gaze and doesn't say anything. Boogs and I catch eyes and he gives me an 'I have no clue' look.

'I'm going to look at the YA,' Santi says to Boogs and walks away from us.

I follow her with my eyes. 'What's up with her?'

Boogs shrugs. 'She's been quiet for the last couple of days now. She's saying everything is fine, but I know there's something on her mind.'

'Hmm. Anyway, is Marcus still cool to DJ for the showcase?'

'Yeah, no doubt. Have you picked the acts? I can't wait to show off my routine,' Boogs says with a grin.

I nod. 'We've got carol singers, solo singers, dancers and a magic act for the kids. It should be fun.'

Boogs holds his hands up. 'Now, before you ask, my dance piece is already looking fire, so you might as well tell all the other performers to take a seat.'

I laugh. 'Okay, okay. I like the confidence.'

'Speaking of confidence, are you going to sing?' Boogs raises his eyebrows at me.

I snort. 'In front of all of those people? No way.'

'You spoke live on TV though,' he says seriously.

'Yeah, but Blair was there to help me through it.'

'So have her come on stage with you.' Boogs nudges me. 'Come on, man. Wonderland is pretty much all everyone talks about these days, so you know we're going to have a lot of people at the show. It's the perfect opportunity for you to show off your sick vocals in real life.'

I know Boogs is right, but the idea of actually singing in front of a crowd makes me feel like a spider has just crawled down my back. I don't even know why I have such an irrational fear of it. Deep in my soul, I know I'm a good singer. But that's the problem with fear – it doesn't make sense.

'I'll think about it,' I say eventually. I don't mean it at all, but at least now Boogs will drop it.

But as my shift continues, I can't get what Boogs said out of my mind. I know I'm not confident enough to sing at the Christmas showcase, but maybe I should put my New Year's resolution into action and start to look into a smaller talent show. If I can get up on a stage without feeling like I'm going to throw up and then actually manage to sing, that would be a good start.

Wonderland's now closed and the bookshop's empty apart from me and Ariel. I finished cashing up ages ago, but I feel weird being out on the shop floor alone with her, so I'm waiting in the office until she's finished. I've watched the video of me singing a few times now. I sound really good. The more I watch it, the more I think I should definitely bite the bullet and enter a talent show. What would I sing though? Do I pick something that's current or old skool? I'm so lost in my thoughts that it takes me a second to see Ariel, who's just walked into the office with paint specks on her face and hands. She puts on her coat, green scarf and bag before she looks at me.

'I'm done. Can you come and look?'

I don't say anything as I follow her to the mural and I'm not prepared for what stares back at me. The only way to describe it is that it's a masterpiece. It's beautiful, vibrant and full of so much history. I walk closer, careful not to get too close because it's still wet, and I notice a face in the painting that weirdly looks like my dad. Then I see another face and it's my great-grandad who started Wonderland. I gasp as I see my grandad ... Mum ... Reon ... me.

'This is ...'

I don't have the words for how the painting makes me feel, but it's like I'm filled with happiness and pride seeing my family legacy amongst greatness. The detail in my grandad's face makes me miss him so much. It's almost as though he's right here, living and breathing. How did Ariel find these photos? I blink quickly because I don't want her to see how emotional it's making me feel.

'As much as this is about celebrating iconic Black writers, your family is Wonderland, and I felt like they needed to be honoured too,' she says.

I clear my throat. 'Thank you.' I can't believe Ariel's done this for us. My parents are going to love it. I want to frame it and take it home with me, but what makes it even more special is that Ariel created this not because we paid her, but because she wanted to gift us this amazing art. All my earlier frustration and anger have disappeared, and as I look at her now, I realize all I want to do is hold her.

Ariel smiles at me, and my heart thuds. She takes a step towards me and I don't move.

'Trey,' she says softly. Just hearing my name on her lips makes me feel like I could float up and touch the sky.

Her hair is falling in front of her face, and without thinking

I brush it away, but she catches my hand and holds onto it. I look down at our brown hands wrapped around each other's. She doesn't say anything as her thumb moves gently up and down my skin, and everything in me feels alive. I want to kiss her so badly.

She takes her hand back and it's like all the warmth leaves my body. I look at my hand now alone.

'Trey,' she says again with more force this time, and I look at her. 'You need to ask Blair what happened on Friday. Wait –' she holds up her hand as I open my mouth to speak – 'I like you, Trey. I really like you, and I think you like me too. You need to know that I would never not show up for you, so please ask Blair for the truth.'

She lets out a deep breath before walking out of Wonderland, leaving me alone, wondering what the hell is going on.

FIFTY-SIX

Ariel's playlist: 'All I Want for Christmas' by TLC

I told Trey that I liked him and the ground didn't open up and swallow me whole. I didn't die; he didn't look disgusted; he didn't laugh at me. I told Trey that I liked him and I feel ... happy.

FIFTY-SEVEN

***Trey's playlist: 'Sleigh' by Smino,
with Monte Booker and Masego***

I'm sitting outside the square by the bare Christmas tree. Hackney Council are going to get the community to help decorate the tree at the showcase. My head is banging and no amount of walking has made it stop. Ariel likes me, and I didn't tell her I like her back. I do like her but . . . Blair. I love Blair and I thought things were getting better between us, but am I just kidding myself? There's no way Blair locked Ariel in a classroom and took her phone on the day of the interview. She wouldn't do that.

Would she?

I shake the voice out of my head. No, she wouldn't.

Are you sure?

'No!'

A couple hand in hand look at me startled and quickly walk on. They probably think I'm crazy.

Why would Ariel make it up though? She could be trying to split us up, but then why would she have waited until now? We've been alone together a lot. I can't put my finger on why Blair would do it either. I rub my throbbing temples. I need to ask her, but she's going to flip out that I'm even questioning her. But then if she did do it, that means I've never known Blair at all, which really scares me. I've been with her for almost two years and I thought I trusted her, but Ariel's explanation seemed completely authentic and that's what's concerning me. Ariel wouldn't ask me to confront Blair if she was lying . . .

I need to talk to someone about this, and the only person I can think of is Boogs. He knows all three of us and can give an outsider's perspective. I send him a text to let him know I'm coming through, and with my hands buried in my pockets I start walking.

I ring the bell when I arrive and Ms Deton opens the door. Boogs is literally her twin. They have the same light eyes and skin. She's already got her coat on and her handbag over her shoulder.

'Hi, Trey. How are you, darling?'

'I'm good.' I give her a hug.

'He's in the living room. I've got to head to my cleaning job now so I'll see you later.' She brushes past me.

'Okay, stay safe.' I give her a smile.

When I walk into the living room, Boogs is lying on the sofa with his arms behind his head, watching the football.

'What's good?' he says, not looking at me.

I sigh. 'I don't know, man.'

I sit on the chair opposite him and Boogs glances at me. He reaches for the remote and pauses it so the football is in mid-air. Then he sits up.

'You okay? What's going on?'

I tell him what Ariel told me. 'But it's crazy, right? Blair wouldn't do that.'

I'm expecting Boogs to say something like *Nah, man, Lil' Mermaid is acting up*, but he stays quiet.

'You think she would do it?' I ask, confused.

'I need to show you something. Pass me my bag over there.'

His dark blue backpack is near my feet and I pick it up and throw it at him. He unzips the small pocket on the side and pulls out a crumpled-looking card. I lean forward, peering at it as Boogs puts it on his lap and uses his hands to push the creases out.

'Here.' He hands it to me and it's still pretty crinkled, but it's clear enough for me to recognize Ariel's distinctive artwork.

A window fills the card and it has snow and frost on it. Inside the window are bookshelves, and I instantly know it's Wonderland from the placement of the till and the little display tables. In the middle of the bookshop is a couple sitting opposite each other, holding hands. The girl has red hair and glasses. Opposite her is a guy with a secretive smile. He's muscular build with wavy hair. The girl is definitely Ariel and the guy ... *Is this me?* I look closer at the drawing, and now I can see the little details, like the guy – well, me – has headphones hanging out of his pocket attached to a phone that's propped up on the table. 'O Holy Night' is on the phone screen. I look at Boogs.

'That's what Blair saw when we were at The Grotto,' he says matter-of-factly.

The card Ariel snatched out of Blair's hands and threw to the floor.

'I took it cause I wanted to see why Ariel was acting weird. It's obviously you two,' Boogs continues.

I trace my finger across the two of us. I have no idea when Ariel drew this, but it's not something Blair would have gone crazy over.

'Do you know what I think? I think Blair saw the card, flipped out and then really did lock Ariel in a classroom.'

I scoff. 'Over a card? Ariel and I have never sat and held hands.'

'Look at it, Trey. Look properly,' Boogs says seriously.

So I do, and I realize the couple look so into each other, almost as if they're in love. I think about all the time I've spent with Ariel recently and how I've been smiling at her just like that. I suck in my breath. 'Shit.'

'You and Blair aren't vibing, but you and Ariel are. Ever since you told me that you liked her, I've been watching both of you, and I've seen how the two of you give each other come hither looks.'

I frown. 'Come hither looks?'

'You know what I'm saying! Even at the twins' birthday party you were trying to touch and dance with Ariel. I think

Blair wanted to get one up on Ariel and make her look so bad that you wouldn't fall for her.'

I shake my head. This is crazy! I know Blair and she wouldn't do that.

'Blair always acts out,' Boogs says, as if he's reading my mind. 'Look at the pink party we threw and how she acted. Blair is always on some emotional shit and, to be honest, I don't know how Santi remains unbothered by it.'

'But ... Blair knew this interview was important to me, to my family. Would she really do that?' I stand up and start to pace the room. Blair had no idea what the news segment was even covering. For all she knew, Ariel and I could have had a speech planned together, so locking her in a room would have sabotaged everything. I stop pacing and Boogs is staring at me.

'Does Santi know something? Is that why she's acting so weird?'

'Oh, she definitely knows, but she's not going to snake her twin. What you need to do is talk to Blair. You know her, and you'll know straight away if she's lying.'

'And what if she did do it?'

Boogs sighs. 'I don't know, man, that's up to you. But if Ariel is telling the truth then you at least owe her an apology, right?'

The mood at home is completely different to how I feel. I walk in and Chaka Khan's playing through the speakers, and loud laughter fills the room. I hang up my coat and walk into the living room to see alcohol on the table and Mum and Aunt Latrice dancing. Dad's attempting to dance from his chair but all he's doing is a shoulder bounce. I cross my arms, surveying the scene. What kind of behaviour is this on a Sunday night?

'Trey!' Mum sashays over, her hands reaching out to me.

I roll my eyes and allow her to drag me to the dance floor. Aunt Latrice whoops when she sees me and then downs her glass. Mum starts two-stepping and singing at the top of her lungs.

'What are we celebrating?' I shout over her.

'Us, baby!'

I gasp. 'Wait, did we hit the target?'

'Not yet,' Aunt Latrice says.

I frown. 'So what are we celebrating exactly?'

'The fact that the bookshop is busier than ever; we were on the news; actual celebrities know who we are.' Mum cups my chin. 'And you.'

I smile. 'Thanks, Mum.'

'Come on, Trey, loosen up!' Aunt Latrice says.

It's pretty hard to stay miserable when your mum is pretending the remote is a microphone and Aunt Latrice is trying to show off her 'breakdancing' moves. After three songs, Aunt Latrice starts making more cocktails in the kitchen, and I make a T shape with my hands.

'I call a time out!'

Mum doesn't even pay attention. The stereo is now playing Dawn Penn's 'You Don't Love Me'.

'Remember this, baby?' Mum says to Dad. 'That night in Jamaica on the beach?'

Dad grins. 'Ooh, that bikini.'

I shudder. I do not need to hear this! 'I'm going to check on the boys.' I assume my cousin Cayan is here, not that anyone seems to care.

I shut the door behind me and head up the stairs to find the boys awake and reading comic books.

'You're meant to be asleep,' I say, taking the comic books from them.

'Mum didn't come to say goodnight,' Reon replies, like that's a legit reason to be up at ten p.m. before a school day.

'Bed.' I point to the bed and the boys groan. Once they're in, I kiss them both on the forehead.

Cayan moans, 'I'm not a baby,' which makes Reon say, 'Yeah, me too.' I side-eye him. He's more than happy to accept my goodnight kiss when he's alone.

I turn off the light and go back downstairs to the living room. 'You know there are ten-year-olds that you created upstairs trying to sleep.'

For some reason that makes the adults laugh. I don't know why I'm the only one with any sense in this house. I turn down the volume and notice Dad's got a drink in his hand.

I point. 'Are you even allowed that?'

'Hush now, boy,' says Dad, waving me out of the room.

I lie on my bed, close my eyes and think of Blair. I was planning on calling her, but I think talking to her face-to-face makes the most sense. It's my last day at college tomorrow before Christmas break, so I'll speak to her then. I need her to look me in the eyes and tell me that she didn't do what Ariel's accused her of, because I honestly don't know how we can be together if she did.

FIFTY-EIGHT

Ariel's playlist: 'What Do the Lonely Do at Christmas?'
by The Emotions

I call Annika as I'm walking home and she answers on the first ring.

'I told Trey that I liked him,' I say quickly.

Annika screams so loud that I have to move the phone away from my ear.

'Shut the fuck up! Are you serious? What happened? Tell me everything!' she shouts.

So I tell her about the mural reveal and then about Blair, which is when Annika stops me.

'You told him to ask Blair? What did he say?' she questions.

'Well, nothing. I didn't really give him a chance to.'

'Right. Okay. Carry on,' Annika says.

'So, I told him that I like him—' Annika squeals, making me laugh. 'And I said I think he liked me too.'

'Shit! What did he say back?' she asks.

I cross the road towards my front door. 'Erm ... well, I didn't really let him respond to that either. I just walked out.'

Now the high I was on starts to disappear. Yes, I told Trey that I liked him, but I have no idea if he likes me back.

Annika groans. 'Ariel, why didn't you just ask him?'

I lean against the brick wall by my house and look up to the sky. 'Cause I just wanted to say my piece and then leave, but, now I'm thinking about it, I should have asked him straight up. And what if Blair still lies and he believes her? Then I've just gone and confessed my feelings to him while the two of them walk off into the sunset and—'

'Girl, you need to calm down,' Annika says loudly over me, and I take a deep breath. 'I'm proud of you for telling Trey how you feel. And you know what? I do think he likes you. But Blair is a whole other situation. We've just gotta pray that he sees through her bullshit.'

I sigh. 'Yeah, you're right.'

If Trey and I are meant to be, he'll get the truth out of Blair. I suddenly hear someone yelling in the background through the phone.

Annika tuts. 'My mum's calling me, but, girl, I'll pray tonight for your man!'

I laugh. 'Thanks, Annika. I'll speak to you later.'

We say goodbye and hang up. I stand outside for a

minute longer looking at the Christmas decorations in our neighbours' houses and offer up my own silent prayer. *Please, God, let it all work out.*

FIFTY-NINE

Trey's playlist: 'Christmas Without You' by Xscape

Five days till Christmas

The adults are hungover, so guess who has to take the boys to school? Thankfully, Cayan's school isn't far from Reon's and his uniform is in his sleepover bag. I deliberately bang about in the kitchen until Aunt Latrice shouts from the living room, 'Trey, quit that noise!'

I drop the boys off and catch the bus to college. I wanted to get there early to talk to Blair, but now it'll have to wait until later. We're pretty much left to our own devices during business studies, so I finish up some work and hand it in to my teacher. It's my last class before Christmas.

'Thanks, Trey. Merry Christmas and good luck with Wonderland.'

'Thank you, and Merry Christmas to you too, Ms Clayton,' I say.

I head to the lounge and see Blair in deep discussion with Bebe, which is odd. They're never together unless they're in a group. It's cold outside, but Blair has on a miniskirt and furry boots, which is typical of her.

'Hey.' I walk over and pull a strained smile.

Blair's eyes light up when she sees me. 'Hey, babe. You done with college?'

'Yeah, you?'

'I've just got to hand in some work for media, but then I'm done.'

'Ah, okay.' I rub the back of my neck. 'Bebe, do you mind if I steal Blair for a sec?'

'Yeah, of course,' she replies, curiosity clear on her face.

I look around the lounge, which is busy with students. Some are wearing Christmas jumpers and others are exchanging presents. There's even a decorated tree in the corner.

'Let's find somewhere private,' I say.

The closest classroom to the lounge is the art room and I go in when I see it's empty. Blair gives me a weird look.

'What?' I ask.

She frowns. 'Why did you pick this room?'

I look around. 'Cause it's near the lounge ...'

She looks relieved. 'Sorry, yeah, of course it is.'

Then it hits me. Was this where she locked Ariel? I sit down, so I'm sitting backwards on one of the chairs, and she sits opposite me.

'You bring me here to do a Bebe and Jerome rendezvous?' She smirks.

Damn, I closed the door behind us.

'Nah, I need to talk to you about something important,' I respond seriously.

She shuffles in her seat before crossing her legs. 'Okay, shoot.'

I take out the creased Christmas card and hand it to her. I watch her carefully and I see her eyes widen slightly as she recognizes it.

'I know you saw this at The Grotto, and that's what Ariel crumpled up. You think it's me and her?'

'Ariel has a silly crush on you. It's whatever.' Blair rolls her eyes.

'What makes you say that?'

'She told me she likes you. Look, Trey, you're just too nice sometimes, and girls like Ariel get the wrong idea when you act that way.'

I nod my head, like I'm taking in what she's saying. 'Did you tell her that?'

'Yeah, I did, and I'm onto her. I know she's only working at Wonderland cause she likes you. I reminded her that you're my boyfriend and not hers.'

'Is that why you locked her in a classroom?' I ask bluntly.

'No!' she snaps. 'Is that what she said?'

I shake my head and lie. 'Someone saw you.'

Blair falls quiet and my heart drops.

'Why did you do it?' I search her face for the truth.

She leans back in her chair and looks out of the window. 'Cause we were fine before she came along.'

'Oh, Blair.' I put my head in my hands. Ariel was telling the truth. How could Blair have done that?

I feel her warm hand on my shoulder, and I look up at her. She doesn't even look sorry.

'That isn't okay!' I snap.

Her face screws up. 'But I planned it so I'd be there with you to do your interview.'

Can she not hear how crazy she sounds?

I get to my feet. 'How did you even get a key?'

'Bebe got it for me,' she says in a small voice.

'Bebe's in on it too? You don't even like the girl. You knew how important the interview was to me and my parents. And Ariel's been nothing but helpful since she started at Wonderland. How could you think it was okay to treat her like that?'

'Oh, she's been very helpful!' Blair says crossing her arms.

I frown. 'What's that supposed to mean?'

'I heard you danced with her at my party, then you went to the cinema with her and didn't tell me. What the hell, Trey? I'm your girlfriend.' Blair stands up and glares at me. 'To be honest, now I think about it, it all seems to point to one thing. Are you cheating on me with her?'

I screw up my face. 'What are you on about? Of course I haven't cheated on you!'

'Really? Is that why you wouldn't have sex with me the other week?' she yells.

'Blair, just stop! I'm not sleeping with Ariel, okay?'

'But you fancy her,' Blair challenges. She searches my face and I don't deny it. 'I knew it. What's so good about her anyway? There's no way you think she's prettier than me.'

'It's got nothing to do with looks. You should know me well enough by now to know that I would never cheat on you. But let's just get real for a second – you don't give a shit about what I'm going through.'

Blair jerks her head back. 'Trey, how can you—'

'Let me finish. Everything that's been happening with Wonderland has been by far the hardest thing me and my family have ever been through. On her first day, Ariel was there helping my dad when he injured himself. She helped when the bookshop flooded. She came up with the idea to do a fundraiser – even the book club was her idea. She's painting a whole mural for free, for fuck's sake. And where have you been? You haven't even checked in on my dad. I've tried to tell you about the bookshop and you don't listen. You don't care about anything but yourself.' I take a deep breath to calm myself down.

Blair scoffs and turns her head away from me, but she doesn't say anything. Suddenly, it feels like a massive weight has been lifted off my shoulders. I don't think I realized quite how much I needed to say that.

'You didn't tell me about half the stuff going on,' Blair eventually says.

'I tried to. You've barely showed any support for Wonderland, despite random strangers helping out. All you've

316

cared about are the stupid thirst comments from girls on my posts.'

Blair laughs. 'If you think so low of me, Trey, why are you with me?'

'I don't know!' I yell, and Blair freezes.

'You don't mean that,' she whispers.

But I do mean it. I don't know why I'm with her. Yes, I love Blair, but that's not enough, not any more. I can't be with someone that I can't confide in and that I definitely don't trust. She hasn't supported me, or my family or Wonderland, and I know, if it was the other way round, I would have been there for her every step of the way.

I swallow and push out the words. 'This relationship isn't right for me any more. I need more than this.'

'But I can do more,' Blair says, walking up to me. 'Trey, please let's just talk about it.' A tear runs down her perfect make-up, and I want to reach out to wipe it away because I hate when people cry, but I close my fist and stop myself. 'Look, I may have made mistakes, I can admit to that, but it's not like you've been perfect either.'

'I know I've been shit in this relationship recently. I've been so consumed with work and trying to be there to help my parents out. This month has been rough. I embarrassed you at your party; I don't have time to hang out; I haven't checked in as much as I should have. I get that.' I pause and gather my thoughts. 'When you were there for me during the interview it meant so much to me. It made me realize we've got a good thing. But now I know that you were only there cause you pulled that stunt on Ariel. It's not a good look. You weren't there for me when you should have been, and I don't think we can come back from this.'

'Why don't we take a break and think this through?' Blair suggests, wiping her eyes.

The door swings open, making Blair yelp.

'Doors open!' Mr Idris, the drama teacher that all the girls fancy, shouts at us before walking off.

Blair and I have broken up a few times, but it's never been final. The breaks have lasted a few weeks and then we've always wandered back to each other. Before, I thought fate was the reason we kept getting back together, but now I'm realizing it's just toxic. We never resolve things and so the same behaviour continues. Blair has been complaining about me working at Wonderland since we got together. She's always on my case saying we don't spend enough time together, but my parents, unlike hers, don't have loads of money and they need me at the shop. This whole situation with Wonderland has put everything into perspective. I used to resent the bookshop and all the time it took from me, but the idea of losing it has reminded me that the most important thing is family. Wonderland is part of my family, part of me, and, whether I work there or not, I want it to be around for as long as possible.

'I'm really sorry, Blair, but I can't see a way past this. I don't want a break this time,' I say.

Blair puts her hands over her face and starts crying uncontrollably. I don't know what to do, so I just stand there silently. There's a box of tissues on the desk and I grab one to offer to her. She takes it and wipes under her eyes, her mascara smudged.

'But I love you, Trey.' Her voice breaks when she says my name, and I swear it's the most heartbreaking sound I've ever heard.

I reach out and hold her hand, and she squeezes back tightly. 'I love you too, Blair. You're amazing, but we have to be honest with each other. This relationship isn't working, and breaking up is better for both of us in the long run.'

Blair sniffs in response. We stare at each other, and even though this feels shit and weird, I know I've made the right choice. We both need and want different things that neither of us can provide the other with. I wish she'd been by my side throughout this Wonderland drama because I think it actually would have brought us closer, but I guess it wasn't meant to be.

'Just please promise me not to walk around college flaunting a new relationship with someone else in my face. Especially if it's Ariel.'

'I'm not going to date Ariel,' I say truthfully. 'I don't want to date anyone for a while. I'm just gonna do me.'

I wasn't planning to say that, but now that I have it feels right. I've been in a relationship for almost two years. Even when Blair and I were on a break, I didn't date anyone else. I never wanted to. The twins are by far the hottest girls in college. But then Ariel came along, and for the first time I was looking at another girl in a romantic way.

'I'm gonna go,' Blair says, taking her hand away from mine. 'I've got to sort out my face before media.'

'Okay,' I reply. This might be the last time Blair and I are alone together like this, and for a second I question whether I've made a mistake. Should I take back everything I've just said and try to carry on as normal? But instead I watch Blair pick up her bag and walk past me. She pauses at the door, gripping the frame tightly. I wait for her to say something, but she doesn't. She walks out of the room, not turning to look back.

SIXTY

Ariel's playlist: 'Little Drummer Boy' by Lauryn Hill

Four days till Christmas

Yesterday, after my last class before Christmas I went to Wonderland, where Gita had sent over a photographer to take pictures of the bookshop and my mural for the *Hackney Gazette*. I watched on like a proud parent as they photographed my art. I'd expected Trey to come, but he'd texted me to say he wasn't feeling too good and was going to go home after college. Hopefully, he'll be better in time for the Christmas showcase on Friday.

After I left Wonderland, I spent the rest of the day trying not to stress that Trey still hadn't said anything to me about liking me or what Blair had said, so to distract myself I edited some photos and videos of my mural for social media. It took way longer than I thought it would, but I figured if I wow someone at the Artists' Studio open day they might go snooping online, and at least now my social will be poppin'.

Today, Mum and I are in the grounds of the Artists' Studio, and it looks even more impressive than the last time I visited with Dad over a year ago. If I'm accepted onto the course, I'll get to study painting with the legendary tutor Malcolm Tzitchey. He's taught some of the best modern artists, so I can only imagine how far he'll take my art. Maybe all the way to Art Basel in Switzerland, or even the National Gallery if I'm the one lucky student who's selected. Imagine, me – a professional artist!

'This place is fantastic,' Mum whispers to me.

I nod in agreement and watch as two girls walk by us – one with bright pink hair and the other with a rainbow ombré. Unlike college, where my red hair looks so out there, here it's normal and it feels like I belong.

The head of the course, Rachel Morden, a silver-haired, very sleek, Black woman with rings on her fingers is speaking to various potential students and parents. We hover around, waiting to be seen.

'Hello. It's nice to meet you,' Rachel says with a smile when it's our turn.

'It's so good to be here.' Mum shakes hands with her. 'This is my daughter, Ariel Spencer.'

'Ariel Spencer?' Rachel raises her eyebrows. 'Why do I feel like I know that name?'

'Her father came here – Michael Spencer,' Mum adds.

Rachel's forehead crinkles. 'Oh my, of course. Michael was such a talent. I am so sorry for your loss.'

'Thank you,' I reply, feeling a pang in my chest. But, for once, it doesn't feel as heavy as usual, and I know it's because being here is the closest I've felt to Dad in a long time.

'I think I know you from something else though.' Rachel taps her full lips with her finger.

I laugh. 'Probably Wonderland – the bookshop that's gone viral.'

Rachel clicks her fingers. 'Yes! You're creating a mural of Black writers? I can't wait to see it.'

'It should be in the *Hackney Gazette* and online in a few days,' I explain.

Mum puts her hands on my shoulders. 'Ariel also did a painting for the Corden College courtyard that was in the local paper.'

'Wow, you're a very impressive woman, Ariel! Have you sent in your application form yet?' I shake my head. 'You know, I grew up in North London too – Tottenham to be precise.'

'Really?' My eyes sweep over Rachel's expensive tailored clothes. I'd never have guessed she was from Tottenham. Her whole vibe looks more Knightsbridge to me.

'The Artists' Studio is one of the top art schools, so we get thousands of applicants from all over the world. But I'll tell you this: it's very refreshing having a local girl in the mix.' Rachel leans in close to me, her silver hair brushing against my cheek. 'I, for one, will be looking forward to your application.

I'd suggest trying for the scholarship.' Rachel gives me a knowing look, and I almost burst with happiness right there on the spot.

She thinks I could get in on the scholarship! Me!

'Thank you so much,' I say, and we shake hands.

'I hope to see you next year. It was good to meet you both.' Rachel waves at us and goes to talk to another family.

'Mum! She thinks I can get a scholarship!' I squeal.

'I'm not surprised, darling. You're so talented and you deserve it.' Mum puts her arm round me, and I rest my head against her shoulder.

Next year I could be here walking the same halls as Dad did. I take a deep breath and smile. It's all coming together.

We get back just after six. From the bus stop, Mum goes to pick up Noah from a friend's house, and I walk the short distance home. I turn the corner and stop. My heart leaps when I see Trey standing outside my house, his hands deep in his pockets and his face buried against his chest.

'Trey?' He looks up and waves. I walk towards him. 'What are you doing here? I thought you were sick.'

He gestures towards my house. 'Do you mind if we go in? I'm freezing.'

I fumble for my keys. 'How long have you been waiting out here?'

'About an hour,' he replies sheepishly.

I look at him bewildered. We go inside and Trey rubs his hands together. It's so cold in the house, so I decide to do something we haven't done since Dad passed away because it was his favourite thing to paint in front of – I put on the fire in the fireplace.

'You know, I've never seen one of these in real life,' Trey says, standing in front of the now crackling flames.

I'm still wondering what the hell he's even doing here, and because I don't know what to do with myself, I start fluffing the pillows on the sofa. I sit down and, after a moment, Trey joins me. He starts tapping his foot on the floor and I glance at him.

'I broke up with Blair yesterday. That's why I didn't come to Wonderland.'

'What?' There's no way I heard him right.

'Blair admitted to locking you in the classroom. I'm really sorry that I didn't believe you, Ariel. '

I take a deep breath. I can't quite believe that there's no more Trey and Blair. Trey takes something crumpled out of his pocket and hands it to me. I open it up, and it's the Christmas card I drew of us. Shit, how did he get this? I bite my lip.

He taps the card. 'This is us, right?'

I glance at him, trying to read how he feels, but his face is blank. Eventually, I nod.

'At first, I wasn't sure if it was me, but the more I looked at it, the more obvious it became.'

He seems calm about it, but Blair was calm at The Grotto – and look how she acted afterwards.

'It was never meant to be on the stall. I must have packed it by mistake. It was just something silly I drew,' I say, avoiding his searching eyes.

'It's not silly,' Trey says softly.

Our eyes meet and my heart starts going crazy. The thuds of my heartbeat feel so loud that I'm surprised Trey can't hear them.

'Ariel, I like you too,' he continues.

There go the butterflies whizzing round in my stomach. A smile spreads across my face. Trey likes me back. All this time of having feelings for him, and now he's here telling me that he LIKES ME BACK!

'But . . .'

Have you ever seen a balloon floating and minding its own business, and then some kid comes along and pops it and the balloon instantly shrivels up into nothing? Yep, that's how I feel right now.

'I've just come out of a long-term relationship and it wouldn't be fair to any of us if we jump into a new one straight away. But I do want to keep getting to know you and hanging out, if you want to?' Trey says. 'All I'm saying is, let's take our time.'

Take our time? That doesn't sound so bad. I can deal with that.

I swallow. 'So, kind of like if we're meant to be, we'll be?'

Trey smiles. 'Something like that.'

As much as I'd love to be with Trey right here and now, I've watched enough romcoms to know that rebounds are a real thing, and what Trey and I have, I think, is more than that. I can wait.

'I'm cool with that,' I say with a small smile.

'You sure? I'm not going to see you on Darren Acre's arm going to some fancy book awards any time soon?'

Darren Acre? What has he got to— Then it hits me. I *knew* Trey was jealous!

'It's Darren Acre though,' I say, and Trey's face falls. I playfully hit him. 'I'm kidding. Come on, why would I want a bestselling author when I have you?'

'Wow, thanks,' Trey says gruffly, but then he grins at me.

I lean in close to him and he wraps his arms round me, rubbing his hand gently along my arm. I want to kiss him so badly. Yes, we're taking it slow, but I can't wait to feel his lips on mine. Does he want the same thing? I pull away from him and his eyes drift down to my lips. Maybe he does . . . He puts his hand on my lower back and gently pushes me forward to move me closer to him.

'We're home!' Mum calls from the hallway and I jump up. Damn it, all I needed was five more minutes!

Trey stands to his feet just as Noah runs in followed by Mum.

'Trey!' Noah skips over to him and gives him a high five. 'Is Reon here?'

'No, not today, little man. Hi again, Mrs Spencer.' Trey reaches out a hand to her and Mum shakes it. She smiles but gives me a quizzical look.

'Trey came by to talk to me about the showcase on Friday.'

'Erm, yeah, there's just so much to do.' Trey points at me. 'So I'll see you tomorrow at work?'

I smile. 'See you then.'

Trey waves as he leaves.

'You put the fire on?' Mum asks.

'Yeah, it was cold,' I mumble, and Mum grins at me. 'What?'

'It just seems a bit . . . I don't know . . . romantic.'

I roll my eyes, but I'm smiling. I look at the flames and I realize there's another family tradition that needs to be brought back.

'Hey, Noah, we should definitely watch *Home Alone* on Christmas Day.'

Noah looks at me. 'Really?' His whole face comes alive and he runs into my open arms. 'Thanks, Ariel. I wish Dad was here to watch it with us.'

'Me too, but, hey . . .' Noah pulls away and stares at me. 'He's always here, right?' I point to his heart. 'And when we start discussing what we'd have done better than Kevin McCallister, we know Dad will say—'

' "I'd just call the police"!' we shout at the same time and burst out laughing.

It feels so good to think about a happy memory of Dad, and I realize this is the first time I haven't felt any sadness when I've remembered him. From now on, I hope we continue to laugh and smile when we think or talk about him. Dad truly was the best.

SIXTY-ONE

Trey's playlist: 'Kiss Me, It's Christmas'
by Leona Lewis and Ne-Yo

Three days till Christmas

I'm woken up by the sun seeping through my curtains. I was having the best dream about me and Ariel. We were in some kind of woodland with mistletoe hanging off the branches and a roaring fire next to us. Her lips looked so full and inviting and I was leaning in closer and closer . . .

Man, I wish her mum and Noah hadn't come back yesterday at that very moment. All I needed was a few more minutes and I could have finally kissed her.

I sit up, resting my head against the headboard, rubbing my eyes with one hand and opening up Instagram with the other. Emily Thomas, the photographer who took the pictures of Wonderland and Ariel's mural for the *Hackney Gazette*, has tagged me in a post. The photos came out amazing. I screenshot them to repost, wishing I could have been there to see it all in action. But I definitely needed that time to myself after everything that went down with Blair.

There's an article link in the *Hackney Gazette* Instagram bio and I click it. I read it quickly to make sure everything is accurate. Hopefully more news outlets will pick up the story as the day goes on. I send the link to the family WhatsApp group and to Ariel, in case they haven't seen it.

Blair and I still follow each other on Instagram, and I hesitate about whether to post the mural on my feed. Everyone knows about it, but is it insensitive to Blair to post something connected to Ariel?

'Trey, I made pancakes!' Mum calls from downstairs.

'Coming,' I shout back. I'll deal with the post later.

I put on a T-shirt over my shorts and walk down the stairs, simultaneously checking Twitter, where the article is already being retweeted by many accounts. *Please, God, let people donate after reading it.* Dad and Reon are already eating when I reach the kitchen, and Mum drops a few pancakes on my plate as I sit down.

'Thanks, Mum. Did you see the article?' I ask.

'Yes, it's brilliant, isn't it?' Mum says, sitting opposite me. 'Can you believe the showcase is only two days away? It will be so nice to see everyone come out to support us. Will Blair be there? I haven't seen her around much.'

'Yeah, about that ...' I put down my knife and fork. 'I actually broke up with Blair on Monday.'

'What? Why?' Mum and Dad ask at the same time. Reon just stares at me as he continues to eat his pancake.

'I didn't feel the relationship was working any more, and I dunno ...' I shrug. 'We're just not good for each other.'

'I'm sorry to hear that, baby,' Mum says, reaching across the table to place her hand on mine. 'Do you think it will just be a short break?'

I shake my head. 'No, we're done for good this time. I know you really liked her, so I'm sorry.'

'I did, but, Trey, we're always going to have your back,' Mum replies softly. She waits a beat. 'Did it have anything to do with Ariel?'

'Ariel!' Reon looks at me wide-eyed. 'Is she your girlfriend now?'

'Trey, you can't be going from one girl to another that quickly,' Dad says, looking at me disapprovingly.

'I'm not! Ariel isn't my girlfriend, but ... I do like her.' I can't help but look at Mum. She called me out on it weeks ago and I dismissed it, and now here I am admitting she was right. I can't tell from her face what she's thinking, and it feels like for ever before she speaks.

'Ariel's a lovely girl, and what she's done to help us is incredible,' Mum says.

There are no words to describe the relief I feel that Mum's okay with it.

'But,' she says – and of course it was too good to be true – 'you're young, Trey, so just take your time. If Ariel is the one for you, she won't go anywhere, okay?'

'I hear that, and I thought the same thing.' I flash a smile at Mum. 'I was expecting you to say, "I told you so".'

'Oh, baby, I saw this a mile away! I definitely told you so.' She grins.

'Whatever, Mum,' I say, laughing. I knew she wouldn't be able to help herself.

We spend the rest of the day at Wonderland going over the line-up for the showcase on Friday, double-checking that we have all the timings correct and Marcus has everyone's music. A big box was delivered to the bookshop, and, when I opened it, it was filled with black canvas bags that had *#SaveWonderland* in gold writing on the front of them, courtesy of Hackney Council. Everyone who purchases a book on Christmas Eve will be given one. I take a picture of the bag for the Wonderland account and the comments quickly clock up with people desperately asking for one.

I try my best not to check the GoFundMe page, but the last time I looked we were seven thousand pounds away from our goal. We've still got time, and I'm not going to let myself think about David Raymond, who I'm sure is watching our every move, waiting to pounce. I wish I knew what our fate will be, but I'm hopeful people will come through for us. I really don't want to be proved wrong.

SIXTY-TWO

Ariel's playlist: 'Christmas in the City' by Mary J. Blige and Angie Martinez

Two days till Christmas

I skim through the newspaper, accidentally ripping a page in my rush to find the article. When I see it, I scream.

'Ariel?' Mum rushes into the living room with Noah behind her.

'Mum, look!' I thrust the *Hackney Gazette* into her arms, and she gasps.

'Wow! This is amazing, darling,' she says.

'Let me see, let me see!' Noah begs, tip-toeing to get a better look.

Me. Ariel Spencer. Officially has a double-page spread in the newspaper! The article is all about Wonderland, the Christmas showcase and my mural – and to see it in print feels like a dream.

Mum wipes her eyes and Noah puts his arm round her waist.

'Don't cry,' I say snuggling up to her.

'They're happy tears, honey.' Mum kisses the side of my head. 'I'm so proud of you, and I know Dad would be over the moon to see this. Oh, it's times like this that I miss him so much.'

I wipe away Mum's tears. 'He can see us, and he'll be throwing a party in Heaven to celebrate, I'm sure of it.' Mum laughs and nods her head. 'But look at us,' I say. 'We've made it through the hardest time of our lives, haven't we?'

'So Dad can see my art too?' Noah asks, and I give him a big hug.

'Of course he can! And we're going to make sure the Spencer name continues its legacy. This is just the beginning.' I kiss Noah on the cheek before Mum holds out her arms.

'I couldn't have got through this year without you both,' Mum says as we squeeze each other tight. 'My two talented superstars.'

I smile to myself, knowing that if Dad was here he'd be calling his entire phonebook to tell all his friends about my article, then he'd be running out to find more copies to keep. I know I'll never stop missing him, but moments like this remind me how lucky I am that I had him for seventeen years. He moulded me into the girl I am today. The artist. And knowing that he'll always be with me, cheering me on, makes me believe I can do anything I put my mind to.

SIXTY-THREE

Trey's playlist: 'Sweet Little Jesus Boy' by Tyrese

Christmas Eve

I wake up feeling the lightest I've felt in for ever. Today's the
day. I shower and get dressed as Mum helps Reon get ready.
Dad is already in a snowman Christmas jumper and jeans, and
he gives me a big smile when he sees me. My parents and Reon
will be there for the actual showcase, but I'm going a little
early to check on the set-up, which Gita has kindly organized.

'You ready?' I ask.

Dad reaches his arms out and, on the count of three, I
take all his weight for a few seconds as I transfer him to the
wheelchair that Aunt Latrice dropped off last night. It's a
friend of a friend's. I have no idea how she knows someon
with a spare wheelchair, but I couldn't be bothered to as

'Woo! This is more like it,' Dad says, pus'

wheelchair forward with his hands. It goes straight into the side table, knocking over the vase, which breaks.

'Clive! You better not be making a mess down there,' Mum shouts.

Dad gives me a sheepish look.

'I'll get the broom,' I say.

Once I've finished tidying up and said goodbye to my family, I meet Aunt Latrice outside Wonderland. She's agreed to cover the shop while the showcase is happening and she's wearing the loudest Christmas jumper I've ever seen. In the centre of it is a Christmas tree that has flashing multi-coloured lights wrapped around it, and when she presses the star it says 'Ho, ho, ho!', which makes no sense.

'It's Christmas!' she says excitedly. 'You ready for today?'

'Yeah, I'm looking forward to it.' Aunt Latrice kisses me on the cheek. I raise my eyebrows at her. 'What's that for?'

'For being a good son, a great brother and an annoying nephew.' She nudges me and I laugh. 'But seriously, Trey, what you've done to help this family is amazing, and I'm so proud of you.'

'Thanks, Aunty. Right, you know how to work the till?'

'Boy, please – I worked here before you were even born.' She gives me a look but then her face turns serious. 'Whatever the outcome is today, enjoy yourself at the showcase, okay?'

I make my way to the square. It looks like all the small businesses in the area have showed up to help. Marcus is onstage setting up his decks; Mrs Avard, who owns the flower stall, has these amazing Christmas floral displays scattered on the tables, which are covered with food, donated by the local bakery and restaurants; and Mr Green came through with the chairs, which are stacked up ready to be put out. We're not due to start for another hour, and I can't wait to see the square packed out with people.

I spot Ariel and Boogs on the other side of the square and walk over to them, stopping to say hi to various people. Once I reach them, I notice they're standing in front of a wall covered in pictures with black frames. There are a few photos of the mural, some of the courtyard and a picture of Ariel with a paintbrush in her hand that I recognize from her Instagram. This must be the artist spotlight that Gita was talking about.

'Very cool,' I say.

Ariel looks at me and smiles. 'I know, right?'

'I'm going to start doing art again, just to get on this wall,' Boogs says.

I laugh. 'You're stupid. Besides, you're going to get your moment today during your dance performance.'

'Speaking of performances, what's up with your singing?' Boogs asks.

Ariel's eyes light up. 'You're singing today?'

'Nah, I'm just going to enjoy the show.'

'Boo!' Ariel and Boogs say at the same time.

'Ah, whatever,' I shoot back.

'I found this.' Boogs shows me his phone, and on the screen is a post about an unsigned showcase for singers. It's almost as if he read my mind and knew I was already thinking about entering a couple of low-key competitions. Maybe this is a sign. 'Before you say anything, just think about it, okay?'

Ariel leans over. 'This looks sick. You should go for it, Trey.'

I zoom in on the date and see that sign-up closes at the end of the month with the auditions and showcase in January. Apparently, an A&R from a prestigious record label will be at the show, and they're bound to attract hundreds of singers. This probably isn't the 'small' show I wanted to start off with, but, then again, what if I won and went on to be the next big thing? Look at Ariel going hard for her dream. She's so fearless and is doing amazing things ... That could be me.

'You know, I've been thinking about entering a singing competition. I guess the video you took of me boosted my confidence,' I eventually say, and Ariel looks at me, surprised. Who could blame her?

'Why didn't you tell me?' Boogs asks. 'That's dope, man!'

I shrug. 'To be honest, I didn't want the pressure.'

'So, in a weird, roundabout way, you're saying I helped you?' Ariel says, looking so pleased with herself that it makes me laugh.

'You'll definitely look into this showcase?' Boogs asks.

I nod. And I mean it.

We walk towards the centre of the square where people are putting out chairs in front of the stage and we help out. Ariel sees someone she knows and goes to say hello.

'Is Santi coming later?' I ask Boogs as we pick up a chair each.

'Nah. Blair isn't doing so good,' he replies a little awkwardly.

I'd hate for my relationship with Santi to dissolve, but she might not want to remain friends after everything with Blair.

Boogs must read my mind because he says, 'She's cool with you, though. She said she had a go at Blair for pulling that stunt on Ariel.'

Sounds like Santi.

'So, are you done done? Or just done?' Boogs questions.

I put the chair down at the end of a long row and lean on it. 'I'm done properly this time, but I obviously still care about her. Maybe one day we can be friends . . .'

Boogs gives me a look, and I burst out laughing. Okay, 'friends' might be a reach.

'And what about Lil' Mermaid?' Boogs asks. 'Are you two gonna give it a go?'

'We're taking it slow, but . . .' I look around and everyone is too busy to pay attention to us. 'We almost kissed the other day at her house.'

'Damn, Trey. My boy don't waste time!' Boogs laughs. 'What happened? She changed her mind?'

I side-eye him as he continues laughing. 'Nah, her mum came home. I was pissed though!'

'Can all performers and helpers please come over to the stage?' Gita says through a megaphone.

Next to the stage is a table that has loads of passes on lanyards and red T-shirts on it. I can't believe this started as a small local show for Wonderland, and now it's a full-on event. Look how far we've come!

'Keep these passes on at all times. It will allow you to go

behind the stage or to the performers' area if you need to.' Gita points to a small tent. 'Those who are helping out, can you please put on the red T-shirts?'

She starts to hand them out, and I see they all say *#SaveWonderland Xmas Showcase* on the front.

'Thank you again for helping us. It means so much,' I say to Gita as I unzip my coat.

'Oh, of course! The press are on the way, so we'll get lots of exposure. Have you seen Ariel?'

I look around the square and spot her on the phone, not too far away from us. 'Over there.'

Gita walks off and I shudder as the cold hits me. I quickly put the T-shirt on over my long-sleeved jumper. Only thirty minutes left to go.

SIXTY-FOUR

Ariel's playlist: 'Little Christmas Tree' by Michael Jackson

I hang up the phone just as Gita walks towards me holding a clipboard. In her other hand is a red T-shirt that she hands over.

'Thank you,' I say with a smile.

'What do you think of the artist spotlight?' Gita asks.

'It's incredible! Thank you so much again for choosing me.'

'Of course!' Gita says before lowering her voice. 'Is everything still on for later?'

I nod. 'I'll come onstage at the end of the show for the big reveal.'

Gita makes a note on her clipboard. 'And the Andersons still don't know?'

'Nope, and we've got to keep it that way.' I grin. They're going to lose their mind! I can't actually believe I've managed to keep this surprise quiet for so long. 'This is going to change everything!'

The community really has showed up for us. The showcase is rammed with people, and I don't think I've ever seen so many Christmas jumpers in one space. People are wandering around, drinking mulled wine and eggnog, or eating cake and mince pies. I see some holding the #SaveWonderland bookshop bag that Hackney Council printed and I smile. The Hackney Community Choir are singing a melody of Christmas songs and their magic fills the air. It's perfect.

Mum and Noah are here, and he and Reon are putting decorations on the lower half of the tree with all the other children. I notice Mr and Mrs Anderson, and I wave at them as I walk over.

Mrs Anderson gives me a warm hug. 'Clive, this is Ariel.'

'Ah, the famous artist.' Mr Anderson shakes my hand. 'Thank you for helping me on the day of my accident. I hear you're quite the treasure – and that mural is one of the best paintings I've ever seen. How did you even manage to find images of my family to base their portraits on?'

'Google,' I say, and he laughs. 'I had a lot of fun painting it. Wonderland deserves all the good things. I really hope we reach the target.'

Mr Anderson's shoulders drop. 'We've tried our best, but what will be will be. I had the pleasure of meeting David Raymond today.' He pulls a face.

Mr Raymond's here? I look around, but it's so packed that

there's no chance of me finding him in the crowd. 'Does Trey know?'

'No, I don't think so. Hopefully they haven't crossed paths. Trey didn't react well the last time he was sniffing about,' Mrs Anderson says.

'In other news, I have something for you.' I pull out the sparkly customized Christmas card from my bag and hand it to Mrs Anderson. She takes it out of the envelope and gasps. It's a picture of the Andersons in front of a heavily decorated Wonderland.

'This is gorgeous!' Mrs Anderson holds the card close to her chest.

I'm so happy she likes it. I have a present for Trey too, but I'm going to give it to him later today. My phone buzzes and I glance down at it. Ah! She's here!

I look back up at the Andersons, trying to hide my excitement. 'I just need to do something quickly, but I'll be back. Enjoy the show!'

I hurry through the crowd, but it's hard to get through when it's this packed and people keep stopping me.

'I heard this was your idea.' I immediately stop and turn at the sound of the familiar voice, and see Bebe walking towards me, with Yarah and James next to her. She has that stupid smirk on her face that seems to only be reserved for me. 'I'm shocked.'

'Yeah, cause you could never,' I reply calmly, and Yarah and James burst out laughing.

Bebe's mouth drops open and I walk off, mentally giving

myself a high five. A couple of weeks ago, I wouldn't even have been able to form words to shoot back at Bebe, but so much has changed since then. I've changed. And I refuse to let girls like Bebe or Blair make me feel small.

'Ariel!' Annika and Jolie appear in the crowd and wave at me. I hurry towards them.

'You missed it – I just gave Bebe a read!' I click my fingers, and Annika laughs.

'You didn't? Oh, why do I always miss the good stuff?' Annika looks around. 'This is really something.'

'Amazing,' Jolie adds. 'I can't believe it was only a couple of weeks ago that we came up with this idea. How are the Andersons doing? They're *so* close to the target. I really hope everyone is feeling extra generous today.'

'They're staying optimistic, so fingers crossed. Listen, I've got to do something before the showcase starts, but I'll catch up with you guys in a bit.'

'Hold up, you never told me what happened with Trey,' Annika says, and Jolie gasps.

'Wait? What happened with Trey?' Jolie asks me.

I laugh. 'I promise I'll explain everything, but let's just say your prayer worked, Annika.' At that, Annika squeals.

'Prayer? What are you guys talking about?' Jolie huffs.

Annika links arms with her. 'I'll fill you in, girl. Where are you going, Ariel?'

I put a finger to my lips and wink at her.

SIXTY-FIVE

Trey's playlist: 'All I Want for Christmas Is You'
by Mariah Carey

People keep wanting to take pictures with me and telling me
they've donated – some more than once, which is brilliant,
but we're now five thousand pounds away from our goal.
David Raymond has given us until six p.m. to accept his
offer, and I'm sure I saw him walking around earlier in
one of his expensive suits. I tried to follow him, but I lost
him in the crowd. He probably can't wait to get a front-row
seat to watch us fail at saving our bookshop. It's so shit.
We've worked so hard and done everything we can to save
Wonderland, and I'm praying with everything in me that we
hit our target.

Bebe, Yarah and James are by the mulled wine stand, but I
don't go over to say hi. I definitely want to talk to Bebe about

her involvement in locking Ariel in the art classroom, but not today. We've worked too hard to put this showcase together and I want to enjoy it.

I'm standing in the crowd, watching the last of the performers bring their A game, and I feel so proud that we pulled it off today. Boogs is closing the show, and then Marcus will play music for the next few hours so we can all dance and chill out together.

The crowd is buzzing and cheering loudly, and a part of me wishes I was onstage singing. Who knows? There may be a showcase next year, and I'll have no excuses to not take part then. I take a sip of my mulled wine and turn my head, searching the crowd for red hair.

Where is she?

I look back to the stage and Boogs comes on in a Father Christmas outfit and sunglasses. I burst out laughing. I've never seen Santa with swag before. Everyone is clapping and laughing before he's even begun, and, as soon as the beat kicks in, Boogs starts to move, gliding across the stage. Everyone goes nuts! I take out my phone and record it so I can send it to Santi. I know she'd have loved being here to watch. Boogs' dance ends too quickly, and I've enjoyed the showcase so much that I wish it was going on for longer.

As Boogs leaves the stage, Ariel walks on holding a microphone. What is she doing onstage? I wave, trying to get her attention, but she can't see me. Beside her is a Black, middle-aged woman with a neat bob …

Wait a second, is that Estee Mase?

People start gasping as they realize who it is. *What the hell? What is Estee Mase doing here with Ariel?*

'Hello, everyone, I'm Ariel Spencer,' she says into the microphone and everyone cheers loudly for her. I'm in too much shock to make a sound. 'Thank you to everyone for all your support for Wonderland bookshop. With your generosity, we've raised forty-five thousand pounds for this brilliant, Black-owned, independent bookshop.' She pauses as everyone applauds. 'I have some special surprise news to share with you all today. Bestselling author Estee Mase will be doing a signing of her new book in Wonderland in thirty minutes!'

I clap in a daze. How did Ariel pull this off? Estee Mase didn't even respond to my messages! Ariel passes the mic to her.

'Hello, everyone. Just like all of you, when I found out about Wonderland and this beautiful family fighting for it, I fell in love with them,' Estee says. 'I'd like to call up Mr and Mrs Anderson and their sons, Trey and Reon, to the stage.'

It's a struggle getting through the crowd. I try to spot Mum, but I don't see her until she's climbing the steps up to the stage, looking just as confused as I am. When I join her, Mum grabs my hand and squeezes it tightly. Dad rolls up the ramp with Reon behind him. Ariel beams at all of us.

'Mr and Mrs Anderson,' Estee says, 'I have so much admiration for the lengths the two of you have gone to in order to support your family. Trey, I've been in awe of everything you've done to save this wonderful bookshop, and, Reon, you're the cutest little thing.' Reon laughs and looks up at me as if to say 'She ain't lying'. 'And that's why I contacted Ariel to see how I could help.'

What? How did Ariel keep that secret from me? I glance at her and she winks at me.

'Wonderland is too important to be lost. I've donated already, and I made a promise to myself that, if Wonderland didn't reach the target, then I must intervene.' Estee pauses, and Mum, Dad, Reon and I look at each other with wide eyes. I'm waiting with bated breath to hear what Estee will say next. 'So, for that reason, I'm going to donate the remaining five thousand pounds!'

There's a split second of silence, where it feels like everything pauses, and then the crowd is going mad, jumping up and down and cheering and clapping. I look over at Mum and she's burst into tears. This can't be real life ... We've reached our target! We've done it! We've saved Wonderland! I grab Mum round the waist, lifting her off the ground, and she laughs through her tears. Dad is punching the air, and Reon is jumping up and down cheering at the top of his lungs. Ariel is clapping, a huge smile on her face. She must have known about this all along! Estee hands Ariel the microphone before walking over to us, and I put Mum down.

'I don't know how I can ever thank you,' Mum says, wiping her wet face.

'It's my pleasure, Mrs Anderson.' Estee hugs her. 'And, going forward, whatever I can do to support Wonderland, you just let me know.'

I gulp, feeling a lump in my throat. 'Thank you so much.'

'Oh, Trey, how could I ignore you, with the messages and the call-out on the news?'

I laugh. 'My bad.'

'Everyone? I have one more surprise,' Ariel says into the mic, and we all look at her. The crowd goes silent. 'Today is all about celebrating Wonderland, but it's also about celebrating Christmas! So myself and Gita from Hackney Council, who helped us put on this amazing showcase, thought it would be fun to have a sing-along with the Queen of Christmas.' Ariel takes a deep breath and sings the first line of 'All I Want for Christmas Is You'. Her voice is high and smooth and pitch perfect. She stops. 'I don't think it's really Christmas without some Mariah Carey, am I right?'

Everyone cheers in agreement and someone shouts, 'I know that's right!'

Gita waves at the crowd as she comes onstage and hands me, Mum, Dad, Reon and Estee hand-held mics. I look down at it, my heart racing.

'Hit it, Marcus!' Ariel shouts.

The iconic music starts and the audience immediately start singing and swaying. It's like a scene from a film. Mum and Estee are laughing as they sing off-key, Dad is singing in a deep smooth voice and Reon is singing all the wrong words. I'm gripping the mic so tightly my hand starts to hurt. I close my eyes to block out all the people.

Come on, Trey, just sing, I tell myself.

I'm sweating and my body is hot, but then I feel a soft hand on mine.

'You don't have to join in,' Ariel whispers. 'But open your eyes. You have to see this.'

So I do, and the crowd are fully dancing now, singing at the top of their lungs and looking like they're having the time of their lives. Mum and Estee are dancing together in the corner. Reon is sitting on Dad's lap, laughing his head off, as Dad spins them round in his wheelchair. And Boogs and some of the other dancers from the show are onstage throwing down their best moves. This isn't scary. This looks ... fun.

I look at Ariel, who's staring at me and searching my face, and slowly I raise the microphone to my lips. Ariel's eyes widen as I open my mouth and start to sing.

At first, it doesn't feel like I'm doing it, because, despite the microphone, I can barely hear myself over the hundreds of voices, but then it feels like the music starts to fill me up and the need to let rip gets bigger and bigger ...

'"All I want for Christmas is you,"' I sing as loudly as I can, adding these crazy riffs because I'm extra like that.

And then I really can't hear myself because the anthem fills up the whole of Hackney. I'm hitting all the Mariah high notes and ad-libs, and it feels like I'm onstage at my own concert. It's the best feeling ever. When I think of Christmas from now on, I know this moment is one I'll always remember.

Once the song ends, Mum pulls me into the biggest hug. I can't believe I did it. My heart is racing, but in a good way, and to be honest I could do it all over again.

'Wasn't that amazing? I've never seen you sing like that, Trey!' Mum says.

My cheeks flush. 'It was really fun.'

'Being onstage suits you,' she says, holding my chin.

I hesitate before asking: 'Do you think I could do it ... professionally?'

For a second my heart stops, because I desperately need Mum to believe in me.

Mum slowly smiles. 'Baby, you can do anything you put your mind to. You've already proved that.'

'Thank you, Mum. That means a lot.'

She's right ... and I'm going to go for it. Next year, I'm entering as many singing competitions as I can.

We walk down off the stage, Dad leading the way, and he almost rolls into an unwanted guest waiting at the bottom ... David Raymond.

'The nerve—' I start to say, but Mum is already marching up to him.

Mr Raymond flashes a smile at her, but it starts to waver when Mum points at him.

'We are not selling Wonderland, Mr Raymond,' she hisses.

'Mrs Anderson, come now – think about it,' he says quickly. 'We've offered you an amazing deal. You won't get anything better than this.'

'You heard what my wife said,' Dad growls, and Mr Raymond takes a step back.

I stand beside my dad, and Mr Raymond looks from me to Dad to Mum. He straightens his tie.

'You probably can't see it, but you're making a huge mistake,' he mutters.

'No. The mistake I made was thinking you were our only option,' Mum says. 'Now, if you don't mind, we'd like to enjoy the rest of our day, and you're not welcome here.'

Mr Raymond's jaw tightens. 'I see. Well, in that case I'll let my partners know your decision. You have a good Christmas.'

'Yeah, right,' Dad says as we watch him walk off. 'He'll always be sniffing around.'

He might, but he'll never get his hands on Wonderland, that's for sure.

'Trey, you sounded like a pop star!' Reon says, clapping his hands.

'He gets his voice from me,' Dad butts in, and I roll my eyes. He playfully punches my arm. 'Amazing, son.'

I grin the cheesiest smile. 'Thanks, guys.'

I look at my family and think back to that Sunday night nearly two weeks ago, when we sat talking round the dinner table. We'd already come up with several ways to save Wonderland before Reon suggested the GoFundMe. Wonderland has only brought us closer together, and I can't see myself not working at the bookshop now. I don't know how long it will take for me to make it as a singer, or if I even ever will, but now that I know I have the support of my family, I'm certain it's all going to work out.

I bend down to hug Dad and see Ariel standing to the side watching us. 'I'm gonna talk to Ariel. I'll be back in a bit.' And as I turn to walk away, I see Mum and Dad share a knowing look.

SIXTY-SIX

Ariel's playlist: 'Winter Wonderland / Here Comes Santa Claus' by Snoop Dogg and Anna Kendrick

Trey and I walk round the corner from the square. I can still hear the music and the crowd, but it's a little bit more peaceful here. Trey is walking with a bounce in his step and a smile so wide that it could light up the world.

'That was amazing!' he says for the millionth time.

I'm sure there are hundreds of videos by now on social media of Trey onstage, and I can't wait for him to see them so he can hear how brilliant he really is.

I take out my phone and text him over a link. His phone beeps and he looks at it and frowns.

'It's your Christmas present,' I explain.

He clicks on the link and it takes him to a playlist called 'Ariel & Trey's Winter Wonderland Playlist'. It has 'O Holy

Night', 'All I Want for Christmas Is You', 'I Saw Mommy Kissing Santa Claus', 'Rocking Around the Christmas Tree', 'Cold December Nights' and, of course, the entire 'Confessions' album by Usher. All of these songs are a memory of Trey and me. These songs are us.

'I figured we can keep adding to it . . . together.' I smile.

'Ariel, this is . . .' He shakes his head. 'I love it. It's perfect.' He takes my hand in his. 'I can't imagine Wonderland without you now, and seeing as we've saved the bookshop, would you like to stay on permanently?'

My heart leaps. 'Yes! I'd love to.' This is honestly the best Christmas Eve ever.

'I, erm . . . I actually got you something too,' Trey says.

'You did?' I wasn't expecting anything from him – getting a permanent job at Wonderland is enough in itself.

Trey takes a folded-up card from his coat pocket. 'Well, I made it actually.'

'You made me something?' I've never had anyone apart from Dad and Noah do that for me.

I unfold the card and see a poorly drawn Christmas tree with the words *Merry Christmas* underneath it. I glance at Trey, and he's biting his lip. Is he nervous?

I open it up.

Ariel,

Thank you for everything. You helped me more than you'll ever know, and I will forever be grateful. Our first proper encounter may have been you spilling a drink

on my fresh white tee, but very quickly you've become
someone extremely important in my life.

You are by far the best gift I could ask for.
Merry Christmas!
Love, Trey xxx

My eyes start to well up. This is the sort of gesture I've only read about in books. I lift up my glasses and wipe my eyes, not caring that my make-up is probably ruined now.

'Thank you, Trey.'

'There's something else I wanted to give you.' He takes a step forward and I don't move. 'And I don't think I can wait any longer.'

I know I can't. He pulls me into him and I tiptoe and purse my lips. I'm so ready for this. I've been waiting so long. But then I feel something wet fall on my face. I wipe it away and it happens again. Light snowflakes land on my coat and specks of white shine in my red hair.

'What the—?' Trey puts his hands out to catch the snow and he tilts his head back to face the sky. 'No way is it actually snowing on Christmas!'

Noah and I have a tradition of playing in the snow until our feet get so cold that we can barely feel them. Snow is one of my favourite things, even though it never snows in London on Christmas. But right now, snow is the last thing on my mind, and I can think of something I'd much rather be doing.

I put my hand round Trey's neck and gently nudge his head down so our lips finally connect. They're a perfect fit. The snow has nothing on this kiss. Every part of me, from my toes to the hair on my head, is alive and buzzing. In any moment, I'm sure I'll start floating up into the sky, above the clouds, all the way to the stars. When I think of Christmas from now on, I know this moment is one I'll always remember.

ACKNOWLEDGEMENTS

Wow! Where to start? *Love in Winter Wonderland* came about in such a strange way. An editor who rejected a past manuscript suggested I write a love story and my immediate reaction was, 'Why would I do that?' But then my agent and I spoke about it, and we realized there was a massive lack of Black love stories in YA, especially set at Christmas time.

To be honest, I didn't think I could write a romance book, despite it being one of my most read genres. I'm a middle-grade author by nature and I didn't think I could write YA, but I'm not one to back down from a challenge. What I did know was that I wanted to tell a story that was about love and not race, and it had to be based in Stoke Newington. I've lived in Stokey for most of my life and my dad lived here from the moment he moved to London, so a book celebrating Hackney was a must!

I'd only written a few chapters when my dad passed away, and as soon as that happened I couldn't write any more. When I felt somewhat ready to try to write again, I got on my knees and prayed to God to help me write this book. It's by His grace that I was able to write it in five months with a broken heart. I believe that writing this book stopped me from falling into a dark place.

First of all, thank you to God for helping me to write this book and giving me the strength to stay up until three a.m. listening to 'O Holy Night' on repeat so I could reach my deadline. I prayed for years for this deal and I kept pushing despite my circumstances. Thank you for answering my prayers.

My agent, Gemma – there are not enough words to express that you are the greatest agent of all time! Thank you for encouraging me to write this book, supporting me when I couldn't and then getting me the best book deal! I'm making you a #SaveWonderland Christmas jumper!

My editor, Amina – what an angel. Your love for this book from the get-go is something I will never forget. I prayed for a quick deal the day before my manuscript went on submission and you got in touch the day after. I knew fairly quickly that working with you would be the right move, and it's one I don't regret. Thank you for backing me, Trey and Ariel. I'll buy you the best seats at the O2 when J Hus tours again.

Thank you to Lucy – I love that you read the book in two hours while on holiday. That's the biggest compliment ever. Between you and Amina and your enthusiasm for the book, I couldn't say no! I'll always remember the Christmas jumpers you both wore for me on our first Zoom call. Epic!

Thank you to all the team at Simon & Schuster – what an

honour to be one of your authors. You made this Hackney girl's dreams come true and brought joy to my family during our hardest time. I am forever grateful.

Mum, Gboli and Lola – I love you all so much, and I hope I've made you proud! Thank you for encouraging me through this journey. Special thank you to Mum for staying up with me every night to keep me company as I wrote this book. Daddy, I did it!!!

Thank you to my friends – Anneliese, who took the time to read the first draft of *Love in Winter Wonderland* because I was too numb to have an opinion of the book. When I saw your response in capital letters, I knew I'd done something right. Helen, my partner in crime, for always backing me and believing that I can do anything. Kate for telling me I better have a six-figure deal when I told you I had important book news. When I said I did, you burst out crying in the middle of our favourite French café, making me cry. It's a memory I'll never forget. Leanne, Zarah and Aleta for consistently telling me that I deserved this deal. You guys have backed me for so many years. It was very hard to take in everything that was happening, and you guys were so happy for me that eventually happiness came for me too. Thank you to all my friends and family for keeping this book deal a secret. I love you, guys!

Massive thanks to Helen from Wonderland Bookshop who helped with all my bookshop questions. I love that there's a real and beautiful Wonderland bookshop, and I cannot wait to hold my Wonderland in your Wonderland.

Lastly, a massive thank you to all the readers, booksellers, bloggers and press for all your support over the years. I hope you all love my love story, and I'm excited to continue bringing all the feels.